"Michael Cisco's works immerse the reader in worlds that are not simply dreamlike in the quality of their imagination but somehow manage to capture and convey the power of the dream itself."

— Thomas Ligotti

"Michael Cisco is of a different kind and league from almost anyone writing today."

— China Mieville

"With Michael Cisco doing things like this, sometimes it feels like the rest of literature might as well get up and head home." -- China Mieville on Cisco's novel CELEBRANT.

"Fans of stylish and thematically sophisticated weird fiction should seek out ... Cisco's visionary genius." -- Publishers Weekly

"*The Narrator* is not a subversive fantasy novel. It eliminates all other fantasy novels and starts the genre anew. You must begin your journey here." -- Nick Mamatas

"An extraordinary story of war and the supernatural that combines the creepiness of *Alien* with the clear-eyed gaze of *Full Metal Jacket*. Like *The Other Side* if it included soldiers who could glide over the water, a mysterious tower right out of early David Lynch, and infused with Kafka's sese of the bizarre. Destined to be a classic."

— Jeff VanderMeer on *The Narrator*.

"A rivetingly strange novel in which Cisco mixes game theory, serious philosophy, SF, and dark fantasy into something at once unreal and really entrancing. Kind of like what might happen if Wyndham Lewis decided to write like M. John Harrison and had Martin Heidegger as his editor. *Member* is a complex, compelling work."

— Brian Evenson

"To miss the humor in Cisco is to miss Cisco. Even though the plight of the characters is dark and the reader feels the dire nature of things, the general absurdity of what happens is at the same time unnervingly funny. I don't mean out loud, laugh-a-minute funny like the jokes in a TV sitcom, but humorous in the way that Poe's stories are or the stories of Borges."

— Jeff Ford, on *The Traitor*

" He is absinthe in a world of Pepsi."

— Jeffery Thomas

"The alchemy of words ceasing to be words, words seamlessly melting before our eyes into grandiose imagery, into soaring halluci-nation, into fever dreams that tap directly into our subconscious and perfectly describe emotions that cannot be described is something no author achieves with more effect than Michael Cisco."

— Paul Tremblay, on *The Golem.*

PEST

MICHAEL T. CISCO

CL◢SH

Copyright © 2023 by Michael T. Cisco

Cover by Matthew Revert

CLASHBooks'Troy, NY

clashbooks.com

-- LIKE THERE'S A WINDOW OPEN SOMEWHERE LETTING THE cold in ...

... The other yaks stand around me, on the slope.

... Like haystacks. Haystacks on short legs.

... Like collapsed tents, with huge heads sticking out, into the cold. Stunned.

... I can't see properly. How am I supposed to see with eyes facing different directions? I see more in back of me, but not what's directly in front of me. It's like there's a big post right there, but it's just my head. And the fringe of hair hanging down I can't brush away. I want to, but I can't bring my hands up to my face.

... I don't have hands. My hands and feet are just stumps, but I can still feel my thumbs, my heels with nothing beneath them. I'm standing on all fours, with my head out and down, nothing beneath my head. My body is behind me, like a caterpillar.

... I feel in my body very light. Huge and light. Sometimes painful. When I turn or bendI get pain, not exactly here, around here, but somewhere. I feel about as big as a house. An empty house.

... One eye sees up the slope and the other down. No horizon.

... The rest of the herd are is dotted around, numb. The smell of that august company is doused in icy dampness. Their breathing murmurs around me like a still bigger body I'm wedged into. The wind is pretty low. Just a drowsy, even slide downwards. Sliding off the shoulders of the mountains. I can feel my ears flap in it.

... Color columns in the center of my head above my mouth, in internal chimneys. My head around me is like a horror mansion. My hands and feet ... or, just feet ...feel pressure, and my balance on top of them ... but nothing else ... no texture, no heat really.

... I can tell when I stand on rocks and when I stand on grass.

... My head is like a horror mansion, but there's never any horror action apart from me being in it. There's no ghosts, just blanks ... like time that doesn't pass. Or arrive.Like I have parts that are immortal even though I'm not.

... It's not just my head. I can't really turn and look at myself, so I can only look back through myself, down my neck. My neck is as big around as my head almost. My head neck and shoulders are heavyand my back parts are so light I feel like I could somersault without trying.

... Hungry. That hasn't changed.

... The night is ending. The sun's dim light is somehow everywhere and the slope and valley below the black peaks vibrate pale blue,the thin frost making the blue iridescent and the whole landscape hums as it sighs with a premonition that the sun will be breaking in on everything in a little while.

... A dry cough from up the slope. One of my fellow yaks takes a step and stops again. We'll do that for a bit, like motors sputtering into action.

... Grant's gone, I know that somehow. I think AC is gone too. Long gone, both of them.

... I hear the wind, and that might be the Cathedral demons, the "book people," whistling. But then I've never not felt that feeling the whole time I've been a yak, however long that's been -- that's the kind of thing that takes so much getting used to that you can't believe how little time it takes.

Dr. Achittampong tosses his cigarette into the green weird plastic butt collector in back of the clinic and enters again through the electric door, which gives one chirp. You can't be seen smoking out in front, even now. Even now, with the world falling apart, you have to do it in back. Why not? Bored and exhausted. Sleepy. With a weary sigh he nods at the new day nurse waiting for him by the reception desk.

He says"Hi" and holds out a hand like a half-wilted celery. The nurse's nametag says "Fort" on it. Her name is Fort?

"Oh hi!" she sings. "I'm pleased to meet you!"

Chipper. Incongruous under epidemic conditions.

He shows her into a room at the end of a dim hallway with polished floors of perfectly flat greenish tiles. A dark-skinned, huge man in a coma, his head swathed in bandages, is the sole occupant of this room. Tufts of long curly black hair emerge from the bandages onto the pillow. Somehow the bandages and the angle make his face impossible to perceive as a face. It's just a pile of features, like unmanned instruments in an orchestra pit; just a heap of bizarre objects, the nurse thinks, looking at the broad nose, the full lips, the round cheeks, the drooping eyes. She notices, too, a scar that starts high on the forehead and extends into the scalp.

"He must have been just shaved."

Dr. Achittampong is retrieving the man's chart. His back to her, he says "Mm."

The man's name, she learns, is Chalo Detto,thirty three, six three, three hundred and three, age -- height -- weight. He's an engineer.They brought him from Catalina Island two days ago, unconscious,his skull fractured. Somebody told someone the patient had been working on a construction project out there. Something happened to him at the construction site. Something heavy fell on his head. He wasn't wearing a helmet. Dr. Achittampong shows her the chart. Brain damage.

"No visitors yet," Dr. Achittampong sighs. "I don't know who's paying for this."

"Catalina? Does he have the syndrome?"

She's thinking the doctor looks hung over.

"It's hard to tell," he says, his voice rising a little. "He gives no sign of it, apart from this scar here."

He examines the heavy arms.

"More scarring here, but nothing new. I think they're still trying to scare up some family, if only to pay the bills."

Dr. Achittampong pauses a moment before he leaves the room, looking steadily at the patient as if he's trying to remember something.

She is to keep him under observation.

⸻

... The sky is clouded over. A few preliminary flakes of snow drop around me. Now that I'm already starting to soften for the spring, all my winter hardness and deadness has faded. The unexpected cold fastens its jaws on to me and I'm suddenly miserable.

... On the bright side, I can feel my fleas freezing off. More importantly, the trafficking urge in my testicles is diminished. They can either cool it or dangle in the snow, it's up to them. The snow has granted me a reprieve from my testicles, but more importantly it is putting my terror to sleep, blurring the other bulls. Is that a flicker of eagerness I get, though? Fight and get it over with, why not? Fucking snow.

... Gallantly we bulls hang back and let the cows take shelter by the rock face. Perhaps they are also availing themselves of this respite. The mountain pours snow down on top of us, but also shields us from the snow. Every now and then I take a bite, and shiver violently. I don't even have to lower my head, the drifts are piling up that high. My massive, puffing body begins to glow from within.

... Chalo the man was not all that susceptible to cold, because I had my share of fat, but nothing like this. Even as the terror and horniness dwindle, my intellect and senses sharpen. I can hear the little pricking sound my fleas make when they freeze and pop out of my skin. I can hear the ominous warbling of the yak uterus nearest to me as it slips back into a light sleep. Chalo the man was massive, inert, full of sourceless shame. Diligent when someone was tapping a foot, waiting for the clean lines and efficiency reports, but otherwise moving and doing as little as possible. No wife, no children. A history of failure with women that could be recounted quickly, but filled all of space.

... Actually, we don't seem to be mingling much. I think we bulls are our own thing, and the cows are their own thing. But those cows are still related to us in some way. We recognize each other instantly, in a way we wouldn't recognize an outside yak. Sowe are a herd of yaks, even if we spend a lot of time apart. Only now, we're nearing each other, like a planet entering perigee.

... Chalo the man could barely keep his mind on anything. He was able to work only the way a painter on a merry-go-round could, by dabbing at this painting over here as you swing by, then switch out your brush and dab a second painting a little further on, and keep going, adding to each painting in alternation, dab by dab, round by round, until they're done. They did get done, though. Chalo the yak can't keep it all together either. I can see all the topics spin and try to hold the wheel, somewhere in the pliant, brownish void between my eyes. This life is more complex, but there's a monastic retirement to this giant head I'm in that makes contemplation of these complexities less harrowing somehow.

... If the grass is going to freeze, you might as well eat it. The furnace inside won't lose steam no matter how much ice I eat. Using my nose and horns, and pawing from time to time, I can clear away snow and reveal the blazing green-shocked-green beneath it.

... The mountain creaks and groans. It's a sound below the range of hearing, but I have what I guess all yaks have -- a secret nerve in each hoof that "hears" the mountain. With this hoof-ear, I can hear when the mountain creaks in a strong blast of wind, and I know when there's a rock slide anywhere. It's like a toothache and a shiver; it's purple for some reason and it almost has a flavor, like grape juice. Lightly carbonated grape juice.

... Almost flat, just a fizzle left. The mountain cracks and rumbles like a big man flexing and stretching. It holds itself up, much as we yaks do, on hard feet with laces that penetrate the earth.

... My head nods when I walk. I don't like it. So, when I walk, I try to hold my head steady as long as I can. It's really exhausting. And it still dips a little anyway.

⊏⊐

The patient is sitting in the middle of the patio, where the wheelchair-bound are rolled on sunny days. From here, they can gaze out over the hills and rooftops, all the way to the Pacific. Now, however, the scene is marred by clouds of smoke from burning buildings, sirens wailing, stern voices amplified by loudspeakers, whirring helicopters, and a more diffuse and uncertain sound produced by unnumbered human beings in distress, shock, and pain.

In addition to the brain trauma that put him here, examination of his body unfolds a history of burns and contusions, some of which must have been incapacitating, extending back over a period of several months at least. All this is consistent with what has come to be called "Catalina Syndrome." No one knows how the syndrome is contracted; it isn't associated with any bacteria, virus, specific injury, or toxin. Nakedness is by far the most common symptom; patients automatically disrobe without seeming to be aware of it. So far as anyone knows, the syndrome does not harm the patient directly. However, since it entails spontaneous movement or activity of parts of the body, particularly the face, without the patient's conscious intention, the syndrome is a serious danger to life and limb.

No somatic problem is ever discernibly the cause of the movements. It is the gestures and facial expressions themselves that are "sick," rather than parts of the body. The gestures and facial expressions are often inappropriate to the patient's present circumstances. In many cases, these facial expressions and gestures produce injuries, either through unwonted or wildly violent motion or through self-inflicted harm, and so open wounds and scars are secondary symptoms. Patients tear and hammer themselves convulsively, screaming in agony, often masturbating at the same time. Patients are, however, either not aware that they are doing anything unusual, or choose to pretend that they are not aware. A handful of patients do become psychologically remote, although this may be an intenser or more obvious manifestation of a remoteness that all those infected experience, or, contrariwise, an augmentation of abstractedness as a pre-existing condition. This remoteness takes the form of an exaggeratedly intense concentration on an unknown thought, as if patients were trying -- with every fiber of their being, every ounce of strength, every last watt of willpower -- to remember, or to imagine, something. Those who exhibit this symptom will also often make spontaneous floundering movements. A doctor with a penchant for sailing claims to have recognized in these movements the actions of someone desperately treading water, struggling to avoid drowning. Since the first outbreak occurred in a religious community on Catalina Island, the syndrome was given "Catalina" as an ad hoc name.

One of the most peculiar attributes of the syndrome, and the one perhaps least well understood by physicians, is the apparent coordination of gestures among patients. It's as if the personal conscious control of certain body parts were being supplanted by communications between bodies, as if the different parts of different human bodies were coordinating amongst themselves, in a kind of conspiracy against the brains or personalities of their respective owners. So, one might observe, for example, a patient in one room stiffly waving a left hand back and forth to complement the similar movement of another patient's right hand in another room, like disarticulated applause. One patient shrugs while the face of another patient adopts an exaggerated, agnostic frown of uncertainty, and neither patient can see the other. It's as if gestures were being distributed among the body parts and faces of different persons, even as their own control of their bodies and faces is diminished, or altogether lost.

... This clinic is an island of calm, more or less, compared to the mayhem out there. I've been sleeping here at the clinic for almost a week now. It's too much trouble getting to and from my house. There are now three checkpoints, and it takes the better part of an hour to clear each one. The better part of an hour under the stupidly hostile gaze of soldiers and thuggish cops. Who needs it? What are they checking? With whom do they do their checking? Does anyone really believe that anyone is keeping track of anything anymore? Why they don't commandeer this place, I don't know, but it seems as though the powers that be are more interested in interring patients with the syndrome, than they are in treating them. I've heard rumors of quarantine camps, patients strapped down in cages, forced feedings, forced dopings. The usual, in other words. Some benign spirit has sheltered us here. We've been forgotten, which is probably for the best. Our patients may die due to lack of medicine or other supplies, but we don't dare to do anything to draw official attention to ourselves.

When this particular patient, a huge Indian man, isn't nodding to himself, which he usually is, he lets his head slump over onto his left shoulder. His eyes are always shut. His mouth blubbers from time to time. He can't speak, and the doctors have concluded that he is at best only minimally aware. The sunlight probably registers, but he is unresponsive to people. Somehow the scar on his forehead has reopened, so now there's a sizeable wad of bandage running down the middle of his forehead and anchored between his eyes. Occasionally, one or another hand will stir, and the nurse on duty will stop and watch it carefully. Will that hand casually reach up and tear out an eyeball? Will it grope the penis out? But the hand only opens slightly and closes again, the way you do when you are hoping to receive something, and then disappointed when you don't.

I swear he hears, though. I'll bet his ears are sharper than anything.

⊏▭⊐

... It's human eyes I miss.

... Sometimes, as I'm going about my yak business, a pair of human eyes will flash past my mind, a fragment of a remembered face breaks off and a powerful current whisks it away. The current is eating away at a crumbling island of memory. Paralyzed by longing, I stop where I am and raise my head.

... Never again, everything around me says.

I snuffle, and I cry.

... The sound that comes out of this enormous, hollow, rigid, badly-clogged nose when I cry is at once such a strange noise that if it weren't for the exact coincidence of the powerful vibrations I wouldn't believe I was making it, and then again it's almost a word, like a human voice speaking.

... My old life. My human life. What was it? What do I remember? What persists is more the cyclone of events around AC, Grant, Catalina, the Annex. My childhood, my education, my many, many failed loves, my long humdrumness, are barely visible from here.

... My nose and ears are picking up special radio waves from the cows as they go into estrus.

... The rut is coming. It will engulf me when it comes. How do I know there will be anything left of my human memory after that passion?

... I sigh. With my lips, I brush the grass at my feet ... my forefeet, where I suppose, as a human, my hands would once have been ... brush the grass with my lips, without eating any. I swing my head up and take in the bright vista of green valley, high Himalayan peaks, the wandering blue and white, the sharply glinting rivulet, wind steady broadside of me.

... My human life, as Chalo Detto the engineer, my casual, unimportant human life, my insignificant, disposable human life, the one I had been barely aware I'd been living, the one I'd squandered with mystifying indifference, now seems like a precious dream. Not, to be sure, a lost paradise, but a lost life. My life. How is it that my livingness made so little impression on me? How did it become a chore? Why did I allow that to happen? Did I allow that to happen? Or was there no choice? That was what Grant really cared about, wasn't it -- that there was, for human beings, in that place and time, no longer any choice about whether or not life, human life, could be allowed to become a chore. That was what he wanted to change.

... The snow is all melted now and the heat is beginning to pick up a bit, so that the wind comes booming up to us from the canyons below, maddeningly ripe with green already. The waves -- it's like those stories about tooth-filling antennas I always wondered about -- the waves buzz like horseradish right up at the top of what I guess is my huge yak sinus, and there's a mustard-humming along the top of my range of hearing. It's like my ears are both hot and burning cold, my eyes are tearing the way they do in a persistent wind, and I feel like I'm about to go crazy and my body will fly out of control kicking and floundering. My nostrils suck air greedily and my lungs start to boom, and I want to smash my head against something as hard as I can, knock the mountain over, run down the slope faster and faster until I'm nothing but a streak of onward momentum and then shatter headfirst against a skull or a boulder or the rim of the world, but I can't feel my sex at all. My genitals flap listlessly in the wind.

... I have only my shadow really to tell me how big my horns are, and I have no idea how to use them. Some of the younger bulls spar, not far from me. Only playing. They act on each other unaware, with a kind of aristocratic hauteur. Their blood is only just beginning to blaze, and they already have moves that I don't know that I can reproduce. When I let my body alone, it does fine, but when I try to think about what my yak body does, a lot of the time I phrase motions with my human schematic out of habit I guess, and my body starts trying to lunge back onto its hind legs, my head drives back into my shoulder hump and stops there, and I nearly sprain my wrists? -- ankles? -- trying to make my arms -- legs? -- act like human arms. I can actually feel the thick, clumsy nerves spasm as they try to translate my fiddly human hand and finger impulses into yak, and it's like trying to play Vivaldian filigree on a two by four. The nerves just bunch together like jammed typewriter keys, while my front hooves try to bend the joint, and all I manage to do is hove over onto the ground.

... Now and then, like a voice heard beneath the ground, I'll notice a faint message of hunger or fatigue, but to my mind I'm just a head, a pair of testicles, and four -- feet? -- attached to a vortex. Now even my testicles seem to be out of touch, and I'm receding into this head, so I might be dying. But if I am dying, then why do I have this cow-rut radio frequency riveted to the top of my sinus passages, buzzing and vibrating and driving me mad?

... I get along so-so with my fellow yaks. Even as a yak, I haven't managed to drop my old coy habit of withholding things from others because I want them dragged out of me with cajolings or demands that never come. So I wander away from the others a bit. My -- feet? -- have a strong tendency to keep me rolling along the landscape. Actually, this is a bit more like walking on my hands, more like having four hands than four feet, but four hands without fingers. They want to find the spots to stand where their inner sense receptor nerve strings go steady. When that happens, the mountain jumps out knife-edged at me, I feel myself firmly planted on the landscape, and it wants to be the scene of me mounting a cow, jump up and be that, the vivid greens and blues and stone colors of my mating.

... Water runs down grooves in the mountain, the sensation is borne in on me with the sound, making me quiver, making me jumpy. I have a nagging feeling. Nag nag nag. What is it? Something to remember.

... I'm alone now, grooving on the streams and the wind throwing green up in my face from the heathery valley. I get a mouthful of whatever this is, and the green blasts up between my eyes like I'm eating sunbeams. But still no news from my hindquarters. A rumble, now, from a stomach of mine, I guess I have a few. Turn my head into the wind, let it ride on the gust like a green pillow under my chin, cold with slobber.

... Standing stock still in the sun I start to think of you. Remembering you out of a kind of waking dream, the pillows of breath that clouded around you. Distinct lips and eyes and a cloudy body that began to coil around like the earliest turning of what's going to be a tornado. You breathe down skeins and blue white foam that fall on me and slide off me like silk scarves. Breathing breathing breathing, pushing open the crack in a shell, to you-with-live a whole landscape of green moist breath and trickling streams, whose breath rubs edgeless banks and waters dim stones, and flickers with transparent dapples in the diffusely milky sunbreath above the earthbreath, the sullen deathbreath ribboned into the escapading thick sexbreath, to touch a whole livingilluminatedlandscape at once and live a whole landscape with you. The long breathing we did, branched air in an upsidedown ionic column that pools its coils against us two. Breath is one sky, the airblue I can see through the clear of the bubble, you taught me this, your face turned lovesullen and solemn, blueblanketing me alive in dusktempered cold, breath grates as it gushes in and out so hard my whole body rattles with breath, and your solemnly violent breath blows my breathskin away layer by layer, a breathpowder coating lifts and folds and becomes a talc mist, between breathdusks you taught me this power, to explore a breathmute liftslumber gliding among skytrash furnaces of dusk.

... My human life. AC, Grant, Catalina, Wilson, the demons, Carhartt and Tarti, the "migrants," the Annex, my legend. Those things are important. They are my having-lived. What nags at me is the real, organic need of mine that they be important, and remembered. So, standing here, in the grass, batting away flies with my tail, feeling the impending rut, gazing over the roof of the world, I will try to reassemble those memories into a story I can hold.

I go into the health food restaurant and meet Grant in a glass corner right up against the highway, headlights in daytime swarming all around him.

The headlights balloon out, detach from cars and swoop past him like blazing, pale cyan spirits. Meanwhile, he's tranquilly dipping his thin lips in purple-brown pu-erh. He is, it turns out, a real pu-erh connoisseur. One time AC came in while he hads a hot cup of pu-erh steaming in front of him. She pointed right at it and said, "That tea smells like horseshit." She points so emphatically her finger nearly is in the cup.

Grant is wearing grey and white in the health food restaurant, and in time I learn that he never wears any other colors. A loose, shapeless thing that isn't light enough for a shirt but too heavy to be a jacket, white linen with the sleeves rolled up, and a grey t-shirt underneath. He's fifty years old and tan, with a dzi bead around his neck. The strands of hair on his head alternate grey and black. It falls in a lustrously supple curtain to his shoulders. It floats, lifts, and glides like the hem of a velvet gown. As he moves his head you would expect to see a woman's face inside that hair, but instead you see a creased, salt-cured middle-aged surfer man, his pale eyes tight with neutral intensity in a tranquil, laconic expression.

I blunder up to the table.

"Are you Mr. Grant?"

The hair slides forward a bit as he nods, then he raises his face to me, and his hair falls back like viscous satin. Like a bird dipping its wings in salute.

"Just Grant."

His voice is a little hoarse, and buttery.

I stick out my hand and he takes it perfunctorily, with a little puff out the nose and a trace of a grin, because we humans are so funny with our funny handshakes. The hand I take in my clammy, oversized paw is long and lean, warm and dry, like a paper hand, with sparkling, perfect fingernails that bode well for his teeth.

I wedge myself between the tube steel armrests of the chair opposite him.

Now ...

Here we are, Grant and me, here are we, sitting together, him and me.

... *Our helll is a travellling sky slicing through space and we are all in there*

... swingging like censors on long tethers among the structcures -- oh look! -- witch have been coordinindated to form the Celestial Disordering Machine.

Witch resembles:

a flecxing bullb of hwirling snowe,

a flock of white starlings,

an ameoeoba in a column of whater,

a representmentation of a series of math problems.

And witch articuliates the skyunits of our hell like bricks in a wall. Witch "brickes" are infinitely flat, clear, reflecting laminae that crash together and grind in patterns which scissor shut on us daemon book people cartoons with a fusewasp from Gilshrakes embedded in each of us. The fusewasp twists snarls whickers and arghues so that eatch and every single one of our number here present is filled with a voice-atmospheare witch is incessantly bickering with our grainy, dully golden outlines.

A whispurred call shakes the air harder than a screame, in a voice made of dashing cascades; dismembered, the slurrying stump of it gushes hallucinogenic ichor, fast sprouting funggus and dancing slimes with hackles that shivver up in merangue piques ...

That whisper is the sound that the garment of the humaen beings makes as it slips, that little abrasion ... of humaens ... against ... fate ... and the world is presentting.

Hurtling around in here as our sky moves through The Sky, the calling of the humaen psiren opens its blazing sex bright as gold in our indigo darkness, and I and every other daemon in the place swarm ruttishly toward it, clamber seethe and swim in around over and through each other to get to it, my volume growing bigger and emptier, the lamplike glare of my bugling eyes, my steadily engorlongating pointed nose, my dilatriangle grin, the spreading points of my urns and hordes and chains, my long rubbery hands flapping over corntrorted fraces and brodies, spinting with feet pesnis tongue and tail and tongue, termbling all over -- and then alley-oop!

All others thrawn down.

I myself I come through I I careen down the sunblazing chute cartwheeling over the abstwracked landscape of black peaks and planes, hardwhite-edged, traversed with giant wurds, cackling and bickering I tumble along the surface whose reverse side is the hueman world-facturdry. The resonacion beneath the membraen that shows me firming up, slowing, filling out, more and more enjanglled. When the snarll is bad enough to generate a vault, I'll translaid over in seveval persons, and staert to waerk on the humaen baeings, rubbling my haends, gnaeshing the old heard lead teathe in my Messerschmitt heaed.

Immediately I'm a convert.

Grant is explaining. His voice is the hoarse caress of a rough hand, like a former smoker's. There's something about his hands that makes you see a cigarette flicking in its fingers, but there isn't any. He doesn't hold me with his eyes, in fact he keeps casting asides diagonally in the direction of a dimension of slow-motion gracefulness, almost as if he were getting pointers.

"So Chalo! Let's talk. I'm really excited to experience your vision."

... He needs me. I'm a structural engineer, and his dream is to erect a huge structure, a whole religious apparatus, on Catalina Island. He objects to my use of the word "religious."

"Religion is killing and dying. I'm not a killer, Chalo."

We discuss my past work, such as it is. I try to explain to him that I'm not an architect. My involvement in architecture is entirely confined to explaining to architects why they won't be able to do most of what they want to do. Grant wants me in both capacities.

"Haven't you ever wanted to design something yourself?"

That was the bait that hooked me.

He looks over my resume.

"What's 'FARTP'?"

"Financial Advisors Regional Turnkey Program."

"What did you think of New York?"

I shrug. I have nothing to say. What comes to mind is a mishmash of impressions and recollections, a blur of pointless haste and tension, a lot of sitting and working.

"Have you ever noticed that the space in California is uniformly good, even in the worst locations?"

"... No, I can't say I have."

"I don't mean the places. I mean the space. Space on the east coast is generally inferior, unless you're on the water. Don't you think?"

Uh-oh.

"It's not the amount of space I mean," he says, as if I had said "uh-oh" aloud. "It's the quality."

I shrug again lamely.

"Space is space."

He grins.

"Westerners have an innate sense of space that easterners lack."

"I was born in Dhaka. Does that make me eastern or western?"

His eyebrows lift slightly.

"What was Dhaka like?"

"Hot. Flooded -- wet. Brown water in the streets half the time. Ankle, sometimes knee deep. Congested. ... Traffic jams all day long. People shut down their cars, get out and schmooze. Friendly."

"When did you leave?"

"When I was about six."

"Where did you go?"

"Burbank. Do you think people from Dhaka have even less of a sense of space than easterners do?"

"I don't know, Chalo. I've never been to Dhaka. I think you are the first person from Dhaka I've met."

"You have something against easterners?"

"Everyone gives us something to work with. I have no biases against people, but I seek out those who have the right senses. For our part, we westerners lack intensity. We're diaphanous."

I mentally review random people I know, trying to remember where they're from and whether they're diaphanous.

"What about southerners?"

He spreads his hands, indicating Los Angeles.

"This is southern, Chalo."

"South-easterners."

"... Not sure. Do you surf?"

"Do I look like I surf?"

"I don't know what a surfer looks like, Chalo" Grant says, and there's an odd note of (what sounds like) genuine warmth in his voice. "You might be an excellent surfer."

"Well, I don't surf."

"Just so."

He beams at me.

———

... There's a lot of tension in the club. The club is us bulls. I don't know if yaks are normally as uptight with each other as we are.

... The problem is a lot of the males are about the same age and the same size. If there was only one good-sized bull, a champion, the herd would be more you know kind of bland, because that scenario has zero uncertainty. Everybody knows who's going to be doing most of the mating. If it isn't you, that's too bad, but you're not moving up or down, you don't have to care about that.

... The normal, easygoing, everyday attitude we've had up until now, shouldering our way through blizzards and roving around grazing the scant fare up here, gobbling melica grass, licking rocks and dreaming for hours without moving, that's all fraying at the edges now.

... A daydreaming bull ambles up and then sees me and starts, whipping his horns around on me. I pivot to get a better look at him, surprising myself with my speed. I'm jumpy. He's jumpy. But his eyes are glazed, half-awake. The next moment he forgets what he's doing and stumbles away, through a mind portal, back into his daydream.

... Out of a dream of rhododendron and box myrtle, apples and juniper. Wild garlic, clematis, cedar. Impatient asters. Orchids with sweet, hand-shaped root tubers. Daisies, good for fever. Moon primrose, firethorn, pearly everlastings, bedstraw and gentian, frail with garlic and daphne ... and snow lotus, rare as diamonds.

... Into a dream of vaginas. A yak's vagina, with precisely regular folds, symmetrical, red, with a gleaming blade of urine sluicing from it. In this image, ever more distinct in the mind, all is contained. I know this intuitively. It makes me think of a cathedral, or of mysterious columns standing half-splashed in golden sunlight among the ruins of an ancient shrine. When I relax my mind, I naturally begin plotting its geometry using estimated measurements, determining surface area, degrees of curvature, criss-crossing it with the beautiful abstract lines I used to love when I was a man and could draw up plans and blueprints.

... Whether or not I've ever actually mated with a yak cow is not something I can call to mind, but given my age and size, I suppose I have. I don't think I'm a virgin yak. However, none of the club members is any offspring of mine. We all know exactly how we relate to each other. Just by listening to the sound of his grunt, noting the particular sway of his testicles, and, most important, the peculiar character of the notch where the bottom of the ear attaches to the head, I recognize the bull who just shied at me as my second cousin. This won't stop us from fighting each other, any more than my recognizing a cow as my mother or sister or daughter would stop me from mounting her -- or her from allowing it, for that matter -- but we'd know. We wouldn't care, but we'd know.

... My head is pre-stocked with exact information. Most of what I think of as my mind is only slop, but there's one corner where everything is neat and well-organized. It contains two items: family recognitions and grass varieties. At a glance I can distinguish between countless types of grass, using a sort of compound label that involves sweetness, bitterness, saltiness, chewiness, moisture, length, degree of greenness, scarcity, primary and secondary stomach feels, and likely stool consistency and odor. I gobble it all indiscriminately, I peruse the glume industriously, but I know what I eat, leaf by leaf.

Meanwhile, Grant talks ... Headlights nuzzle the edges of his face and crowd past his features, sort of muscling the pliable image on its way to me.

"The word 'world' has at least two meanings, Chalo."

Oh boy, I think. Oh great.

"One is, everything that is. Another, is, the idea I have, of what it is. By and by, as you go through life, and you come up against the limitations of your ideas, and you encounter people coming up against the limits of their ideas, and of your own, you realize, that your world, and their world, are not the same. Then, if you don't freak out, and start insisting you alone, are right, you will eventually arrive at an idea, of the world, that includes, other people's ideas. Some people, find, this idea, of the world ... disconcerting. Unstable. Most religious, or spiritual, seekers, are moved by the impulse, to find a more, stable world, all mapped out and thoroughly delineated, with their role in it, clearly marked. More importantly, once they have their, concept, in place -- whatever that means -- they believe they're ballasted by, all the others they can recruit, to it, since they are no longer alone, with their ideas.

"However, you can, Chalo, confront, the idea, that any world is unstable. Accept it, or convince yourself you've accepted it, take your stand, go it alone, like a bold nihilist advancing on the void. So --"

He gestures with his right and left hands as he speaks now, forming two sides of a balance with himself in the middle.

"-- you have your believers over here, and your skeptics, over here. One side, is supposed to be living a fantasy, the other side, is supposed to, reject fantasy, or to,at least confine it, to some kind of, lesser role in things."

He lowers his hands.

"Well, none of that interests me, Chalo. It doesn't seem to me that the world is split into fantasy and reality. It's all the world. There is no escape into a fantasy. But that's because the fantasy is also real, and so, it's still part of what you are trying to escape. Some people hope for that, that escape, all their lives, and that's as far as they get. Just hoping. Some kill themselves, either all at once, or inch by inch, in order to die into the better world. Maybe they get there. But who knows?

"Living with hope is enough for some people. As far as I'm concerned, though, dying to live makes no sense to me, and living with hope, is still too much like, waiting to live.

"People think in terms of worlds colliding, or in rivalry with each other. They want to replace one with another, as if there had to be only one, or maybe they want to turn the clock back, and live in the past. I think people are too hung up on worlds. What they really want, is something more than any one world could possibly give them."

The quiet intensity that has been running steadily in the background of his words takes a step toward me now.

"It's a kind of life that has no name, just like your typical love song is a monologue, not addressed to someone by name, but only to some *you*. Who listens in silence. Chalo, my whole fantasy is the real world, and what there is to reach out to is that *you*; it's the silence that listens when you call, not knowing."

Grant gazes at me neutrally, pacifically. That's the way he must scope out the wave as it folds up on top of him, watching to slip the hook and slide out along a nice long glassy lawn of seawater. Coming out the chute without wetting his hair.

"I still struggle trying to think of what name I can call the project I'm asking you to help me with. Giving it a name is only slightly less bad than not giving it a name, but for starters, I would call it an annex. Whatever it's called, I always end up having to explain and explain.

"... We can't be, quaint. It can't be just another hippie, new age commune. What I am going to accomplish requires a place that is at once real, and yet, not welded to the rest of reality. Only annexed to it. It has to be open, and new. It has to be a community, and a place where all kinds of experiments can happen -- technical, psychological, social, artistic -- any kind. It should have the maximum experimental potential, like a research lab."

"Expensive."

"I know. The toughest ... angle, to it, is that the thing has to be ... a kind of machine. It has to ... remake the people, who come to it, and remake the world, around it, but it can't be a world in itself. It has to be only, partially connected to the world. Those who confront the world -- confront it head on -- are destroyed by it, naturally. It's because the world is powerful, but also because there is no place to strike from, or to retreat to, that isn't in that world."

"That's been tried a million times, though."

"Well, I'm trying it again."

"So, what are you going to do different?"

"... A ... being ... is coming ... to earth, planet earth, Chalo. To Catalina Island. ... I am going to get some people together, and we are going to be there when it comes."

"A being? What being?"

"ASpecial Guest. An Ancient Newborn. ... If that's too religious-sounding for you, you might call it an embodiment of what physicists call 'work' ... a being of infinite joules. ... On a field sable, the letter W, joules."

Must be a private joke. That's not off-putting at all.

"... And this thing's coming?"

"It's coming."

"When?"

"... Within my lifetime."

"To do what?"

"... To set events in motion, that can't get started any other way. To get things going in the right direction, toward a kind of healing that isn't just a restoration of the way things were before ... but a real healing. ... A Special Guest will come to Catalina Island; that I know."

"How?"

"... I know it the way I know other things that have happened after I knew they would. ... A Special Guest is going to come to Catalina Island. It will do something that sets in motion, a sequence of events, that will balloon to vast proportions in the human world. Then it will go. Some human beings will have to be there, will have to bear witness, to it, and then help it -- be a part of that sequence of events. ... The annex must be built in that place, and there must be people there who are prepared and ready."

"You're crazy."

Grant smiles.

"Does that bother you?"

"Nothing bothers me if I get paid, I guess. ... No, I'm not bothered. I think you believe it, and as -- well, are you bothered if I don't believe it?"

▭

... From time to time a bluesy, scintillating deliciousness comes to me on the mountain air and stops me in my tracks. I blip away from time and I can't feel my body. All there is of me is a floating warm helix of golden cinders until it ends. I almost completely forget about it when it's over. It passes, going on somewhere else, too fleet for me to catch. I don't imagine it's the same one every time. It seems to me more like a smoke ring, a scrap of creation, of the big bang, perversely keeping its original nature and gambolling around in the universe for its own enjoyment.

... I fall in with the other stoic bulls and we file down into the valley with the floor of green spread out like a vast pizza of living grass. As we descend, the air becomes heady with ephedra and valerian, indigo, white mountain roses and Russian sage, purple blue salvia and a funny kind of asparagus, wine-black wool grapes and wild ginger. As a man, I could barely identify grass, but now my nose is a roomy botanical index that can distinguish automatically between over seventy different varieties of sageretia, with notes that make as plain as black and white the age, vigor, and ... charisma? Some plants are inherently more charismatic than others to me, and that registers as distinctly as the difference between hot and cold.

... I lower my head and graze in my sleep, half-awakening every now and then to find myself a number of yards from where I last knew I was, at the end of a barely discernible ribbon of cropped grass, now churning inside me like a load of cold green laundry. A trickle of green vitality in my turgid blood perks me up, but part of me says to keep it, put my head back down, stop thinking ... graze on, sleep, my lips working until they ache, scraping my eyeballs with bone-dry lids, unloading whopper turds on the cropped ribbon behind me. No whiff of females, but a blurry yak vagina satellite orbiting my mind slowly ...

... ok ok I get it. There's more to life than this, but not much more. There's imbroglios to come, crazed sex agonies after, then exhausted bewilderment in a shapeless period before the snow comes down on us, the bull clubs reform and stagger off, looking for a break from the smell and closeness of the cows -- who won't be sad to see us go either.

... I stand on the high rocks and remember. I don't know what's making me remember. You met me at the train station. Looking up from the floor, I see long hands stroking each other, silhouetted against the light background of the hall, the white walls, the white smears of light on the pale floorboards. A flash and it all turns to moonlight. I hear the sandy whisper the skin makes, and there's a shudder in the air and in me that's like a guttering candle, slumping down and bobbing up in deep pulses around a filmy hollow blaze, somehow tired the way I'm tired, windless, with a halo of tired around my head like a crown of cool, dead air.

Your word out of the gloom sounds like a throbbing note rung on a dish of water, with a taut waterhead, fully automatic in the way it returns its bent vibrations from the rim and collapses in the middle of the circle like a sort of self-kiss. The parcel of your voice drops like a sugary blob of ink into some obscurity, the air it displaces slides along one side of me, heeded by a warmth I carry for you that compasses me in toward the source of your voice, scattering veils of breath that settle back into the surrounding air while you and I wait for something.

The dark suppleness is going to pick us both up like beanbags and knead us together, all in one ethereal, shapeless palm that fills the room, and is wired by sinews to the cushion the world always sways on. That is bound to happen, one of these minutes. But for now, it's your one word, and the shadows of long hands stroking each other, your shadow stroking my shadow, and blending unmixed with the bulb of gloom encompassing us both, without up or down, or any direction at all except together, where the diaphragm underneath dimples and settles, funneling you and me into its middle, to slip among each other like yolks. Floating around a warm thumb of interstellar space, exploring the room toward each other. The day sinks like a baffled sun through the heart of the room and everything is made of sleep and time gone by. I'm still looking up at your hands from the floor, and I know that it's almost too late for me, there's so much time in your hands, the way they rub together, cascading time between them.

This is the time of you and me, that's why it's so strange, because my groping brain can't find the pronoun that means you and me at once even though my body knows exactly where it is and how to find it. Just now, at the lip of the slide, barely above the tipping point, feeling time lift and shudder in me, hesitating, wandering, losing itself.

Then ... much later ... the same threadbare old stomach of shame of being me, is going to close around me again.

⊏⊐

"This ..."

Grant gestures at the world.

"... is bullshit. Everyone knows that. Not everyone admits it. But everybody knows it. What you want to work with is dreams, and you want work, that dreams."

"What about the dreamer? What does the dreamer eat? What roof does the dreamer dream under?"

"I'm not sure yet. They aren't dreamers though, they're workers. The work is what dreams."

"Dreams about what?"

" That's a problem, Chalo, because, I would say, heaven ... but all the ideas of heaven that I know are just that it isn't hell. I know it's real, but apart from its being good, and populated, and eternal, I don't know what it is."

"So do you want, like, an artist's colony?"

"Sort of, but not quite. That's closer, though."

He doesn't seem to know what he's talking about, so why does he seem to know exactly what he's doing?

"I don't really see people caring that much about that kind of thing anymore. I'll be honest with you."

"It could be the best time, then."

Two waiters pass our table. One is saying -- "So it's going to be Desiree's tomorrow."

"Let's talk about your work. Show me some of your designs."

He points to one of the sheets I've slopped out on the table between the bean sprout burritos and the matcha kombucha.

"Do you have any pictures of this finished?"

I do. He studies them. He taps one picture with a corner of the other.

"Have you done any more like this one?"

"I'm just implementing other people's designs right now."

"Do you feel held back by that?"

"Nope. ... Our designer is pretty touchy. He's easily offended. So, I don't make changes."

"So giving you design work makes your designer feel threatened."

"Pretty much."

Now Grant wants to show Catalina to me. He doesn't drive, but he does ride, so I'm picking him up at the Equestrian Center. The site I'm working at now is swamped all that week in unseasonable rain, my car is so splattered with mud dried right up to the windows, and not a little on the windshield, too, you'd think it was a rally car.

"Sorry about all the mud."

Coming down concrete steps, Grant just smiles. His gait is loose and easy, and he swings into the passenger seat in one fluid motion. He's all in white, again.

So now comes the long drive down to Long Beach. Suddenly he tells me he needs to make a stop downtown. I pull onto the off ramp.

We stop at a light and he tells me to turn right, even though that's not the way to go. I'm in no hurry, so I turn.

"Now turn here ... no -- next street ... put your hazards on ..."

"My hazards?"

"Go slowly ..."

He's looking down the street, which is lined with parked cars. A bank truck is double-parked in the middle of the block, back open. I'm about to say something when he tells me to pull over and let the two cars behind us pass. Next thing I know he's hopped out of the car, leaving the door ajar. He walks up to the bank truck just as one of the uniformed guards steps around to say something to the other one on the sidewalk, and I see a money bag drop out the back of the truck and land on the street just below the rear bumper. Grant is two strides away.

He takes those strides, crouches, reaches under the open door, snags the sack, straightens, and keeps walking toward the front of the truck, sack in his right hand and behind him, left hand fingers flipping at me to pull forward which I do, and he tosses the sack into the footwell and slides into the passenger seat, pulling the door to without shutting it and nodding me to pull on.

"He won't come around until we turn the corner if you keep moving, but don't speed up."

His eyes have a hard, excitable light in them, as if he were spoiling to be accosted, like there was more he could do in this line if he were given the chance.

"Don't hurry ..."

I reach the corner and mean to look back but, passing a parked van, a bum is suddenly revealed, standing nearly at the corner, wrapped in rags from head to toe and standing perfectly still.

The next thing I know, I've turned onto Las Palmas and Grant is regally letting his breath out through his nose. At the next intersection he finally shuts his door. At the intersection after that, he casually reaches down and shoves the money bag under his seat and out of sight.

"Is that thing going to blow up?"

"It would have blown up by now if it was going to."

"I don't want that thing blowing up in here!"

"It won't blow up."

"... You see?" he says a block later.

"Well don't open it in here -- could the driver have seen my license plate?"

"He was leaning across the seat. He was talking to the other one."

"What about cameras?"

"Most trucks don't have cameras."

"Most?"

"You can report the car stolen if you're worried ... But the camera would have to have a trowel attached to read your plates, there's so much mud on them."

"... You're a thief!"

A little smile, a little spill of air from his nostrils. He has the spectre cigarette effect again.

"No comment?"

"It's the people's money."

"I know it's the people's money, it *was* the people's money! Now it's *your* money!"

"Our money."

"You're not paying me with that."

"This is a partnership. Neither of us pays the other. It was going to be turned into hell money. Now it is going to go toward realizing a higher purpose."

"... How much you think is in there?"

"I don't know," he says, as if his not knowing were a little surprising. "We should postpone our trip to the island to another day. Are you free Wednesday?"

I park near Pershing Square, get out, dump the contents of a cardboard box full of papers and plans I have in the trunk, and Grant stows the sack in it. He's going to take the metro.

"You're a thief."

Grant beams at me. Infinite love, infinite love.

———

... The club is angling down along a green ridge lushed up deep like green flame smoking with mist, but the smell isn't getting through to me. My nose is cloggy. Come to think of it, I feel kind of lousy -- do yaks catch colds? It doesn't seem as if a yak should be susceptible to colds. But, yeah, I have that same feeling, like there's a small spotlight of heat at the back of my throat, and sluicings and teemings going on in my enormous sinuses. It's like a fancy fountain in there. And capsule elevators travelling up and down like at the Bonaventure Hotel. There's also a hard, possibly metallic ledge lightly denting the backs of my eyes.

... A muddy, trampled field, pockmarked with bootprints. Seepings. Mucus, in at least a dozen varieties and consistencies, is all I can smell. It's demoralizing to stand here having a cold. The wind tugs at my long, chewed-up pelt, but it can't worry its way closer to the skin, and I'm uncomfortably warm.

... A memory comes back to me. A man I worked for, Mr. Denigas, endlessly harassed about his name which he pronounced DEN-gus, rejected a proposal I put together for a strip mall. Maybe the idea was no good: breaking up the outline and canting the store-fronts outward so you didn't have to walk right by it to see what each store was -- or maybe it was an OK idea badly presented, but he never told me what was wrong with it. He claimed he was swamped, exhausted, but I knew he was fed up with me. The next few jobs he gave to some of the others, including an engineer he'd quarreled with. I knew there was nothing seriously wrong, that I wasn't about to lose my position, but it nettled me, not being told anything. Taking another look, now that I'm a yak, I notice how my employer's spine was just starting to bow forward, and how much grey there was in his hair. He was turning into a papery old man.

... Did I live to get old? I don't remember it.

... So now, is this me dead? And no memory of getting old, or of anything particularly deadly happening to me?

... I remember a life choked with shame, unaccountable shame, then Grant, Catalina, working with AC, being there when the book people were summoned, but ... dried and curling, infinite love, and no old folks' home, no social security check, no high-contrast violent scene or accident. ... Is Chalo dead? Is he dead, *and* having a cold? Or dreaming that he's a yak with a cold? Whose dream is this?

... The chill mud beneath the grass is making my front left hoof ache. When I lower my head, I can hear the gristle in my neck popping like a wet rubber wheel rolling on fine gravel. When did Mr. Denigas forgive me for whatever it was I did? When can I lower my head directly into the earth and sleep, vacantly watching the forever of the horizon?

... Will somebody ever forgive me for anything? All I want to feel is forgiven. A turd flops out of my hindquarters. It has made its contribution to the poetry of the moment. I would do something to get myself in trouble, if I had the spirit for it, just to be able to get a bit of that motherload of forgiveness Grant had unlimited access to. If I could get forgiven for being sick I wouldn't stop being sick, but I'd wake up refreshed. Everything is a mystery.

... Forgiveness as permission to sin. I won't hold it against you, old pal, old chum. Buddy.

... I notice something lying among the rocks at my feet. As a yak, I don't know what it is, but as a former man I know it's a piece of glass edged with swimming-pool blue, with that smoothness that can make glass look soft as ice with its own meltwater still clinging to it. What a thing.

... The upbuildingness I always needed, that feeling of "on and up" I got from my work with Grant, is gone. Now my life is one vacant moment after another, standing up and falling down. Nothing's happening. I'm a yak; like any other yak. Doing all the same things, not special at all. I should feel completely satisfied, then, right? I should feel my days as full as can be. Why me? That's not the question -- I mean anyway who else? -- but ... a yak? Why a yak?

... From between my sickness and my tiredness comes a sharp feeling of grief over my bygone purposes, because I guess animals don't have destinies. But then, I don't feel ashamed of myself anymore either. That old companion has abandoned me. My vade mecum of glum resignation at being just Chalo is gone with the wind.

... I never know what time it is. Even the darkness and light of the sky aren't really night and day, they're only similar to night and day. The cold is retreating. The warmth is advancing. But I don't experience the change of seasons, just "now hot" and "now cold." With a glimmering memory of the one while I'm feeling the other. This isn't time that's passing. It's space, like the edges of space slipping down around me.

... But I look out over the fiery green valley, see the sturdy bulls and cows, all the resolution of the landscape and the plants and animals and all the symphonic anarchy of striving that shrieks and laughs in the grass blades and hard shrubs, of privet and anisodus, luculia and jasmine, gastrodia mating with fungus on a rotting log, and mulberry, and wallichia triandra, and birds going off like rockets, flickering bugs and little bounding animals, pikas, I think, in the tufts, and big old yaks mincing and chewing over them, swaying massive heads like stormclouds over the forest of grass, turning for a moment to regard without thinking the white ribbon of meltwater siphoning between the rocks to fall into a frothing pool, white on black, and ringed with stones, pouring out to swell the brook there, travelling.

... If Chalo is dead, and his former person reincarnated as a yak, a yak with a cold, or dreaming this in his coffin, then I've outlived my destiny and this is ever after. If I were stronger just now, that would make me feel free.

━━

Grant is nothing but voice mail for a few weeks after he snags that money sack, then the one Sunday I forget to turn off my phone at naptime he rings me up.

"Hello Chalo!" he says, as jovial as a grandfather. "What would you say to a trip to the bank with me tomorrow? I'm going to California Fedality and I would really appreciate it if you were on board."

I can hear children playing in the background. Great whoops.

What I'd say is "balls" but for some reason I don't, I agree to pick him up at a Tibetan restaurant in San Gabriel around noon and drive him all the way downtown. He skips out the door briskly, greeting me with a toss of his head. I notice I'm getting too accustomed to his profile against my passenger window. He talks, and I glance and glance again.

The Sorbente Group occupies a few levels of a glass box high rise, trying to camouflage itself against the sky, hiding in plain view like the banks. An open floor plan with Richard Serra derivative metal dividers like battleship bulkheads. Everything else is white stuff or glass, with an even refrigerator glare boring down from recessed LEDs, creating tech islands in a sort of mysterious labyrinth.

There's a receptionist but no reception desk. The receiving zone has slab benches of some white material, embedded in white planters filled with smooth white stones and raked white sand. The receptionist is a skinny white woman with a thin layer of white fuzz covering her scalp. She wears a tastefully bland blue t-shirt, very crisp, with creased white trousers and grey sneakers that all look brand new.

"Have a seat, gentlemen," she says, gesturing to a bench.

There are a few other people sitting there, and she pays no attention either to them or to us, keeping her gaze calmly and steadily fixed on the door, her hands clasped in front of her as if she were leading herself in a waltz. A portentous stillness sifts down from the decor onto us, like white soot from white chimneys over white furnaces burning white phosphorous, cold as ice. Somehow the name of the company floats in ectoplasmic grey light against the partition facing the glass doors, only subtly contrasting with the grey background. Occasional bits of graphic snow float down across it and gleam.

As if she had been counting down a set interval, the woman turns to us at last.

"What can I help you gentlemen with today?"

"We're here to discuss a loan," Grant says.

"Mm'all right then just a moment I'll get you set up. Can you tell me roughly the amount you are looking to borrow today?"

"I would prefer to discuss that with a loan officer," Grant says, apologetically.

"I understand perfectly sir. But, we do not actually employ loan officers; we have loan originators. Are you familiar with the term, loan originator?"

"I'm afraid not."

"Loan originators have more direct contact with loan genesis agents -- you might remember them as underwriters. May I ask whether or not the loan is personal or --?"

"Again, that would be something for me to discuss with the one you refer to as the loan originator."

"I understand. Someone will be with you shortly to discuss your loan. Is there anything else I can help you with right now?"

"No, thank you."

"Mm'all right then I'll just be right here if you need anything and please don't hesitate to ask."

She pivots back into her original position and replaces her eyes on the door.

Grant leans a bit over to me.

"-- I don't think you should mention your work with Financial Advisors."

"But that's some of my best work. Leave that out, I haven't got much else."

"Nothing anyone does in New York is going to interest a California banker. -- You haven't done any playgrounds, have you? California playgrounds?"

"No, sorry."

"Tell him you really want to."

The woman turns to us again.

"Mr. Browlshweer is free."

As she speaks, an arrow of blue light appears on the edge of one of the metal dividers, pointing toward an opening. We follow a series of such arrows to a circular office area, and, as we enter the enclosure of the Serra walls, a faint circle of blue light appears on the floor, outlining the "office." The circle grows steadily brighter, then fades abruptly without entirely disappearing. There's no desk here either, and a man is now standing in the middle of the circle, smiling and waiting for us. The moment we cross the circle, he steps forward and extends his hands.

"Hello, I'm Steve Browlshweer."

The hand I take is just a neutral member.

He's wearing casual slacks and casual jacket, polo shirt, with no necktie. The absence of the necktie has a stealth-wealth way of calling attention to itself. His eyeglasses are almost invisible, and seem to contain small points of autonomously moving light.

"Will you both be comfortable walking with me?"

He gestures toward a fold in the barrier. I get a cold pang. No I will not be comfortable walking with this person. I am not comfortable standing with this person.

"Sure," Grant says.

"So, what brings you to us?"

We are in an irregular passageway that's scalloped like the Sydney opera house. I see a few people, dressed more or less like Steve Browlshweer, drifting up and down, gazing at the metal partitions like patrons at an art gallery. The partitions are crawling with projected displays in muted, low-contrast light. It's as though the walls were decorated with a lot of mirrors of all sizes, drifting, and flickering. They are screens, full of light, captive and articulated.

"We need to fund a construction project."

"I see. What kind of project?"

"A campus."

"A college?"

"Collegial, but not a college."

So now we're walking, but I feel like we're on a conveyor belt, and everything here is on conveyor belts or turntables, everything's gliding. Always gliding, gliding, gliding. Nothing's fixed relative to anything else. Makes me a little nauseous and a lot suspicious, all this glide glide. Why is everything gliding? When you glide like that, not like on the wind, not like in an actual glider, but this way, it's because you're actually very firmly rooted to some moving belt or wheel. You glide because you're fixed to glide, and all the stuff that glides isn't gliding to any destination but just gliding, gliding in place. So the gliding is really a way of giving fixed elements an illusion of lightness and mobility.

"What *is* college?" Grant asks.

"Where will you be looking to build this campus?"

"Catalina. Do you know the island?"

"And how much are you looking to borrow?"

The Loan Originator is steering us with an occasional point of his finger. He does not look at either of us. It's as if he were talking to us on a speaker phone. He has a white ring on the middle finger of his right hand, and there's a piercing blue light where the stone would be.

"Two million. We would start small."

The Loan Originator begins to walk more rapidly, touching luminous spots on the partitions with his middle finger as he goes by. My body hops strangely as I accelerate to keep up with him. He makes a spiral gesture with his middle finger and spreads open his left hand. A panel of feeble light the color of a raincloud appears in his left hand like a floating sheet of paper. Still walking, he makes flourishes over the panel with his middle finger.

"Two million," he says to the panel. "I'll need your credit information. Just send it to me from your phone."

Grant holds out a piece of glass, as if he were beaming data from it to the hand of the Loan Originator.

"I'm not getting anything," he says. He never takes his eyes from the panel above his hand, but deftly weaves around people coming the other way and follows the irregularities of the floorplan effortlessly.

"Hm," Grant says. "Must be an incompatibility."

He puts the piece of glass away.

"Should I just tell you what you need to know?"

"Start with income."

"I have no income at the moment. Only assets."

"Assets in what amount?"

Grant produces a bank statement from the inside pocket of his linen jacket, or shirt -- jacket, I suppose -- and offers it to the Loan Originator, who doesn't seem to notice it at first, and then jerks aside when he does, as if he'd mistaken it for a poisonous insect.

"I'm sorry, but this is a no-paper establishment."

"Oh, I beg your pardon."

"That's all right," Steve Browlshweer says, briskly resuming his walk and returning his attention immediately to his hand. "Just tell me the value of your assets, verbally."

"Two hundred thousand."

The Loan Originator seems to be waiting for more. Grant is gliding along with him, taking in the surroundings.

"I really like this space. The openness is refreshing."

This is bullshit. The floorplan is open but there's no openness; Grant's calling attention to it only makes me notice its various suffo- cations working around me, withdrawing air through screens.

"Thank you," the Loan Originator says, and with what might be a little spasm of impatience he asks -- "Uh can you tell me please the breakdown of the assets in terms of how much in stock, how much in property, and so on?"

"Oh, it's all cash."

"Cash, thank you."

More finger flourishing.

"Now Mr. Grant I will have to ask you some security questions in order to ascertain your credit history."

"Just Grant, please."

Nameless little swirlies and streaks, throbbing logos, are all a gaze without the eyes, an expressionless gaze without the eyes that settles coldly down on you. They watch me, but they don't see me.

"With us, a voluntary disclosure is an automatic process. You've made an unclear statement that needs further clarification."

"I'm ready to cooperate in any way you require."

The Loan Originator's screen flickers with a steady seething crawl of information. His eyes widen and his face, made ghastly by the light from the panel in his hand, lengthens. He looks up at Grant, at last.

"You have *no* credit. ... You have no rating, not even a zero."

For a moment I wonder if he's going to have us thrown out.

"Do you see?"

He turns the screen in midair toward Grant, who doesn't even glance at it.

"I can't read screens. I can't even see images on screens."

Grant gestures at his eyes.

"All the sun I get off the waves, it's affected my vision."

"To determine reinsurance, customer expenses resulting in decreases are ceded to companies and reinsurance companies and expenditures must be evaluated with priority given to the enhancement of a.) providing insurance protection in the donation amendments and the actuarial gains in capitalized statements of net cost --"

We are walking faster and faster. The Loan Originator speaks galvanically.

"-- which is an unclear statement that needs cash estimations and the useful life of the furniture for example reported separately with a whole range of protections to the end of each lease term, with remaining costs for any shortage, not including the administrative operating costs, but restricted to the specific functions of life as it should be clearly stated that securities --"

We're zooming through this endless open floor plan at a quick march, our feet all hitting the floor in perfect sync. A flicker of impatience crosses the Loan Originator's face when we don't respond to the light cues, and he steers us by pointing with that blazing middle finger, raising his arm in a way that makes me think of old cartoon stoplights.

"-- issued by the department to the unearned premium reserve associated with the company's operations in order to maintain accordance with market demand while including operations for which the capital equipment lease committee has been set up to maintain prudent underwriting b.) consolidating the value of the items the company is underwriting notwithstanding and assigned to operating investing and financing activities --"

Where are we going? It's like we're flying into another dimension. Hell. I glance over at Grant. He seems like he's surfing, his face relaxed, neutral, his hair rippling in an ocean breeze.

"Nice for *you*," I think, panting. "You *are* a surfer."

"-- from inception date through the assistance in the expansion of previous years recorded from health and pension plans by the board of directors, the office of personnel management, in a forward-looking policy as always, trying to disclose any of the treasury and equipment assets at the inception held by the public as part of the lease or the leasehold improvement and depreciation recognized by each agency at cost amounts in the interest, c.) exerting efforts to maintain explanations of any items that the current year's program allocated to their user agencies for which the statements of net cost are amortized over the straight-line reserve we always attach, including the company's charges to operations upon retirement, for further clarification from the external individual agency regarding non-federal net payment of cash on hand, which is five years, while the estimated useful property plant and equipment claim costs and unearned premiums of administrative operating costs in reinsurance programs are maintained as transparently as possible while net cost amounts will differ in --"

I am beginning to think that the Loan Originator isn't taking us to any specific place.

"-- consequence of this policy because the net cost is originally assisting management with the determination benefit program costs and eliminations respecting the general services administration, such as are classified into accumulated depreciation eliminations and recorded at cost leasehold improvements of the future minimum lease payments, which are the present value of factors that decreased profit flows present in the receipts and buy/sell revenues, and imputed costs for which it is reasonable as this situation is presented in an accrual basis for the estimated useful growth of premium income results and losses, if applicable, for property plant and equipment reinsurance protection which will enable the company's risk insurance capacity, upon the end of the useful lives of the assets, to sustain the 'credibility' and 'service quality,' whereas the net statements of cash, because of the importance of good corporate governance, are recognized for the receipt caused by below-projected profit, that is the negative deemed as an unrestricted increase in incurred claims lower than that of the goods and services financed in automatic processes by an engagement resulting from any matters related to the company, as adjusted for buy/sell costs and related revenues returned to the lessor individual agency, the company and the dollar amounts involved needed for insurance protection primarily because of allocations of net cost amounts because providing agencies are added to in addition for imputed costs to be met for the purpose of global competition d.) minimising the operating company's liquidity and earnings, including our commitment to transparency --"

▭

The sun is going down, the wind is rising. At night, the fires become livid rents in the darkness, and the screaming, the sirens, the helicopters, the wind become more frightening, more intimate. They get more inside you, like a dream.

Chalo's blanket is cold. A chill breeze pours steadily over his face, drying out his drooping mouth and his eyes, tousling the crazy tufts of hair protruding at random from his bandages.

"Hold up! ... Almost forgot one!"

A big pair of hands grabs the handles of Chalo's wheelchair.

"Wouldn't want to forget you, buddy, yeah?"

The glass door, the dim room, the veil of shadow thrown over his face as he bumps and rattles toward the hall.

"Would you get the lights?"

A funnel of despair: the vague hallway of grey hair, stale chlorine, regular doors, blurry ashes, bogus light that doesn't really come from anywhere, staining whatever it touches. The whole building is carved out of nicotine and it sits in a run-off puddle of soiled time and flaccid space that drips in and drips out lifelessly.

This is not a plague hospital. There's no urgency. No spirit of anxious watching. No battle fatigue. This is just a regular clinic for people with ordinary, uninteresting problems. Problems of no consequence. No cure will be discovered here.

Chalo is wheeled into his room.

Snap. Snap snap.

"Shit."

A burly figure kneels by his chair and thrusts something round into Chalo's hand.

"Power's out again, bud. I got to go check on the dialysis patients. You push that if you need me, OK?"

Footsteps.

"I'll be right back."

No patients on life support. Nothing dramatic. A power outage is not a serious emergency here.

Chalo in the chair. All grey. Allgrey allgrey. The call button tumbles down into his crotch from his limp hand. His tepid blood settles. His pulse ebbs. His diaphragm heaves, his throat clicks and gurgles. Grey breathing. The grey light around the edges of the blinds is frozen in place.

... Yaks always know what time it is.

... Why did I just think that? I have no idea what time it is.

... The sun is high in the sky, so it must be near midday ... but the horizon is also so high, that it might as well be dusk.

... My cavernous insides suddenly go cold. A weird, sourceless horror is welling up in me like icewater. *I don't know what time it is.* All at once I am invisible. I have no shadow, and exist in myself, but nowhere else.

... Where did the other yaks go? What is this mountain? And the plunging valley that seems to snap like a bedspread, motionless, piebald with big wet black glistening patches and green-brown hummocks -- it's not on Earth. It's not on the Earth.

... The sun is the same but the light is different -- or maybe the reverse. The sun is in disagreement with its own light. What's going on? It's like my body is opening up, letting a freezing wildfire in. In my mind, I'm bucking and snorting and flailing my head, but my body is stock still, and actually relaxing against my will. Am I dying?

... The vacant sunlight, the bare slope of the mountain, and the silent valley. I'm not where I was. SoI've been walking after all. I'm here, now. I'm here enough to know that I don't seem to myself to be here. I'm climbing, and the slope folds and turns upwards here in a dry flume that's as smooth as an esophagus.

I'm following the warped crease of the fold upwards now.

... Nothing bigger than grass and wildflowers grows up here, but the light coming down on me is all broken up, as if tree branches roofed the flume over. The soil here is chocolate-colored and damp, but not slippery.

... The flume ends in an incline, evenly-covered with smooth stones. Chalky blue and dull green, whitish-grey and watery pink. They waver, shimmering, even though there is no water there. Fragments of shale and siltstone, greywacke, granite, and schist. Up past this phantom waterfall, the land widens out in a bowl with steep green sides rising nearly straight up to egg-shaped peaks of raw basalt. The mysterious water is doing some kind of work here too; it's like the bowl is littered with invisible bodies sleeping under invisible blankets of flowing invisible water. The blue of the sky is concentrated by the bowl; visibly boundless thickness of blue with tiny dark points in it, like stationary birds frozen in midflight, miles and miles up.

Turning my ears to detect the soft noise of their breathing, I pick my way carefully among the sleepers. A magnetic feeling drags my hooves, so there's an extra tug when I raise them and a slight pull and click when I set them down again, leaving no footprints in the satiny green grass. My every movement creates fragrant turbulences. The perfume is like incense, as if this meadow were smoking.

... Now I see a line -- a descending line -- a diagonal -- where what I thought was the backside of the bowl is actually one slope of my point of view superimposed in front of another one, and there's another way in back of it. That diagonal line conjures in my mind the image of Grant surfing down a huge wave, cutting a drooping white seam diagonally across the concavity of the breaker with his arms held out lightly as a bird in flight, knees bent, his perfect hair hovering around his collected face. So what's up there? Thinking of the wave I am aware of avalanches trembling all around me, like demons on a tripwire; the outlines of the avalanches are already there, already happening, but the mass and the matter of the avalanches is elsewhere. For the moment.

This isn't going to last. That seems true. It isn't possible for me to stay here, although it is possible for me to get lost or trapped here. I infer all this with a certainty I can't explain.

... I round the edge of the diagonal and enter the alley beyond, which is just a rock-strewn, refreshingly ordinary passage up and through, formed by a cleft in the granite curtain. No weird water, no sleepers, no breathing. But still the disembodied feeling. Not knowing what time it is. There's a smell that makes me twist my head around -- I was thinking about how I see, because I've walked up slopes before and, as a man, I kept my eyes on the top without noticing the sides. I would zoom in on the top, then zoom in on the rocks at my feet. Now, without binocular eyes, I see like a still point in the middle of a moving field.

... The smell is jasmine. I've never smelt that so high up.

... It isn't jasmine anyway.

... My left eye locks on to a dolmen against paper-white sky, like an actor alone on an empty stage, and the outline selects me. It singles me out for an announcement that's like being given a new name, changing me so that I'm exactly the same. I know that doesn't make sense, but here it does.

A coruscating, multicolored jumble of smooth shapes flashes down, cutting my knot, and I spring up without moving, like a jack in the box bursting up my weight. The feeling that I even have a body at all just vanishes, and I am young with weightlessness that wants to scramble all over every inch of everything, and fly around ricocheting off myself. I didn't ask to have this feeling and I hate having it inflicted on me like this by the dolmen, which is walking away from me on thick turtle legs, but it's the rotation of the planet that's carrying it off. I haven't budged, but inside there's rushing and flips being performed, gymnastics, wind chimes being blown nearly down.

... Eventually, though, my head droops. I breathe deeply. There's lightness, exhaustion, surprise, disappointment. There's feeling emptied out sweetly, in a way I resent. I have no idea what just happened. The place has a familiar ... something -- it just is familiar, I guess. Not just because rocks are all alike, but the place has some claim on my memory *I guess*, or some place like it. There are no tracks in the soft ground here but mine. I suppose I made them all just now. I lower my head further -- I want to lie down, I want to mash my forehead into black clay and feel it suck the heat from my brow, but my fucking horns won't let me.

I glance down the slope. I'm flying. Instantly. Bolting. No fatigue at all, just boundless force. The sun beams power into me and cracks a crystal flail in the air, lashing me on down the slope like a runaway train, where I barrel around the corner of the alley, lose my footing, and tumble over onto my side, my stupid legs rigid in the air and then down under me, up and charging again, headlong, heedless of the invisible water streams that I dash and shatter and throw up around me in a ghost shawl of magic water, trampling sleepers and beating the shit out of the fucking ground, roaring down the long slope, all the way down -- like an avalanche I'm gonna ram the planet head first, gonna smash it in half!

Wands of daylight graze the tile floor of the day room. A helicopter hovers very low, very near, for a very long time. The day room vibrates dully with its noise. Sirens rise and fall, but there are fewer now.

Chalo sits in his wheelchair and remembers the way that, some-how, hands have contrived to form a bubble, the edges gleaming, strands bulging among interlaced fingers, we the palms, lifting like breath in an upward floating movement, and the unhurried heavy downfall of the sweeps, the coils of the dragon rampaging in the silence and the shadow broadcast by this moment, off the ground, elastically propelling itself through a cindery perfume that smells like silence, and the warm gloom of mouths and eyes opening to cry vertical rays that pry apart dense ethers, unconsciously meticulous to separate each page with probing murmurs, blurred answers that play against the bell of the glass like flames, glowing voices ply fraying beams rippling like flashlight puddles as they sweep over uneven ground, caress the form from it and lave it with air foam, sea shout, bodies molded from inside out, weltering in clear fragrant oil, what we call water, and names us alternately one by one, slipping through every body in us, forming a little streak of motion, spinning like a top where our bodies meet the whir, trembling in both, so hard it's been, so difficult, so unworthy, so let us, why not let us -- gradually the cables slide loose from the knot, uncurling, they knit bundles, borne under and then abruptly switch sides, turn around and link, turn back, return, kiss, knit, go blank, get stern, wear down, grow up, and get rewound, keep waiting, wait, stop!

Wait!

Wounds like folded envelopes, whipped egg whites float up, hover above the body like clouds scudding just beyond the land, tracking the rain's footprints back to the rising eminence of cauliclouds dangling their colorless ringlets, engulfed in fresh air the joints are unstrung, the music vehemently becalmed, the head vast and darkly suffused with bright air, you swept, you felt, you roamed, you stole, you swore, you wailed, you strove, you groaned, you hoped, you sloped, you swept, you foamed, you made.

... Wound down at the end into the sterile old stomach of shame. All this in the gloom of that cavernous head, spreading into the air like a smudge. So vast, and so dwindled. Chalo, one person, a common enough memory, wound of daylight straying around the floor, from north to west, from east to east, going nowhere, already gone, and the remains, and their motionless tears.

A weeiirrd daayyy for AC -- all very very swimmy and like being underwater, but without the weight.

"That's not *educational!*" a woman says into her cell phone. "Why don't you all call me ..."

She feels like a dazed soldier wandering away from cover, taking no precautions where all possible precautions might be not enough.

She should retreat to a safe place and pull herself together.

Sharpen up, or go home.

The people around her ripple and smear the air as they move. The image of the former posture persists with the motion happening inside it, like the bird twisting inside the egg. Then the image firms together, burns in lightly, and the next motion blurs in back of it and through it, smooth and ratcheting at the same time.

As always, her own movements are normal. Her disguise is still perfect. She is a three-dimensional shadow. She absorbs all the glaring, painfully, and that keeps her surface tension together so she can glide along in reality like a bead of water skipping unmixed out to the edge of the surface of the pool. She's wide awake but the light and noise are so overwhelming she can't focus her attention, and her fierce core is balked.

There are two cops standing on the corner, bulky in all their gear, talking cop talk to each other. It sounds like the noises an obese asthmatic would make in his sleep; it's just a groaning, rattling mutter, like sleeptalking. They look asleep. All the cops have the same expressionless faces, eyes half closed in disdainful repose. Even when they pull someone aside to reproach them for something, even when they are angry, their eyes are half closed, their faces slack. One glances at her as she goes by and makes a remark to his partner.

"Awgk'g, 'enhh hunh. 'Glaehn."

The sound makes her want to slam shut like a pillbug.

Numbly she walks across cancer -- campus. Campus. Something down below wants to disrupt her jealously-protected silence. Her personality is getting queasy with her.

If it's motion sickness, then stop moving.

She stops where she is, without raising her eyes from the pavement. After a moment and without any looking around she pivots and walks into the shade beneath the high porch of the administration building. There she stops, half in the light, between the flat, square pillars.

This is a compromise, because she does not allow herself to be completely in any alien shade, because that would mean adulterating her own, special shade with some other shade.

It's bad, she tells herself. She should have the strength to resist daylight on her own yes, but it's worse to succumb -- this is the way to continue resisting right now, now is her autopilot correct? Is she right to go on automatically, or is she forgetting?

There's nothing else on her to-do list.

No nothing, so go on.

Going on to the library she passes a garden, like a tiny park on campus, in a sunken rectangle cut feathery and blackly green in white pavement. She sees the white figure in the park and has stopped and is gazing at him fixedly, something too quick to see brushed beneath her chin and she raised her head to look around -- which she usually would never do -- and the figure emerged from the day and the gloom of the garden, and the intense silence she only has just noticed, to give her attention something at last to focus on. As if he had been waiting there to give her attention to himself.

He's sitting cross-legged on a plain slab of white concrete, surrounded by people sitting in a semicircle on the grass. Over his white linen clothes he's thrown a sheet of white lace that falls down over his face, down to the center of the his back, over his shoulders, down to the breastbone. Around his neck, through the veil, she can see his dzi bead. He rocks and begins to chant in a soft, sing-song, voice, dulled as if she were hearing it through a thin wall --

"amadaraha bin darabai shabti, diya achan chahar diddi nachuya, abindagarala dahin dahinsaha, woyinja degun hashetanka"

-- the voice swoops casually up and down and the hands rise and fall in a routine, signing the phrases in a almost casually.

AC catches herself watching this, and puts herself back on track -- to the library.

The words roll along with her. Like a weightless shotput rolling around and around the inside her crown.

What was that? Was it bullshit? If it were bullshit she wouldn't have even noticed it. She is immune to bullshit. This involved bullshit but without being bullshit, because it can't not have bullshit in it, this day being part bullshit and part not, so the action of the veiled man was a kind of reflection, giving back bullshit for bullshit.

She wants to know if there is anything but bullshit. AC resists bullshit and insists on being separate from it all, like a veiled figure. So, was that her? Sitting there, chanting a language she doesn't know?

... Later that day, she sees the linen outfit again.

The man in the linen outfit has taken off his veil. His glossy half-grey hair only looks too perfect to be real; it is clearly the same man, standing with his back to her, posting a flier on the message board outside the student union. He glides away, giving her only a vague impression of a placid, sunbrowned face.

DO YOU KNOW TIBETAN?
Translator needed. Pay by the hour.

The top of the flier has a snarling three-eyed face on it. She's familiar with the face and likes it a lot, and doesn't like anybody else liking it.

Tibetan language study was one of the courses her expulsion from Cal State had forced her to interrupt. She was taking it again now, not because she was interested in it, but because it allowed her to complete her language requirement without having to attend a regular class, in a room full of *people*. Crowds are good places to hide, but the proximity of other people has a way of driving her gradually frantic. Independent study is not easy either, insofar as it means facing off with another *person* with nowhere to hide, but it was possible for her to get through a *personal session* without needing to rush to the bathroom halfway through. While AC doesn't like her, the Tibetan instructor is a pretty bland, inoffensive soul. AC plans on forgetting all of it, along with everything else she's ever been forced to learn, but she has come to admire the impermeability of the difficult Tibetan writing system, as well as the almost total lack of people to speak Tibetan with. Even Latin is better known, at least around here, and childishly easy to read in comparison.

Soshe does know the sketchiest Tibetan, *the sketchiest Tibetan in hell or heaven*, and she also needs money -- her library pay barely covers bus and lunch. The long-haired man ...

... so later Grant and Chalo are going on campus and ...

"That's not *educational!*" a woman says, her tone half indignant and half mocking. "Why don't you all call me ..."

We set our after-images on sustained decay and disengage from the Loan Originator, who keeps on obliviously boring through spaceintime with his auger of fiduciary douche talk. Sidestepping back to street level is like siphoning through a revolving door into the open air. Grant bending a little forward and extending one hand very carefully, like an E.T.A. Hoffmann character reaching for a doorknob, and we both blip over a moment that will be rejoined later.

"Man!" Grant says, and looks at me. "Whew, huh?"

"I don't want to go back in there."

"Well, we'll have to if we want to get that money."

"We can't fast-forward to the end?"

"Doesn't work that way, Chalo. There is no end to that. But we can pause and clean our ears out. See you later."

He pulls a barrel bag from behind a park bench and walks toward the center of the campus, extracting what appears to be a lace tablecloth from the bag.

⊏⊐

AC's mother was a Christian Scientist who taught her we are all bubbles in the mind of God and all suffering is Error. She used to get crushing migraines and would sit there at the dining room table cutting and pasting photographs together with a facial expression that at first glance seemed neutral but was terrifying to see for any length of time. AC gets migraines too, takes the strongest painkillers she can lay hands on, but they never really work, not well enough.

Riding the bus back to her apartment she stares fixedly at a page she tore from an art book in the library, showing a painting called

Human Nature Two by Rene Magritte. Staring at the blue sky in the painting takes the edge off. It makes the bus bearable. That birdless blue sky is living death. Full of light, placidly stern, soft cloudiness that is also biting, hanging on, the blue probe. Dingy bus light catches on the dents in the page and she has to keep tilting it, while the bus swerves and wallows, and her guts lurch with it and the heavy pillowy human next to her is half lying down on top of her, to keep those fucking reflections from messing up her view.

When she looks up from the painting she sees cops with dripping chrome gloves, people in lockstep, people on the clock, holding clocks that blare prismatic light across their faces, screaming into their clocks and talking prismatic light screams that blink against their chattering teeth. There before her eyes in the window of a second-storey gym, a man is lifting a barbell up and down. The feet in the street go up and down. The passing cars go left and right. That siren wailing up and down. The bus goes up and down over the shattered street. Two young women in high heels are waving their flowing hair up and down, massaging painted glow cavities talking, chrome sunglass sweat etches their faces with pale glitter.

Are they bubbles of God-mind or are they Error?

I'm a machine. I don't stand out.

I'm like you. I'm a machine.

I won't freak out. I feel nothing. I feel nothing.

I think nothing. I feel nothing. I am not here.

My blue-sky program experiences no emotions, has no preferences, is *not* desperate to get home, it is not. It loves everyone, it wants to grab the woman next to me and cut her face into strips with a straight razor, bash the driver's head in with the snotfaced baby swung high in both hands and throw a bomb into the bus behind me, jump with both feet on a cop's fucking face and pulp his shiteating skull on the fucking sidewalk, get his gun, shoot gun, shoot gun, die shooting.

"AC, Chalo, Chalo, AC,"

The translator is a little girl?

... No, just a very small young woman. Not that short, but delicate ...

The architect is a mammoth slob slothmammoth.

... Serious, small face. Her glasses are too big for her. She's wearing a plain black hoodie, drops the hood over plain black hair pulled up in a knot. No luster, no ornament. Grave. Reserved. Hispanic? Asian? Egyptian? Bangalorean?

A flabby boulder.

AC meets Chalo now, almost a month after she first encountered Grant at what he referred to as "The Mexican Tea Room" and which turned out to be a macrobiotic boutique cafe breathily named *Impresiones*, where the idea was Apple Store meets Mexican something. He was there first, blowing steam off his tea. The steam billowed up his chest and floated around his head like cigarette smoke, and he would take piping hot sips and breathe the steam out through his mouth and nostrils.

He asked her what she liked to read, and not what AC stood for.

"True crime," she told him.

There was a reflecting pool in a white plaster basin, as square as a basement sink, outside the curtained window, and lights from that had a way of darting up into the steam around Grant's head like bright fish. They weren't doing that for AC. She studied the menu without taking anything in.

"Can I get you anything?"

"What's the most food of these?"

"The bean sprout burrito is humongous!" the waiter holds his hands around an imaginary breadloaf-sized object.

AC slashes the burrito to ribbons and then forks it methodically into her mouth. Grant drinks his green tea quietly, without a sound, in a barely visible column of green steam.

"How long have you been studying Tibetan?"

"Years."

"Can you sight-translate?"

"Yes."

"Here, let's put that backpack over on this side."

Grant holds out his hands. AC uncharacteristically goes along with him, picking her backpack off the floor and handing it to him.

Grant puts the strap around his left armrest, so that it hangs off the side of the chair, just clear of the ground.

"When you look out over the ocean, how do you feel?"

"I don't go to the beach."

"Mountains?"

"No."

"Desert?"

"... I lived there for a year."

"Deserts are deceptively honest places. Would you do me a favor and translate this sample for me?"

AC has already finished her burrito. She burps softly and stares at the funny owl cartoon on her plate. It wouldn't be there if it weren't Mexican, but there's nothing Mexican about it. The owl isn't wearing a serape or anything; it's just standing there looking coy. No chef's hat. It shouldn't be there.

The piece of paper has lines of Tibetan script printed across it, like a row of little black backbones. AC lied about sight translation, but but but by luck she knows this passage, which opens the *Bon of Magic Power*:

"Then from the dark center heavy quick-spreading obscurity mounted a hearthstone-contaminating deer leading thirteen hearthstone spirits and spirits of what's unclean after burning, and shouted we must destroy the human world and the god world."

"Great -- now I would like you ..."

Here he reaches under the table --

"... to see what you can do with this."

He lifts up a bundle held together with a clamp; handwriting on curly graph paper. She takes it and flips the pages.

"A lot of pages."

"How long do you think it would take you to do it?"

"Weeks. I have a job."

She already knows she can't translate this, but he doesn't.

A waiter hastens past on his way to the large party in the back room, a pitcher slides off his platter and bounces on the floor, spilling a quart of sangria just where AC's backpack had been, before Grant had asked to move it.

"How long to get the first ten pages? Can you do that by next week?"

"Sure. How much will you give me?"

"Ten a page."

"If you need it fast, I would want more."

"Ten is what I can afford."

"OK. Can I have fifty now?"

"I'm afraid I don't have that much on me, AC. But the meal is on me."

In midconversation she closes her eyes against the ranks of passing lights that draw and redraw a kinky abacus of magenta and gold around him.

"Are you all right, AC?"

"I'm fine."

Idiots have been asking her that question every minute of every hour of every day and getting the same rebuff without fail. You will never catch me out answering any other way.

Grant is looking at her very gently -- very detestably gently. An old familiar pang of fear, still a shock no matter how blunted time makes it.

Does he know?

That day should have been magical, with a silver letter emerging from the clouds at the zenith. To-bus-walking she stops for a long time, looking into the vacant lot that she passes every day. Without the slightest motion she looks at what she's looking at for a long time before she takes it.

This was years ago, when she was attending a four-year college. Dance night, the cafeteria is shaking with bass, dark inside and striated with blinking lights, shadowy figures slithering among the lights, arms going up and down. Her roommate is out and AC is alone with the thing she found, loading it, racking a round into the chamber, through a series of doors that punctuate the increase of booming from the cafeteria, right out into the crowd lights and noise pulling the trigger, not aiming at anyone just at *them*, the music going and the lights, the gun barking at the end of her arm like a tethered dog, flapping and bucking in her hand.

Screams in the music, raising arms, students gush from the building, glass is breaking, furniture is crashing, AC is standing still,
reloading without looking at what she's doing or seeming to see
anything, her face frozen. A security guard charges through the double
doors that open onto another world of even fluorescent lighting on
white tile floors, red arrow-slit classroom doors, and steel drinking fountains. He sees AC and her gun, wheels around into the student lounge.
When he pops back out into the hall through the second entrance, by
the exit door at the hall's end, she is standing in the dark just inside the
cafeteria, colored lights zooming all around her, and with the wild lights
and music it's like the hall ends in a frenzied thundercloud gathered
around a young woman the size of an eleven-year-old with a pistol in
both hands that starts popping the moment he breaks for the door. The
guard is a heavy black man in his forties and he can feel all the flesh on
his body lurch and shudder as he pounds through into the sireny,
distraught scene outside, but a bullet etched line just missing him he
also can feel, the puff of its draft and the evil hum of it that will whip
back around on him in random moments of fright for the rest of his life.

Bang bang bang, bang bang bang bang. Breaking glass.

Her brown windbreaker is full of bullets like loose candies and
she starts methodically reloading. Now bright blue and red flashing
lights travel across the tall cafeteria windows. They sweep from the
street side around to the front and stop with a little jerk, then sit and
swivel. She's alone -- no she isn't there's a custodian, a Jamaican
woman she recognizes, scrambling from behind an overturned table
and through a swinging steel door into the kitchen. AC inserts the
magazine, racks the top shell, then refills the other magazine
methodically inserting bullet after bullet as one pair of blue and red
lights passes from the street side to the front, and white light
splashes up one window, stiffly moving up and down a moment
before settling in place. The music has transitioned into a livelier
number. Colored lights twist to and fro and bow up and down.

Two cops in bulky vests and helmets plough through the
double doors emptying their guns sort of toward her and throw
themselves dramatically behind the coke machine, and an overturned desk. AC empties her gun toward them from out of the
phantasmagoria of lights and music -- breaking glass and tiles, splin-

tering wood, ticking steel clonking on plastic -- the cops empty their guns, draw new ones, and resume firing almost without pause -- AC empties her gun and automatically reloads, taking no cover and needing none, and there's more damage and music and shouting and nobody hitting anybody. So the two police clumsily retreat outside where there are now more cops than students and a gang of at least ten charges the door with rifles, gargling police talk to each other.

One brings her rifle up just in time to blow the liver out of the Jamaican custodian in the act of tackling AC from behind. AC's pistol pinwheels into a corner and she goes down under the larger woman's weight. The grimacing face is only an inch from her own, wrung with pain, crying out. Prone and helpless, covered in the custodian's blood, AC is arrested, not shot. An unintelligible blank-faced cop reads her rights as if it were a ritual curse.

She is led out to the car. The cops sitting in the front seat have blank faces, blank voices. Inert as a manikin herself she is swept away to the police station. A female cop leans into her.

"Glka, nghehn ocxhr, nk'eh'ugh, khlheh glkla."

Then, a holding cell.

The first sign of any emotion comes only when she learns that there were no fatalities, with the exception of the custodian, who was policekill.

Not only that -- *not only that* -- there weren't *any serious injuries*. Not *one* student had to spend more than a *single night* in the hospital. Eventually she will learn, despite adamantly closing her ears to any word about that night, that even the most badly shaken students were able to resume classes that semester.

Not one. *Not one.* Six and a half clips. One hundred and six ... one hundred and six shots. 106 potential fatalities -- zero realized, *zero.*

Four hundred and ninety-four days later she is released from the psychiatric facility. She moves, ends up working in a community college library almost the same as before, waking up in the same morning with the bedsheets and pillowcases, the stuff in the arrangement at the time to the ham and eggs, ham and eggs, sausage and eggs and milk milk milk, off to work, off to school, bus bus bus

bus bus bus, wait wait wait wait wait wait wait for what for what for what for what for what for what for what.

I shot a lot of people, she says silently to the other passengers.
I'd do it again. I'd shoot you.
The kids, the old ones, the blind ones.
I shot a lot of people.

▭

... The night wind ruffles my pelt. A gust of wind slaps me across the eyes with my own hair and wakes me. I can't get back to sleep. Most of the others are over there, a herd of dark heaps. They wheeze and snuffle. They stir now and then. More than snoring I hear the turbid rumbling of our vast intestines.

... The sky is clear and there's almost more lights in it than there are dark spaces. I crane my head and crick my neck getting a better look. The upper reaches of the high peaks cut against the paler dark around me, still dappled with patches of snow that aren't stars, but it's fun to think about how they are different. Not much fun. I lie down again. I don't remember standing up but I think I stood up when I woke up. Lying down as a yak is something I can do automatically, but only once I remember to stop trying to figure out how to do it and just let it happen. If I try to fold and arrange my limbs according to a mental image, I remain motionless. The ignition sequence doesn't happen. But if I think about something else and just kind let my weight down a little, the next thing I know, I'm down.

... Now on the ground I roll over onto my right side, my legs toward the lower part of the slope. Yak constellations percolate in and out of the starfield. I pick out a constellation of two yaks doing it and the thought hits my groin. A helical wave of evanescent excitement, or what do I mean, it's like a funnel, a small twister sort of kind of made of ghost fumes formed like a clay cup on a potter wheel, the potter's hands are what I feel, they shape it, like coaxing the foal out of a little bank of mist.

... My eye searches through space, just to see what's there, while sexual longing kneads me and induces swelling and laves me inside, so my eyes are like warm lakes, the upturned one full of probing and the downturned one ready to plop out onto the grass and roll bumping down the slope toward the valley floor. Both together wading through the water reeds of a starry night, very voluptuously clear and still.

... There's headlights over there. I see human beings. Automatically I heave myself upright to get a better look. A little camp by a stream that runs through a flat rocky place in the valley, with some fire and some electric lights, flashlights -- are they looking for something? The motion seems playful. I zero in on one figure with a boxy flashlight -- she's not AC, but almost. AC only looked like an eleven-year-old. This girl is smiling the way AC never did but she has the same puppety, weightless way of moving. She's come to a standstill the way children do sometimes. They don't keep on going like adults do. They halt. Then they go back and forth, and then they do something. Right now she's still thinking, or not thinking but just looking. She drops the beam of her flashlight and looks up at the sky the way I just was but using both eyes, and points at a meteor. I don't know why she got one and not me, maybe she should be the narrator, but she would be anyway, just not in this book.

... Even being in this hulking horny body, thinking of AC, with the smell of the grass I've bruised and the raw earth I've exposed with my rock and roll, the earthy musk of snoozing yaks and the interminable groan from my sixth or seventh stomach just now ... none of that connects concretely to anything I ever encountered in connection with her, so it must be me that's the memory, associating with her what's happening. She had that way of being so still, so that I remember her in profile, not full on.

... She looked like she was in front of a green screen world all the time. I never got to share that with her, but I wanted to. Something about her made me want to. To step out from the screen into AC-space. Silent and shadowy, like heaven inside a cloud instead of on top. She puts her mouth up to my ear and tells me what she wants. I hear that pale, fluting voice tickle my ear like an air tongue.

⊏⊐

Quest for funding: phase two --

Grant as always meets me in a sort of white linen suit, blue sky, ocean breeze, as always. He carries it around with him.

"Hello, Chalo!"

He sits down and gets tea served to him in a water glass and his mane of pu erh steam is restored. Without taking his eyes off me he holds a hand out to the woman sitting at the next table. She takes it, also without looking. They sit holding hands, she's conducting her own conversation and Grant sipping his tea. For a moment I find myself in a gently older other city of quiet and sexuality and a few anachronisms.

"Why should I talk?" someone going by says. "What would I talk about?"

"Are you ready for another round with the bankers?"

He releases the woman's hand and draws his through the air in a magic arc. We go back downtown and he pauses a moment before the glass facade to steady himself in his reflection. Looking through the window, only with difficulty could I distinguish myself from the wall opposite me, only with difficulty could I distinguish my reflection from the glass.

A get a flicker of panic.

Why?

Because I am me. It makes me feel, just now, like freaking out.

I am in a trap. The trap of being me. That can't be cut away from my having become involved in this stupid shit so now I have to go stare down a fucking bank full of bankers. And I have to do it like this. Look at me. How am I like this?

Grant presses my shoulder a moment before we go back in.

"You're a Californian. Remember that."

Those random walls with the screens come up around us. Mr. Browlshweer walks beside us, still talking as our feet slot back into our footsteps. This long run-around walk was already in progress, already in progress before we ever set foot in this place.

I don't know why Grant wants me here. Maybe he just needs the support. I'm willing to back him up -- I don't know why I am, but I am. I glance at Grant. He's not looking at me, but I know he feels me, and it's doing him some good, and that does me some good. It shores me up a little against the feeling that I'm an unnecessary double of somebody else, scrambled together from data which will in time be making autonomous purchases and financial arrangements in my name. Which, actually, will be *its* name, to which it will have the legal-financial claim, because there can be only one of us and it turns out I'm not it.

I am breathing the atmosphere of sinister; like CGI air. Each particle is neat and clear and glossy and it doesn't travel any weight to my lungs, so breathing in doesn't feel different from breathing out.

The Loan Originator speaks confidently about complicated things competently. We have to hurry to keep up.

" ... The company will need a complete report on all activities, as well as an accounting for 100% of what you've done in the past fiscal year, and a thorough record of all your transactions."

"I'll get that right to you," says Grant absently, running a finger along one of the metal dividers.

Grant may be expecting me to chime in here, but I don't want to talk. Like the man said, "why should I talk?" I don't want to talk, or even to move, or to leave, or to do anything; I feel like I'm caught at the bottom of a syphon of depersonalization. I'm trying to make myself remember what humanity is -- my mother's face gouged with worry, squirming around getting grass stains when I was a kid and your face and your hands, the sky of your face and hands, the clashing beach of your face and hands, and these things give me a kind of inner orange that clashes totally with whatever is this shit going on around me, whatever this is, palpably clashing with an indifferently predatory cold that's melting me. The digital wendigo bank incubus.

Now Mr. Browlshweer swivels his head at me.

"You're the design agent?"

"I'm the designer."

It's as if I'd admitted to occupying a lesser position than whatever a design agent is.

Mr. Browlshweer's eyes scan my face as if it were a screen.

"You've assembled complexes on this scale before?" he asks, his voice coming from somewhere well behind his face.

"Only once, and not so large."

"Where was this?"

"I did it for the Financial Advisors Regional Turnkey Program. In New York. New York City."

"New York."

The bank man touches his finger to the glass plate he's been making notes on as if he were about to write it down. He doesn't. Grant was right.

"Uh," I say.

Mr. Browlshweer looks at me. Screen light contracts around his face.

"I'm interested in building playgrounds."

I keep sighing as I bullshit.

"I've been looking into ... like, researching ... playgrounds "..''

Mr. Browlshweer is looking at me and his finger is regularly scrolling down his piece of glass. With each scroll life ebbs out of – -- but Grant intervenes.

Grant and the Loan Originator square off. Mr. Browlshw'er's glasses glint like armor, and Gr'nt's dzi bead growls with subsonic pseudo-Tibetan vibrations. Smoothings on both sides. Mr. Browlshweer snaps his fingers and his animated digital assistant unfolds in the air beside him, forming a diamond that reminds me of those divination paper puzzle things little girls used to make to fit over their fingertips. This thing floats just above his left shoulder, facing his ear.

"Iris," he says peremptorily, "What is Mr. Grant's credit score?"

The diamond folds and unfolds along a criss-cross and murmurs something into Mr. Browlshweer's ear. Grant rubs his dzi bead and a faint musical note hums from behind his eyes as Mr. Browlshweer turns toward us bringing the entire scene with him, as if he were the pivot for a flat backdrop swinging around on us. Grant puts his hand on my shoulder quickly.

"Jump when I do."

We jump together. The moment dilates.

There's more than one emptiness here. The two warring emptinesses clash as we jump, smooth cruising business seriousness versus Zen hippie composure. The dead bank vacuousness harms me by forcing me to make it real, and Grant's there to say nothing but tidal flow is real.

Mr. Browlshweer shows a boardroom with glass walls and a lenticular table lined with sophisticated uncomfortable expensive cheap-looking modern chairs. Grant makes the glass walls stop sterilizing the trees and grass outside, and the room fills with the smell of the ocean, tide pools, hot dogs, cigarettes, and pine needles baked by the sun.

Mr. Browlshweer turns the animated dial by his head and the board room is high in a high rise, the gleaming leaves of the trees turn into the windows of plain glass box office buildings. We're hemmed in -- but Grant turns the wood-paneled wall behind him into a sleepy grove in late afternoon sun. Brown light is caught in the hairnet of the canopy over us and our feet are covered with fragrant dust.

Mr. Browlshweer dials up some more glistening white plastic and the smell of art galleries. The gloss slides off the walls and onto us both, like poison slime. The smell coats my tongue like a leaf of shrink wrap. He's trying to hit us now that we're disoriented with a null blot that's like a diffracted wafer of the art gallery atmosphere fringed with a nauseous, poisoned feeling. Grant nearly blunders into an expensive piece of shitsculpture. Instead, he allows himself to fold into a pseudo-lotus position. I catch myself just a fraction of an inch away from an expensive ugly mobile thing adorned with disembodied stock market screens -- I can't feel my legs, I don't know if I'm walking or standing still. Mr. Browlshweer is asking me for my last five jobs and pay stubs, and it's like I've been painlessly disemboweled, sterilized, and my blood is all gushing down a discreetly-hidden sluice without anyone noticing, including me.

"How many playgrounds have you designed? Where have you uploaded your portfolio?"

Mr. Browlshweer reaches into his jacket pocket and brings out a chrome stylus that puckers the surface of reality -- an instrument of permanent finance magic that traces brokered association links, tracking down toward the signature line and a signature that will cut us off from the power forever.

Then he starts violently -- the ordinary human emotion of

surprise has broken his chi -- his eyes, which have already gone a cold aviator blue, are riveted on the tip of the surfboard it turns out he is holding, or thinks he is holding, because he's fallen under a wave that drops on him, while Grant eases along the hollow of the curl with his hands floating lightly, his hair floating lightly, the fragments of sea froth mingling with the innumerable stars, undiminished by the conspiratorially full moon.

Where I am in all this is more than I can say. I seem to be in the numb center of the action, like the referee at a fight. Grant glides off into the distance and his night wave curls along after him, and Mr. Browlshweer steps briskly from the water into a Plexiglas pyramid, bone dry.

"Whew!" Grant says. "That Loan Originator is tough!"

We're sitting on the edge of a planter on the street outside the bank.

"A pretty tough cookie!" he adds.

"Did we blow it?"

"No, no," Grant says, but he sounds a little down. "It's not smooth sailing, but we're not rejected yet. What we *need* --" and here his tone takes on a bit of a new resolution -- "are reinforcements. He won't be alone next time, and we shouldn't be either."

What do you mean we?

A woman comes out of the lobby with a baby in a fancy stroller. The baby is wearing earbuds.

"Hey!" I shout at her.

I have to repeat it several times before she realizes I'm talking to her.

"That's a shitty thing to do to your kid, making them wear earphones."

"Well, thanks, but I don't think I need your advice on how to raise my baby," she answers caustically.

"Take those fucking god damn earphones out!" I scream, with bulging eyes.

The woman is hustling herself away.

"Fuck you!" she says jerkily.

"I told you to take those motherfucking ears out -- earphones!"

I stand up and lash the air with my finger.

"Take that shit out! Get that shit out of that baby's head! What are you doing to that baby?"

"Get away from me!" she says, from now at least twenty-five feet away. "Fuck off!"

"What the fuck do you think you're doing to your kid?"

She vanishes around the corner to dial 911 and when I turn Grant is beaming at me.

"What?" I bark.

He's still smiling.

"What?!"

———

... There's a funny smell on the breeze today. I think there are people around again, maybe doing laundry in a stream. Might be soap, I'm smelling.

... My front left hoof is a little off; I think there may be a crack in it. No pain, really, just a little wobble. Not much to speak of. I should watch it, though. No one to help me if it fails. Or is that so? Maybe yaks help each other out.

... Not much to say about the weather. The sky is the same marinated blue it always is up here. Some wind. I can actually swivel my ears out of the wind, so the world doesn't sound like fluttering burlap. Eyes a bit dry. Continual gurgling in my cavernous gut.

... Further up the slope now, toward a sort of declivity, if that's the right word, where the ground is torn open to bare brown soil and loose stones. Fragments of gneiss, fragments of pegmatite shimmering with flakes of mica. Am I being watched? No people around. I can't smell soap, or whatever it was, anymore, just earth and grass. I stop moving. I'll move again soon. I seem to have hit a personal lull here in the groove in the ground. I might fall asleep. It wouldn't make any difference if I did.

... A few more steps, but without really moving. I dwindle down. My ghost deflates until it's only a small mound hidden in the spacious shell of my yak form. Maybe this is me finally going yak. All the other yaks are like this, but also slightly less self-conscious, and I'm converting fully now, without a struggle. I'm going to watch my human self-die into a yak like any other. Live and die as a yak. Old grey yak lies down in the snow, never to rise no more, or shredded by wolves, hauled laboriously down by a snow leopard, shot from a safe distance by a human asshole, rolling stiff-legged down into a ravenous knot of vultures. There are vultures everywhere in the mountains here. They're practically part of the sky. You see them every time you look up therethey are at the margins of vision, perched on rocks and cinematic trees, necks out like snakes, complacently scanning the obituaries the wind carries.

-- There's a vulture now, sitting on a white stone that's so regular it could be a carved block. Turquoise is herniated out of the rock like a gleaming loop of exposed intestine, soft and shining amid fluttering saxifrage and dandelions.

"What?"

The vulture is staring at me.

"What?!"

The vulture is still staring at me.

I go cold. The rumbling of my gut stops and my blood congeals. The daylight, the grass, the earth and stones, the flowers, the wind, my banal thinking, are an evil game.

... I come closer to the vulture. A colder wind carries wood smoke to me. The vulture's eyes are flashing like water in the sun. Coming closer, I see there's a hidden track of beaten grass that starts behind the white block and cuts up the slope a bit more, before vanishing into some skimpy trees and bushes that grow beneath an overhang. The track is fresh, looks as though something heavy was dragged along here.

... Like a sleepwalker, I pass the vulture, inwardly paralyzed, thinking I'm going to feel that icy beak rip into me as I come within reach, and I'll feel cold fingers getting a purchase on me, piercing into me.

... The bracken is dense here, but it's been forced aside by whatever left the track. Smaller than a yak but strong enough to shove through thicket tough as iron, that's tearing at me. A tahr, maybe? It would have to have been really determined. Coming around the other side of the overhang I get a feeling I can almost hear, like a big final bass note, and a hiss of time passing. A person framed against the sky in a fold between higher places is motionlessly waiting for me.

-- A person in rags, all faded variations of an original color I can't think of its name right now. It is a living person, not a scarecrow. It stands like a living thing. There's nothing else about it I can describe. Alive, and in rags, and not moving, and waiting for me.

-- This person wants to show me something, in order to change me, because it is a thing with a purpose, like a man-made thing.

The idea of turning back is like inadvertent violence, directed against no one. I could do it.

I come up to the figure, allowing my head to nod. Watching it swing gives me the illusion that it's in the landscape. There's a leathery smell coming off of it. A musty smell -- dried flesh.

... Now I'm only a few feet away, and I still see only knotted rags that look limp but act rigid, motionless in a wind that throws my shaggy pelt around and tugs hard at me.

Crunch of gravel -- it's turned away from me. It's further up the slope now, turned back to me again. Up the slope.

... Now what's it doing? It's kneeling on the ground and doing something with its hands.

... It could be a small figure very near me, or a large figure farther away, and under its hands I can see Los Angeles swimming in a typically sunny day, and the waves on the beach and surfers, Grant -- the Annex -- AC in her fantasies headshotting uniformed and business-attired people getting away on her bicycle to the vacant lots and vacant suburban streets, and there's Chalo, talking to a woman who's into him you can tell -- am I going to see a bunch of yaks on a mountain, and am I going to see one of them having an elaborate inner life, and am I going to see my seeing this right now? Because the image that's there isn't an image, I'm seeing I'm seeing what I'm seeing what I'm seeing like I would see a rock on the ground, or my own foot when I look down, or whatever I see, the sky, the world, the wind shaking the grass. The figure is sort of picking up this sight or washing its hands in the city like a surgeon at a basin. The city is now a bay full of seawater, the shore receded all the way to the foothills of the San Gabriel mountains, just the tops of the taller buildings above water -- and those spectral god-hands splashing in the bay where Los Angeles was before the water rose. The figure is throwing the sight up over its head, and rubbing the rags where the face probably is, and every time it dips down and throws the sight over itself like a curling bedsheet, the figure is more dense and more transparent. It's washing itself into the landscape, but really into the universe, becoming a diamond ghost, becoming everything without disappearing.

... It's not becoming everything. I don't know how I, a humble yak, would know it, but it seems to me it's becoming one of some greater number of versions of everything. And it wanted to show this to me. It wanted me to see it, and to wonder why -- especially to wonder why, as if wondering why was what really mattered.

... The rags around the figure's head are more and more transparent, and through it with a shock I see a face. It looks familiar. It isn't a living face, it's art. A metal bust of a man's head, black, gleaming, smiling, showing all his teeth, and wearing a shapeless sort of a wool hat ...?

... The figure is gone now. Everything seems beautiful. Why would someone fading into a landscape make it more beautiful?

... A cold peak-shadow has crept up on me. I move out into the warmth. In the crystalline light of the low-hanging sun -- well, what else would I do? I saw what I saw, my mind went blank. I started grazing, filling my first stomach. Why not? I'm a yak. Should I commit suicide, or sing, or run and tell the other yaks about it? -- Anyway: in the crystalline light of the low-hanging sun I see the long, even shadows of the other yaks, the standing stones, the tall peaks, the black pines, the eleven million wildflowers, everything trailing flat dark geometrical shapes. There's mine, shaped like a yak, not a man.

... Was I brought here to see the figure in rags orchestrate the story of my life? Could it have been a coincidence, or would anyone, encountering that figure, see their own life? Or would they all see mine? It seemed the figure was experiencing it all too, having an experience that relates experiences, like art without the art.

I don't feel a "passionate desire to know," I'm just confused. I don't have to go on, or do anything, let alone answer any question. Would I prefer to know if there were something I could do, or that I ought to do? Or that someone or something is asking me to do? It's not like I need to do something, to do anything, but I want to know what there is to do, that's it. Mostly it. I don't know how real this is. It only feels kind of real. *"Kind* of, but not *sort* of," like my friend David used to say. He's real.

Maybe I bonked my head or something, and I'm lying somewhere unconscious, dreaming all this. Yeah, maybe, kind of, but not sort of.

———

"It's good to see you again, Chalo," comes at me from an errant tuft of sea mist.

"Have you ever read any occult stuff?" Grant asks a moment later.

"I read a lot of it once."

"And then stopped?"

"It was bullshit."

He nods. His gaze travels to the mountains.

"You're getting ready to tell me that it isn't?"

"I think I might know how to ..." Grant goes on, picking his words slowly. "... get at something real in it. I think there's something real in it, but occultism needs a revolution to be real. Like anything else."

He pauses, and his gaze travels further over rolling hills. I watch him watching a hawk go teetering up the wind into the higher up, flip and sway and dip. Suddenly I have the feeling I'm in love with someone who isn't there. A feeling of absent love. It passes, trailing nostalgic memories of summer park afternoons and girls on the Burbank wind. The space between me and those birds is full of my memories, and emotions I'm too old to feel anymore. They hang all around me, like TV signals falling away into outer space forever.

"Now," Grant says, drawing out the word. "All that tabulating. The prayers. Little tasks. Little ... bans. Things you can and can't do, if you want to make it work ... Little, arbitrary things. Like what color clothes you wear, what you eat, whether you have sex, whether or not you shave your face ..."

He fans his left hand.

"... That's not all just irrelevant, but it isn't the main thing -- the main thing --"

He points with his left index finger.

"-- is the gesture that you're making. It's all gestures. It's all exactly like grammar. The language doesn't come from the rules. Its the rules -- the rules are codifications of everyday practices that are usually taken for granted. That's what I mean by the gesture. Trying to do spiritual work from a book is like trying to carry on a conversation with someone in a language you don't know, using a dictionary. Without the milieu, the language is dead, and without its milieu, the spiritual work is dead."

Grant looks at me, sunset red on his face.

"Does that make sense, Chalo?"

I open my mouth. The little inrush of fresh air that hits my tongue stops me from thinking, and I shut my mouth again.

Grant looks back out at the blue.

"I think it makes sense," he says, as if someone else had been speaking, and he is volunteering his agreement.

⊏⊐

"It's good to see you again, Chalo," comes at me from an errant tuft of sea mist.

"Have you ever read any occult stuff?" Grant asks a moment later.

"I read a lot of it once."

"And then stopped?"

"It was bullshit."

He nods. His gaze travels to the mountains.

"You're getting ready to tell me that it isn't?"

"I think I might know how to ..." Grant goes on, picking his words slowly. "... get at something real in it. I think there's something real in it, but occultism needs a revolution to be real. Like anything else."

He pauses, and his gaze travels further over rolling hills. I watch him watching a hawk go teetering up the wind into the higher up, flip and sway and dip. Suddenly I have the feeling I'm in love with someone who isn't there. A feeling of absent love. It passes, trailing nostalgic memories of summer park afternoons and girls on the Burbank wind. The space between me and those birds is full of my memories, and emotions I'm too old to feel anymore. They hang all around me, like TV signals falling away into outer space forever.

"Now," Grant says, drawing out the word. "All that tabulating. The prayers. Little tasks. Little ... bans. Things you can and can't do, if you want to make it work ... Little, arbitrary things. Like what color clothes you wear, what you eat, whether you have sex, whether or not you shave your face ..."

He fans his left hand.

"... That's not all just irrelevant, but it isn't the main thing -- the main thing --"

He points with his left index finger.

"-- is the gesture that you're making. It's all gestures. It's all exactly like grammar. The language doesn't come from the rules. Its the rules -- the rules are codifications of everyday practices that are usually taken for granted. That's what I mean by the gesture. Trying to do spiritual work from a book is like trying to carry on a conversation with someone in a language you don't know, using a dictionary. Without the milieu, the language is dead, and without its milieu, the spiritual work is dead."

Grant looks at me, sunset red on his face.

"Does that make sense, Chalo?"

I open my mouth. The little inrush of fresh air that hits my tongue stops me from thinking, and I shut my mouth again.

Grant looks back out at the blue.

"I think it makes sense," he says, as if someone else had been speaking, and he is volunteering his agreement.

\#

The Tibetan writing Grant has given AC is impenetrable. She's been poring over it all night, and even the briefest phrases refuse to

come clear. Back and forth to the dictionary, her grammar books --
nothing's coming through. It's as if the whole text were one obscure
idiom. The handwriting is clear enough, and the graph paper makes
the lines unmistakable. She flips forward and backward, trying to
find anything at all she can make out. There is a title, but she is able
to make it out only because it is some kind of European phrase in
Tibetan characters: *Complutensian Polyglot Terma.*

The sky is lightening in the east when she gives up.

So the next day she sits down and just makes up a bunch of
plausible-sounding stuff. He won't know the difference.

Child of an honorable lineage!

conjure the servants of the false king
the red life-master whose red throne stands in a copper cavern
a red river runs beneath the throne
and divides for each of the fourteen emanations of pure pollution
into fourteen red streams
where twenty-eight red birds drink

the rock emanation
the water emanation
the earth emanation
the sky emanation
the slate mountain emanation
the glacier emanation

the emanation of the pollution of the rock
the emanation of the pollution of the water
the emanation of the pollution of the earth
the emanation of the pollution of the sky
the emanation of the pollution of the slate mountain
the emanation of the pollution of the glacier

the obscuration of the rock
the obscuration of the water

the obscuration of the earth
the obscuration of the sky
the obscuration of the slate mountain
the obscuration of the glacier

brother and sister, the hidden coat of mail
screaming
let us destroy the world of men and the world of gods

riding on crows
emptying the vessel of Chinese medicinal water
leading twenty-eight war hordes of killers
dressed in flayed skin dripping blood
dressed in bloody scalps
dressed in garlands of human heads
clashing thunderbolts
clashing red flames
clashing diamond arrow heads
leading twenty-eight war hordes of insane red corpses
riding on yaks and monsters

the thousand-knife saw wheel
the flaming axe
the star cleaver
the diamond bow
that impales with arrows
fletched with red feathers from the tails of red vulture-fiends
the net glowing like sunset
the lance bedecked with silk scarves
the lightning sling with dzi eyes

The sky goer is the wrathful woman of the sky who guides the treasure-revealer to the sacred treasures wherever they may be hidden; the sacred books found in snowdrifts and caves, unspoiled beneath lake waters or hidden in clouds by the treasure-revealer.

The revealer Vatavika fell ill in his fourteenth year. Near to death, his mind became so surcharged with images that it fell into *formlessness, and out of this formlessness arose the six madmen whom he then found and who then joined him, and together with him became the seven warlike madmen. The sky goer showed him the daemon asleep in a book that divides itself in emanations when awake.*

"That ought to do it," AC thinks.

⊂▭⊃

I'm sitting with Grant on a park bench by the beach. There's a discarded glass bottle with the label torn off, lying on the pavement about halfway across the sidewalk, over by the base of a planter. It's caught my attention, because it's there.

A woman on the sidewalk is swaying to and fro and announcing to everybody,

"Right now at Costco they're selling fifteen cans of Progresso Soup for ten dollars! Fifteen cans, 18.5 ounce-ize cans, for ten dollars! Those are the big cans! That's a good meal!"

She repeats her announcement a little further down the street, and a little further, and a little further.

Grant shows me some sheets of curly graph paper covered in what looks like Sanskrit.

"I think this is what the Tibetans call a terma. They're books and things that boddhisattvas hide in the landscape, to be found by later generations when the time is right."

"On graph paper?"

Now he slides some crisp printed sheets in front of me.

"Translation," it says at the top in the center. The first line below it is "... *Child of an honorable lineage!*"

He lets me read it. When I raise my eyes again, he leans over and taps the bottom of the page.

"They're the ones."

I check the spot he points to.

"The seven warlike madmen?"

"A team of seasoned revolutionaries."

Grant looks at the sky. The wind ruffles his light linen clothing. He takes a deep breath, and lowers his eyes to the ocean. Suddenly I realize that I'm going to get up off this bench and walk away forever if he can't explain himself to me, right now.

Grant points to the ocean.

"The gods are the ocean. The demons are the waves. The waves aren't the ocean, but they don't exist without it. ... A surfer doesn't interact with the ocean, a surfer, interacts with the wave. A surfer is part of the movement of the ocean itself as it just sits there. He travels, it doesn't. Like the world. We get high, we get low -- the waves. The sea, is just there. Things rise, things fall. The surfer rises, the surfer falls -- the surfer rises again, falls again. A surfer isn't really separate and making it, like making it on their own, doing your thing. A surfer is just lost in the water there. But when a surfer gets up, gets up on a wave, Chalo, the surfer moves, uses the wave to move, right? Right between active and passive. A surfer has to hook into the between to move, otherwise the surfer is just going in circles, like the water circle --"

He gestures to the sky.

"-- or the traffic circle --"

He gestures to the cars in the parking lot.

"Whatever human circles, circles of friends, job circles, psychology. The only line, not a straight line, but a line, is on the wave in between. It's the gobetween that counts. The source always gets lost in translation, that's the point. You learn to take translating itself as the source. ... But like you say, it's dangerous. The circles are safe. That's why we stay in them. A surfer will wipe out eventually."

Suddenly Grant is beaming at me.

"You *have to* wipe out. But a surfer moves first, then wipes out. The move gets made."

"From one part of the water to another part," I say. "You still end up in the water."

"You were already in the water. You can't help that. You can tread water, right? You can swim laboriously and kill yourself and get overwhelmed by the current and get pushed back. Or hauled out to sea on a rip current. You can try to climb out. But a surfer is going to take and get up on top of that water and --"

He claps his right hand on his outstretched left like skipping a stone --

"-- fly," he says.

The bottle sits on a grey circle, its own shadow.

Irrelevantly, I imagine the captain's voice on the airliner PA.

"Ladies and Gentleman, from up here in the cockpit it appears all our engines are gone, so I'll just go ahead and turn on the seatbelt sign for a bit during our descent as we glide to the ground. We'll get you there in what looks to be about twenty minutes. Until then, sit back, relax, and enjoy the rest of your flight. Talk to you on the ground."

"So -- demons," I say.

"Just do a quick delivery," a passing man says to another man. "Give him the shit and don't talk."

"Why would I talk?" the other man says. "What would I talk about?"

Ocean spray, hot dog with mustard, cigarette puff.

Sunlight stands in rigid spines, up and down, and blue air whips everything at ground level from left to right, right to left. The day is mostly empty, criss-crossed with darting birds and quick human gestures, rolling waves. Sparkling cars. Daylight shatters on the glass in front of me. Why does the fractured light in the clear bottle seem corrupt?

"Revolutionaries," Grant says, as if I had just asked him something.

⊏⊐

So ... Grant has set it all up. We, whoever that is, are going to meet with a representative of his revolutionaries, and now, of course, he can't make it because he's been called in for round three of Loan Originating, and I have to go instead.

"AC should go with you ... You can pick her up at the college."

The idea of seeing AC again startles me. I feel like a well someone's thrown a rock down, and I forget to complain, or to ask what to do.

My hands feel shaky on the steering wheel when I pull onto the campus roundabout. There she is! Drops into the passenger seat.

"Hello."

"Hi."

"... We waiting for someone else?"

"No."

I pivot into traffic.

AC has her hood up and she's looking at her hands on her knees.

"You OK?"

"... Yeah."

It's like we're already bitter and not talking to each other.

Grant didn't tell me much, I imagine explaining to her. He's paying a lot of money for this. A good-sized chunk of that hundred grand he stole that you don't know about.

Brown hills spotted with green brush rise up around us and the road rounds curves. I continue our imaginary conversation. AC is leaning into the air conditioning vent, directing it against her face.

Where are we going? Well, they -- evidently there will be more than one 'revolutionary representative' present -- wanted to meet us at one of the cabins up there.

Shattered sun snaps and bursts over AC like fireworks. I can hear her breathing through her nose, and smell public bathroom hand soap. She barely moves.

It's just like Grant, right? I imagine saying. He sets up this weird thing, this stuff, and then he can't go, and so he -- I trail off. Just now, really, I feel like I'd rather be sleeping.

I pull into a dirt lot and park under the pine trees. Clamber out of the car into a smell of hot asphalt and dry brush. Black sage, white sage, laurel sumac, live oak dust.

"Cabin two."

Together we walk up to the cabin. She barely comes up to my collarbone. Wind in the trees. The air around us rests very light. Like there's no place else in the world. What are we really going to see here, today? I'm expecting, what? Something vague. But the this-is-happening-ness of it is a little nerve wracking. The air and the light, all easy, and behind me a little at my side AC AC AC.

We reach the small cabin. The stingy porch, the cheap store-bought door with the glass panes in it. I reach up above the door and fumble the key down from its hiding place without thinking about spiders, unlock, go in.

"Where there is no more striving."

Where did that come from?

There's no furniture. There's fake wooden paneling, and cheap carpeting that smells. AC is taking small steps, her arms folded, looking all around for the best place in the room.

"Pretty close in here."

My voice booms, surprisingly. I open windows, letting in that helium air. I can feel her behind me like an open freezer. When I turn, she's standing almost in the middle of the room, arms still crossed, looking out through the open door, stoically waiting for the medium.

I hear a voice outside while I'm still in the bathroom. When I come out again, a lean black man in a polo shirt tucked into his blue jeans is in the doorway looking intently at AC, waiting for her to get around to answering his question.

"Hey," he says when he sees me.

I come up and shake his hand.

"Are you Chalo?"

"Yeah. This is AC."

"I'm Holly."

He holds my gaze.

"Are you prepared?"

"No. How should I prepare?"

He sighs through his nose and takes his hips in his hands.

"Well," he says after a moment. "You just relax."

He points at AC.

"You too. Any tension is going to be bad for you. Bad for all of us. You understand?"

He looks first to me, then to AC, sizing us up.

"Are you cool?"

I shrug. AC does nothing.

"Now I'm going to go get Adrien."

He heads back toward the parking area. He's got cowboy boots under the jeans.

AC has retreated to one corner of the cabin. In the gloom, I can see the whites of her eyes as she looks at me.

"Nothing to be afraid of."

Is she afraid or angry?

Here comes Holly. He walks attentively at the side of a woman who's moving like a sleepwalker. On the woman's other side is another woman, with short sandy hair that just missed being pale red. They steer the entranced woman with a light pressure on her elbows. Holly catches my eye.

"That's Meredith," he says, with a toss of his head toward the other "handler."

"Hi," she says a little sheepishly.

"This is Adrien," Holly says, guiding her into the cabin.

Both of them are keeping a close eye on her, as if she might collapse, or make a break for it, any moment. There's a white scarf covering her head, and a white top that reveals the amazing vitiligo on her arms, shoulders, and upper chest, freckled salt and pepper in what looks like exactly equal proportions. She's wearing some kind of support garment, like a medical chastity belt, outside her high-waisted mom jeans.

I fall back to make way. Adrien steps into the cabin, and the day snuffs like a pinched-out candle. I can still see the daylight, but now everything outside is as vividly leaden as a Richard Dadd painting. The three of them pause just inside the door. Adrien seems to be getting her bearings. Holly and Meredith guide Adrien into the middle of the room, taking small steps. Tension rolls in behind her like a train car and presses the air right out of the cabin. Holly stays with her, and Meredith opens the duffle bag, takes out loose colored chalks, big thick ones, and starts marking up the floor and walls.

The impulse to ask questions is gone.

Holly is murmuring something to Adrien. The head under the scarf turns in little birdlike twists -- I glimpse her eyes. The irises consist of tiny points of black and white, like static. Her gaze is so powerful I can't notice her features, except that they are also equally white and black. Holly gently turns her head away from me and I stop holding my breath. The medium rubs her groin absently.

"No," Holly says, pulling her hands away and replacing them at her sides, repeating "no" softly to her.

A shiver travels over her body, shaking her scarf.

"Ha --" she says, tossing her head.

It's like she's dreaming.

The scarf falls back around her neck exposing a boyish haircut. Even her hair is speckled with tiny patches, black and white, like static.

"Adrien?" Meredith says, from the corner.

When Adrien looks in her direction, Meredith points to a mark she just made in pink chalk on the baseboard.

Holly locks eyes with me a moment.

"Stay cool. Relaxed. Work with us."

She goes from one mark to another, drawn in a sawtooth up and down arrangement in pink, blue, green, and yellow.

Adrien starts taking deep breaths, holding her hands up before her chest and lightly touching her breastbone with her fingertips. The room immediately fills with the minty smell of her breath, mingled with a kind of barnyard odor.

Holly is watching her carefully now, while Meredith keeps glancing back at us, to make sure we're behaving, not freaking out. Fear creeps into their eyes. This is heavy. I stand next to AC, crossing around to her left so that I'm not between her and the door.

"Got to look out for her," I tell myself nobly.

Meredith repeats the succession of marks several times. They look like fake Chinese or Sanskrit letters, mixed in with little dangling lines of up and down script. What kind of "revolutionaries" are we dealing with?

Adrien moans and staggers forward, rising up onto the pads of her feet and lifting her arms. She starts to sway from the waist, then folds, flexing backward until she's bent double, then up again, without ever lowering her arms. She repeats this faster and faster, huffing, grunting, and throws off her scarf. Holly hurries to fetch it and she thrusts both hands between her legs sawing wildly. Holly snatches the scarf up and darts back to her.

"Now! Now!" he says in a prohibiting tone. "No! No! Arms up!"

With a frustrated mewling sound Adrien allows him to pull her hands back into the air again. Her arms move like pipe cleaners. Holly throws the scarf over her head again, while Meredith rushes over to get her arms. The intervention seems to throw Adrien off her rhythm and it takes her a while to get back into that flexing back and forth. Each time her hands dive down to her crotch, Meredith lunges to pull them back out and Holly repeats his "now now."

This must go on for the better part of half an hour. Adrien is glistening with sweat, breathing hard -- it smells like a horse barn in here. Meredith catches Holly's eye. They seem to be weighing some decision, maybe to stop the seance.

Adrien's breath evens into a steady panting. Meredith and Holly ease up a little.

"I think she's stable now," Meredith says.

"Wait a little more," Holly says.

They watch her carefully, holding her, for a few minutes. Then Holly says "OK."

Meredith releases Adrien, who staggers a little on the balls of her feet, her head craned back, breath coming fast, as if she were trying to see something through the scarf and the roof.

Meredith goes to the duffle bag and carefully pulls out something I recognize, the Messerschmitt head -- must be a copy -- known as the "The Artist as He Imagined Himself Laughing." A sound of surprise comes out of me, and Holly shoots me a look that tells me not to make sounds.

Adrien has elongated even further, like she's straining up into the air, trying to lift herself off the ground. I don't know if my voice aggravated her, but I think it's the unveiling of the head. The Messerschmitt head is a bust of black lead depicting a smiling man wearing a knit hat. He grins broadly, showing his even teeth. I've always remembered it because when do you ever see a statue with teeth?

Now I hear, from very far away ... from the top of a mountain overlooking a valley where the air is perfectly still ... a bell. One chime. We all heard it. Everyone started at the sound, even AC.

I notice movement around the bust and I whip my eyes over to it with a wild feeling of alarm I can't account for. A wisp of smoke is fanning out across the lead hat. It flows from the left ear of the bust, and melts into the air of the cabin.

The chime hangs, ringing in the air, not fading. I want to hold my breath, but instead I begin panting. I should take myself and AC out of here right now. What's happening to Adrien's ear? Her left ear? The speckled skin at the opening of her ear canal is discoloring; it's as if there was a jet of invisible fire shooting out of it.

Adrien snarls, grabs her chastity belt right between the legs and yanks at it so violently she's tugging her right leg clear of the floor. The animal smell pours out of her and I can hear the sound of heavy canvas ripping.

"Whup! Op! Nope!" Holly says, taking her arm.

"She's off! She's off!" Meredith says, hurrying to the duffle bag without taking her eyes from Adrien.

Adrien jerks. A window sash flies up. Adrien makes a lunging motion and whips Holly around like a crank, so he pinwheels out through the open window which snaps shut after him. It all happens so fast it's unreal -- like he weighed nothing.

"Adrien!" Meredith shouts.

Adrien throws off her scarf, and rips the heavy chastity belt in half. Meredith has a doll she's pulled from the duffle bag and is rushing up to Adrien holding it out and chanting something, but somehow, as she comes up on Adrien, she trips, staggers backwards almost as if she'd run full speed into a wall, and goes tumbling out the now open door of the cabin, which slaps shut after her -- leaving us, AC and I, alone with Adrien, who is masturbating in anguish so violently she's shredding her clothes.

Her entire body is speckled evenly. Her sweat splashes on the floor so that her feet squeak against the bare boards, her whole body flexing, the working of bunched muscles under her skin is so tremendous it's like she's turning into a wolf, as if the rigid sinews were shifting to new positions. Meredith is pounding on a window with a rock and Holly is beside her, both of them shouting wide-eyed at us, but there's no sound, no breaking glass, only the reverberation of that bell, and Adrien, her sobs, her choked and maimed language, the fragments of her clothing snowing down around her. The glass isn't breaking, or even cracking.

"Should we try and stop her?"

"No," AC says.

A wisp of smoke has just extruded itself from the Messerschmitt head. There are more wisps -- coming from where, I don't know.

The ringing has only become more remote, but it shakes space around us with a permeating throb that's like the first ripple of an earthquake. Inside it, there is a more regular stamping, a sense of something rushing headlong in our direction like a runaway train -- what is it? Something familiar about it. Looking at Adrien, it's like she's framed against an image of high mountains, sharp peaks, blue sky, green meadows dotted wildflowers, countless wildflowers, and big animals, milling around, between and among us -- something -- there's one of them, in particular ... whose eyes ...

-- a colossal yak bursts through the wall to my left with a jolt that seems to want to make the cabin slide from its foundations --

-- without thinking, I grab AC and pull her out of its path as it barrels right by us --

-- the walls and roof topple and fall away with a crash, the floor vanishes beneath grass and rocks, a stony slope and huge human forms rushing heavily past and around us, and screaming black birds and figures with cackling girls on their shoulders. The come down the slope with mattocks and picks, banging their feet against the slope like the clop and bang of a rockslide. They converge in one spot just in front of Adrien, who has somehow contrived to get herself up on the back of the yak, plunge their picks and mattocks into the ground, digging madly. The landscape is not the California chapparal -- it's not anywhere I've been, and the air is thin and I can't tell what AC is thinking, she keeps whipping her head this way and that.

A sputtering, rumbling motor noise attracts my attention in time to see a big woman, or man dressed as a woman, big as me, come roaring around a boulder on a motorcycle. This person is wearing a mu-mu and a leather aviator cap. A cigarette is pinched in the corner of a thin-lipped, downturned mouth. The motorcycle has a sidecar, and a passenger. An eighteenth-century guy in a powdered wig, with a serious nosebleed. The motorcycle is towing a miniature trailer. Because I'm hallucinating, right? The smoking head has smoked my head, clearly.

Adrien is lying on the yak's back, the Messerschmitt head perched above hers, grinning down the length of her body and oozing wisps of smoke. Adrien masturbates while the ogres hack open the ground, hauling out huge rocks and clods of cakey black soil. The big person stomps around behind the motorcycles and opens the trailer -- a mob of bright-eyed mental patients in white gowns spill out and scamper over to Adrien on their wasted, hairy legs. They begin masturbating in a circle around her with their tongues hanging out.

A luminous woman all engulfed in gauzy scarves, her eyes like two winter mint blue ice caves and antlers on her head, floats in from trees -- trees? -- densely ensconced in fog and butterflies, brandishing a long titanium scepter polished like a mirror, and some vague figures in the air attend to her, just little independent folds and flirts of mist. Eighteenth-century man walks bent, although he is not old, and his mouth, framed in scarlet on his ashen face, mutters an incessant growling. He looks like Kant. Using a tree branch as a crutch he advances toward the hovering woman without looking up at her.

Where is this landscape of black gravel and huge rocks, dense mist stinking like tar pits?

AC is staring at a point in space out beyond where gauze woman and nosebleed man are, where the mist is churning like the compartments of a kaleidoscope. I am digging alongside the ogres, throwing shovelfuls of earth over my shoulder one after another. I can't see the sky or the horizon but I know we're way up high, in a place where gravity is much less, and the air is electric.

Adrien is getting near to orgasm it sounds like and the masturbating mental patients are producing so much sperm gushing onto the ground around the yak's feet that it forms a bluish-white stream and rolls toward the pit the ogres have been digging. The sperm turns the crumbly coffee-ground loam a sterile grey white like sunbaked dogshit.

I see dead eyes on purple fire just above Adrien's knees. I see the flying woman's tears and the blood from the nosebleed man fall among the threads of sperm as it plunges into the whole. A cathedral soars upward into space from between her legs. I see AC recoil, throw up her hand, start to turn, and I chuck my shovel and run after her.

With a heavy organ rumble the cathedral rams the clearing sky with its jagged outline, looming over us now with a panoply of life-sized erotic carvings, the arclight eyes of the figures crackling to life and fluted stone mouths gushing orgasmic jets of roaring blue flame. As I reach AC, Adrien comes for the first time and the cathedral doors fly open. At about fifty meters away, glancing over my shoulder, I can see the dense, felty blackness inside and the luminous panels of colored light in the windows, the will-o'-the-wisps of the candles standing motionless in angled rows deep within. The smell of cathedrals swoops out on us.

Adrien arches her back and her cries are telling me that she's reached the moment of rapid escalation and as she comes again her cries make the gloom within the cathedral arch vibrate like a vertical pool and the orgasm congeals in it, shuddering the gloom and shuffling it together into a human form -- the Narthex, a brawny man in a blonde wig, face painted across the nose, dressed like a 1970s playboy, swaggering with thuggish hauteur down the steps toward us, and wan in the shadows stands the wiry Close --

Adrien comes again, and the dark deeper inside the cathedral trembles together into the Nave -- a crooked noodle, rolling on one battered wheel in a skirt of hay, the face long, lean, ablaze with conniving, eyes incessantly rolling, long limp hands kneading and knotting together, cooing ingratiation's.

She comes again, wildly thrashing, growling, hoarse, becoming a dirty old man and three gamboling little figures that are like giant mice or pigs, and plump, obnoxious little boys when they're children. They cluster around a deeply-tanned and oiled septuagenarian wearing only a pair of brown leather dungarees with his right hand jammed down the front and furiously jerking at himself as he swings his body after the Nave, wiping his nose on the back of his forearm. That's the Transept, attended by the Triforium.

Another orgasm, the fiercest and most exhausting, and, reclining on a sort of chaise-lounge, the Apse comes after, all in platinum satin with the Baldachin rolled up and tied to the back. The legs of the chaise-longue neatly flick in and out with the diagonal gait of a dog, setting the Apse's moon-nectar martini swaying.

Beside me I feel AC suddenly jump backwards. She must have seen something I didn't.

"Shit!"

She's bolting away from the cathedral toward a heap of high rocks that may not have anything but space behind it.

"Hey! Hey hey whoa!"

Something tells me we can't be separated here and I run after her. She saw something else in the cathedral that I didn't see. If it's that bad, maybe running away is the move.

She scrambles up the rocks.

"Aw fuck AC come on!"

I'm dragging myself up the rocks and behind me the organ is blasting and I'm missing all the lightning, but AC suddenly stops and doubles back -- no path that way I guess -- and gives me a chance to latch on to her. That's when I see something drop onto the stones down below. AC twists in my arms like a fish and it takes all my strength to hold on to her, because, if she went the way she wants to go, she'd fall headlong down that slope and crash into boulders. One glimpse of the thing down there is all I can get -- I see a box made of rib bones laced around a fibrous, pale grey bouillon cube of desiccated meat. I don't think AC saw it. It wobbles there -- I believe it was ejected from the cathedral -- now I know it must be because it just put forth a pale, skinny arm, wrapped in thick purple velvet all studded with jewels, an embroidered bird, an embroidered lion, among other things.

The ground flips on its side.

I jam myself painfully between two rocks and see AC's legs whip against a blackening sky -- I reach out and feel her waist in the crook of my elbow. She's light as paper mache. My free arm and my legs help wedge me further in among the stones, the blue washes right out of the sky and the horizon smokes with gold steam.

When I can stand again we are halfway up a long blue slope that shines white as moonlit snow, dotted with rocks in puddles of inky shadow, sharp as razors, and overlooking an ocean of madman's semen, roilingand slopping against the perfect circle of the shore. A pier juts out into the bay and a whole procession is following Adrien, still on the back of the yak and surrounded by a shuffling retinue of masturbating maniacs, to a power yacht like a cathedral lying face down in the -- well, not water -- its huge engine like a cratered cartoon meteor huffing and puffing, vibrating with pistons. The Narthex is already at the wheel, the Transept is doing something to the engine while the Triforium are shoveling moonrocks into the bluewhite furnace mouths all over it, the Nave perches on the bow like a vigilant figurehead and the Apse slips on a satin slicker and nor-wester hat, then opens a platinum parasol -- paralun I guess -- to shield the Baldachin.

At the mouth of the crater bay, a gargantuan whirlpool is forming -- it's a bizarre bluewhite cavity, like an ice cave of spoiled milk. AC writhes and snarls and kicks at me, but I don't put her down. She's slapping me, shouting --

"Blue light?! Turn around! Turn around you idiot!"

But I'm watching that whirlpool evert and reach up, screwing into the sky like a waterspout. The powerboat has ripped free of the pier in a gout of shocking red flame and is beelining toward the maelstrom.

A secondary, bluish glare, is however washing over us from behind, growing in intensity like the headlights of an approaching car. AC grabs my head in both hands and turns it so fiercely I have to pivot in place to avoid whiplash, and now I see the source of the blue light is the Earth rolling down on top of us from space. So, I start to run.

I run from the Earth, still carrying AC. Behind me, giants roll the earth down on us like a steamroller, pushing it on its axle, thighs bulging, heads down between their massive arms, and there are rows of work elementals pounding anvils all across globe, driving the planet on with their hammers. The world fixes us like a cat's eye, mottled with dead zones where there is no oxygen, and the pupil is California's golden slit all aflicker with raging wildfires.

The cataract of madmen's semen coils directly overhead, rising into space like a huge ribbon of cloudy egg white and coiling toward a spot in the Pacific Ocean, just off the burning coast of Southern California. The buttress-pontooned powerboat, covered in gothic carvings, with evil-looking rocket engines vomiting red fire and black smoke, with a roar that mingles with what sounds like screams of terror -- the Transept appears to be fucking the motor -- charges toward one side of the spermspout, and then begins to climb it along a sort of screwthread ridge around the column. Adrien is visible on the yak, square in the middle of the deck.

We're left behind?

Well, that was bound to happen.

Still running toward the shore, trying to keep my eye on the bucking powerboat as it climbs up the vertical sperm stalk ladling itself now into the Pacific Ocean, making a seething blue-white medallion on the water -- the surface of whatever we're on is folding up saddle shaped, so we're nearly bent double over the sperm super-falls -- AC thrashing and swearing.

Suddenly I catch sight of Grant; he simply slides into view against the void, riding his surfboard along the knife-edge of the semen pillar, just far enough behind the powerboat to avoid the jets of hellfire. There he goes, neat and dry, gliding with one arm calmly raised, reading the crisp wave-edges like a string of prayer beads, his perfect hair floating around him.

Even from this distance he seems to be aware of us.

He throws us a smile and waves with his floating right hand -- come on, that means, you'll have to dive in if you want to get back. Up past the two dead eyes glazed white inside the purple blazes, toward the outline of the cat's-eye slit state of California, burning gold and turning down on top of us, the great sperm slick is also Catalina Island.

So we have to jump into the ocean of insane cum to get away from the planet bearing down on us like a runaway train, or no – to land on it? Because a runaway train is the place to be?

I gaze down into the sloshing white muck below –

Wham – right into the sperm.

Swimming in it. Blinking it out of my eyes, trying to get to that spout, that funnel, tornado, vomit.

... How long?

...

... My weight is being massaged and drawn this way and that in gelatinous salt water, my hands claw sea froth, my fat buoys me – -- my head breaking through but not long enou– --

... On the beach now, finally. I 'an't think.

Wh're's AC? My weight is double' I'm crushing the island still snowy with strong-smelling semen under my sloppy feet.

... No sign of AC.

..' I'm exhausted.

... My arms, my shoulders, my chest and my back are all aching. I must have been swimming and swimming. Kelp festoons me. Salt smarts in my eyes, encrusts me. The sky is blue. There's the moon, faint white in the blue like a fading cum stain. I'm on earth, then. That's good.

Right? Yeah. I mean ... sure, right.

... Nobody around. Panting, I shamble up the long slope from the beach, until I reach a broad, flat expanse of scattered trees below a ridge line.

Something whuffles at me, on my left. What is it?

... It's a bison.

A bull bison.

A whole herd of bison, waiting for me.

"Hey," I say.

... Numbly, I drag myself further up the slope. I think I'm trying to find a vantage point. I crawl up on a heap of rocks and turn around, wincing as a flash of reflected light hits my eye. I think it's the sun flashing off a window in what might have been a tall tower, rising up over the ridge there. Now I can't find it.

Seeing no other likely signs, I get down and start plodding upwards, in the rough direction of the flash.

... There it is again -- another pyrotechnic burst of sunlight, and the suggestion of a white spire now, rather than a tower. But when I blink the glare away, I can't find it. Just pink and green after images swimming against everything.

... Again it happens.

... I'm getting scared -- there plainly is nothing there, but I keep getting these sunbolts. My eyes are still burning with salt and my head is spinning, a flash, try to see what it is, so tired -- nothing but sky.

... I top the ridge and find myself looking down into a little canyon with a broad, level floor. The canyon is open at one end, and fans out to form a natural amphitheatre.

... The shape of the canyon -- makes me think of something -- it hits my mind like lightning.

... Before my eyes I see lines float up from the canyon floor, precise jets of water and curtains of water and precise rising domes and spires like the shapes of fountains, stable, but not solid -- a grand gallery, a spacious plaza, a great hall, ancillary buildings, delicate fountains, graceful spires high enough to be seen over the ridgeline. The spire I saw flash from down there.

... There is a temple complex there and not there, there and not there, there and not there, each time there it is, and a flash of the drafting table and the building plan laid out in front of me and me working on the plan, dotting lines and numbering angles, flash in on the complex more and more constructed, with great cranes, hulking workers carrying slabs and girders, and the light in the canyon swells like sunlight coming from behind a cloud and dimming out again, that heavy ebb and flow of weightless light -- I see through the scaffolding, the activity of construction, through to the concept and its relationships, where angles become black lines and dotted arcs on white paper forming a constellation of thrilling numerical balancing acts whose end result is a structure made mostly out of water arranged in jets and sheets, plumes and screens, waternumbers falling into slots and chutes to help muffle the noise of the falling -- another fallingwater, a literal fallingwater, my fallingwater, where Grant will gather to do his ONE ONE ONE for ghosts doing the meditations, raising and lowering their arms, their heads, and the water funneling their vibes up translucent spires to a mind-beacon concentration focus point, way up in the air over our heads to rain down in pains on the earth again.

... Am I on the ridge?

... Naked in front of my drafting table, my clothes shredded and thrown all over in puddles of seawater and wisps of kelp. I grab something, maybe a blanket? to dry myself with hastily, then sweep everything off my drafting table toss down a sheet of paper and then I throw the plan for the annex on it in great long exact sweeps --

...

... My phone is ringing. The pert voice on the other end of the line identifies itself as UCLA Medical Center. I check the time, but I have no idea when I started. My body is numb, the light in the sky might be day ending or breaking, I don't know.

-- What time is it?!

-- It's time to go.

Grant is in the emergency room.

I receive this information without surprise and begin robotically dressing myself in my seawater clothes. Halfway through this procedure it occurs to me that I am in my home where all my clothes are, and I switch to dry, basically clean clothes.

... Grant is sitting on the edge of an ivy-filled planter outside the hospital as I pull up. I can't be sure, but it seems like someone else is just leaving him.

"What happened?"

Grant is pale; his voice is weak but calm.

"I'm not sure. I guess it was an asthma attack. I'd been feeling funny for a while, then all of a sudden I couldn't breathe. I guess I must have passed out. I woke up here. They say there's nothing physically wrong with me."

The heap of medical documentation rests there on his lap, giving off a bad smell. There's something like a smell dissipating off of Grant too, the trace of a brush with death -- a sort of whisper, a sort of cold? Who was that just quitting his side?

Grant carefully folds his forms together into a packet.

"Hold up here a second."

He gets out of the car at an intersection and tosses the medical bale into a garbage can. When he gets back in the passenger seat, he seems less ashen.

"How did it go?"

I laugh.

But who was that just quitting his side?

So I tell him all about it on the drive to his beach, where he wants to go, and it seems very lame and ridiculous put into words, commingling with traffic lights, litter, and dopey bumper stickers. Grant listens to me with the wind holding his hair up away from his ears, as if it were helping him.

Meanwhile in the suburbs people are sitting down to dinner lit up one family per square. The epidemic hasn't hit yet, so the state of emergency is only ordinary. Home hearthlights flow out on lawns and gardens.

Float like seaweed through those homes and domestic sights until you reach the house with no lights on. Lying low against the ground, ominous beneath heavy trees.

Go through the wall.

("Caen you imaegine being possessed by the body of a teenaeged girl?") the Apse says and clicks her tongue. ("I'd raether be aenointed in oil. HIC You couldn't get *me* in one of those things!")

The Narthex is cleaning his solid amber 1911 automatic with a soft cloth. The upper half of his face is coated with a thick layer of congealed honey. Through it can be seen the false eyes painted on his permanently closed eyelids. His lips and teeth are black, and cigar ash covers the rest of his face, all the way down to his closely bandaged throat. The Transept is sitting on the floor in front of the open stove, drenched in sweat, steaming in the oven heat, and masturbating with his hand down his leather pants. He concentrates fiercely, compelling the Triforium to make the house more habitable -- removing light bulbs, doubling up curtains, blocking drains and keyholes. The whole place must be hermetically sealed. The Close stands in the corner by the front door, a pale face on a wiry body, impassive, watchful. Eyes rolling in her sun-dappled face, the Nave has the end of a spider web wrapped around her thin green tongue and she's tugging gently at it, coaxing the spider down into her mouth. Once its legs begin to play speculatively on her lips, she sucks it in noisily and rattles it around inside puffed cheeks, which light up so the spider is visible, scrabbling wildly around in there. She blows a spider-bubble and flicks it out into the gloom with an index finger.

The Apse sips her martini and looks at the Nave.

("Thaet's some paestime.")

The Nave wheels over to her deferentially, her weird hay skirt hissing on the linoleum.

"Perhaps you would ... like one?"

She gestures at another spiderweb in the corner. The spider hears her and scurries behind some moulding.

("I prefer a mosquito, HIC.")

The Nave wipes the spittle from her chin and dries her fingertips on her sailor's tunic.

The Apse ruffles her slimy hair with a free hand.

("Now, let's do whistles.")

The revolutionaries gather together in the dark and fling their arms around each others' shoulders, eyes burning like angry red stars -- even the painted eyes of the Narthex -- and they whistle in unison, rocking side to side, smoke rising from their lips, and a reedy chord of crumbling friction rises jauntily from them, braided together and twisting out into the suburban time with a subtle warp that slides along the suburban nerves raising the suburban hackles, slides an element of tension and darkness into idle dinner conversations, so that the dusk flattening into night against the windows takes on an ominous weight ... solid black panels on white walls, and at the same time, the outer night is yawning and deepening to infinity, opening to a danger that never fully comes, but which seems to hang, dilating, just above the gleams of tall streetlights. The bright points only intensify the gulfs they make vanish between them, but there is enough light from the sky to show the blue outlines of somber trees and brooding ridge lines. That daemon-warp mumbles and palpates the nerve-haze of the contracting neighborhood, like a speculative predator searching for something. It stirs restlessness in people who are too tired to do anything about it. It numbs and distracts people who are awake. It gives the night an innocence that makes people forget to sleep, makes them want to go out to where the shadows each hide a coyote, a poisonous snake, a serial killer, or maybe even a mountain lion.

Whistle whistle whistle. Even the Close can't help but join in. Rustling in the hidden rafters, between the roof and the plaster, the Crossing draws near -- a grey spiderishness drenching them in an invisible shower of ghoulish cold.

But what's -- ?

... There's something --?

... Something's feeding back along the whiz of the note ... something is sliding back at them along the whir of the note.

There, in the center of the braided whistling, like a funnel of smoke ...

... There he is, headlights swarming around his head, drinking silence with his hot tea, drinking silence with the darkness in his hair, drinking silence with his smug dzi bead, drinking silence with his white linens, taking them on without any holy names or symbols, without any pentangles, without Hebrew, without Latin, with nothing but calm. He surfs their whistles back to them, finding and reminding ... you're here to do a job ... just a little job ... do me a favor, and help me with this one little job ...

Grant and I are on the 134, zooming under green highway signs in the concrete trough.

"We didn't lose our souls, did we?"

"No, Chalo."

"We didn't sign anything, so we're good, right?"

"Right."

Grant has his head back, one arm rests along the lowered window.

"But don't they only work for souls?"

"Maybe. I'm gambling myself on it. Just myself."

"Just yourself?"

"Just myself."

"So you signed?"

"No. I didn't."

"But they're still here, with us?"

I have the feeling they're not only still around, but that they're right here with me, right behind me, back in the back seat.

"With no signature, they are only half-summoned."

"Half-summoned."

"Right."

"And you know this how?"

"From what's happening."

"So you didn't know going into this. You just gave it a shot on spec."

"You were never at risk, Chalo."

"I ended up in the Pacific, man, I think that's risk."

"I thought you ended up at home."

Wind. Hushed whir of freeway traffic.

"I wanted them half-summoned," Grant says. "Trying to pin them down ... it never works out. They always weasel out of any articulated bargain. But with silence, you can get them. You can bring them through enough so that they can't go back -- and they don't want to go back, they want to stay on this side and make trouble -- but they aren't free to act. You pull them in to you by with-holding orders, because they think they can catch you. They're wait-ing; that's just what they're waiting for. -- So remember, don't bargain with a stranger."

"Everything's evil and everybody's a stranger anyway."

"The question is whether these are what you're thinking of as evil demons to us, or to the bankers. What's evil to the evil is good to the enemies of the evil."

I drive on in silence myself for a while, watching the silhouetted hills swell in the windshield. I look over at Grant, and he seems twenty years older, all the color blanched from underneath his tan.

"You're going to handle real demons with logical jugglery. ... Maybe not?"

"I have got the sound of a billion hands clapping."

A smile appears, speaking not to me but to the roof of the car, and the sky above it.

━━━

The Nave leans into a closeup. Her drawn face is streaked with perspiration --

They can handle drumming, they can handle chanting, they can handle beating the ground with hands and feet, they can handle circles and squares and classical languages, but they can't handle this smooth silence. It's like someone following you around every-where you go, not saying anything but just looking at you, waiting.

Of course, that's what the Close does, but the Close is one of them and part of them. They can't handle it coming from outside the church. So the Nave wheels up to the Apse, who is reclining on her divan with her sempiternal martini. The Nave is always quivering, as if she were about to giggle with pain.

"Grant praesses us through the Crossing," she says. "What should we do? You alwaeys know whaet to do!"

("Mm,") the Apse says. She speaks with a midwestern twang. ("Well, he is raether getting on my nerves, too ...")

"Whaet aebout the Pulpit? Aeren't they working on him?" the Narthex rumbles.

("They haenven't had enough time to do much, Narthex. HIC! Not thaet they ever tell me aenything.")

"They took a humaen naeme," the Narthex says with displeasure. "Thaet meaens they aernen't here to plaey baell with us."

The Nave wraps her arm around her head and drags her hand over her face and scalp.

"Grant presses *hard*," she whines. "He shows glide ... claims color. His implacable waeve riding is maeking unfortunaeteness toward us aend it's driving me nuts."

"NUT," the Transept says, biting off the T crisply.

"We aere being nutsdriven by the incessaent mute exortaetion of Grant. He presses us through the Crossing. You alwaeys know whaet to do. Tell us whaet to do."

The Apse lolls her head back thoughtfully on the chaise-longue, rolls it very slowly from right to left, then lifts it again. She takes a sip of her martini, hiccups, then drops her head back and rolls it again. It's still rolling as she begins to speak.

("We're going to haeve to HIC give him something to tide him over, thaet's aell. If we caen get him some of thaet money he's aefter, he'll haeve to go aebout using it, aend that should get him to laey off for a time.")

"Aww thaet sounds like work," the Narthex grumbles.

The Apse's head arrives upright on her neck at last.

("Well, it should buy us some time to figure a way out of this mess.")

The others gather around. The Triforium adjust the lighting, drawing the Apse a little farther into the deeper shadow that hovers about them like a negative campfire.

("*I* tell you whaet, the Nave aend the Transept should head over to the baenk and get them to waeive that credit history.")

"HEAED," the Transept says.

"Would thaet be enough?" the Nave asks eagerly.

The Apse nods her chin down to her collarbone and swings her head up again, her large eyes half covered by her heavy eyelids.

("Enough to maeke work but not enough to HIC maeke us commit. He'll haeve his haends full trying to get thaet loan then -- say ...")

An anti-light comes into her eyes, which fades to two cold points. She barks a cold laugh that makes the Nave straighten up electrified.

"You've thought of something?" she asks impetuously.

("Ho ho ho,") the Apse chortles. ("Haeve I! Gaether 'round fellas.")

The demons converge on her.

If you had second sight then you would see those two demons walking in the door as they are.

(If you had second sight, you wouldn't be working here.)

If you had second sight, you wouldn't see two gymbody business smoothsters in senator suit-and-hair combos blandly flicking cell-phones, you'd see two crazy demons boogie-ing down the hall with eyes like cold stars and cold star-slime-streaked chins, snapping their fingers and bobbing their heads. The Transept veers off course following every ass and the Nave wheels right in behind him to steer him back around with long sure fingers.

"Mmmnnokay this is Mr. Brairbershn, he's our Creditorian and he'll be helping you today," the receptionist says.

The Transept slobbers and rams his dick up and down inside his leather pants. The Nave gently palpates the air near her with her upper lip hoisted. To the receptionist, they appear to be two respectable straight men in suits, rather stupidly standing in front of her instead of going in to meet Mr. Brairbershn.

"Their company must stand on ceremony more," she thinks. "Old-fashioned."

Aloud she says, "Go along in please."

"Aesk us three times," the Nave says.

"I'm sorry?"

"*Our* HR depaertment requires us to be aesked three times before we enter aeny office," the Nave explains, with just the right note of superiority.

"ENTER!" the Transept echoes, pounding himself violently. His comments don't penetrate his cover, although a closer observer might have noticed an agitation of the pink cheeks.

"Oh wow," the receptionist says. "That's super-thorough."

"They're strict aes hell," the Nave says.

"OK well, please go on in."

"GO IN!"

"Thaet's one."

"Please go in,"

"GO IN!"

"Thaet's two."

"And, please go in!" the receptionist says, her voice rising as she gets into the spirit of the game.

"GO IN!"

"Thaenk you very much!" the Nave says unctuously.

The two seep in on the Creditorian, who has been tossing wafers of data into folders on a screen between himself and the window. Now he comes up to them with his hand out.

"Hello, how are you? I'm Steve Brairbershn."

"I'm Warren Navistock," the Nave says.

"ROD FITZTRABS."

"Well Mr. Navistock, Mr. FitzTrabs, what can I do for you today?"

"We're here to discuss the issuaence of a credit waiever in connection with loaen applicaetion 430233."

"Are you representing Mr. Grant?"

"Yes, thaet's right."

If you had second sight, you'd see her blow her nose copiously into a filthy rag and hand it, quivering with snot, over to Mr. Brairbershn, who does not have second sight and consequently sees a power of attorney crisply extracted from the inside pocket of a rather unobtrusively expensive tailored suit and extended to him in manicured fingers.

"Mmnok, just let me call up the application here ..."

Mr. Brairbershn's face works thoughtfully as he reviews Grant's documentation, which is a virtual blank.

"Ehmm, well, I'm not sure we can ... oblige you there ..."

Mr. Brairbershn continues to flip squares on the screen, his back to them.

"You're not sure ...?"

Mr. Brairbershn reaches, without looking, for his pen, which rests like a mercury lancet of cool professionalism on the glass counter before him.

"Let me give those figures one laest little look," the Nave says as she reaches across the desk for the tablet and knocks the pen to the floor.

"Butterfingers! Let me get thaet for you."

Face blazing with concentrated mockery she fixes her gaze on Mr. Brairbershn as she pantomimes retrieving the pen.

"Here it is," she says, producing from the lining of her own filthy jacket a Messerschmitt head, the one misnomered as "An Enraged and Vengeful Gypsy," and sets it down on the desk. She reaches into the left ear, which flexes as if it were made of actual cartilage; wisps of grey smoke rise sluggishly into the air as the Nave pulls her daemon stylus out, glowing orange like an unquenched ingot, and presses it into the distracted Creditorian's limply open hand with a hiss of steam.

Fire shoots through every nerve in the Creditorian's body, sweat bursts from every pore, without looking he scribbles his signature on the credit waiver the Nave holds out to him.

"Thaenk you!" the Nave croons nasally, tucking the waiver into her nose with a small bow.

"Thank *yooou!*" Mr. Brairbershn screeches, his eyes popping.

The Nave links arms with the Transept and they begin to turn like counterweights around each other, bobbysocksing out of the office while Mr. Brairbershn fumbles at his pocket square, which is sewn in place. The Messerschmitt head stares alarmingly at him, teeth bared in a crazed grin, and viscous smoke dribbling slimily from the left ear. The smoke lifts heavily from the bust, and melts into the antiseptically conditioned air of the office.

Arm in arm the revolutionaries sashay out the front door, the Nave half-towing the Transept who sways in space like a magnet, attracted by every rump he sees, and out into the street and into the back of the black maria the Narthex has idling at the curb. In his office, Mr. Brairbershn stares at the head on his desk, transfixed by its wide-open eyes of pupiless black lead. The skin around the opening of his ear canal discolors, as if it were charring. His body begins to jerk and quiver. His face twitches in shapeless, nameless new facial expressions. Suddenly he throws himself to the floor, b-boying wildly.

"Aell's well old boy!" the Nave brandishes the credit waiver where the Narthex can see it. "The Apse's Messerschmitt gimmick did the trick! Now we caen do spells!"

"She's alwaeys right aebout thaet sort of thing."

The Narthex leers around his cigar, the Triforium nose the heavy car out into traffic, Mr. Brairbershn pinwheels in a frenzy of masterful floorwork spraying sweat like a lawn sprinkler -- king flares, air flares and floats, crickets and halos and perfect darkhammers. His body throws off a tainted wind that ruffles the expensive, tastefully flavorless polo shirts of his horrified co-workers. As the revolutionary book people are withdrawing from the neighborhood, Mr. Brairbershn drops into a long spinout on midspine, and explodes in vomit amid barks of disgust.

"Oh -- God!" someone cries peremptorily. "Call housecleaning!"

"You can still see the sashimi!" the receptionist whispers.

⊏────⊐

For a moment, I thought he'd died in his wheelchair with his back to the setting sun, because his eyes and mouth were open and there was a fly -- a big fat one -- rubbing its hands there on his left eye. He stirred when I shooed the fly away, dabbed at his eye, and a tear came out.

⊏────⊐

... These fucking flies won't give me a moment's peace. I roll around in the grass. There's a big pushy one in particular that keeps whacking me in the face, like a belligerent frat boy chest bumping me. Another one keeps hissing in my left ear. There's another one beating off in the middle of my nose, and there's this lazy languid one who never comes near but never goes away, either. I'm moving up into the wind. Is that a spider, dangling from one my horns?

... OK now the mountain wind is giving them some trouble but the little shits aren't giving up! They're clinging to me now. I'm scraping my head against the grass and the rocks.

... Right on the ridge now. I throw my head around letting the air groom me. I want to go up, my feet are taking me up and up, through the little gullies, to the spot I've been to before, where the figure took me.

... A venerable old bull blocks my path. Peering at me, nearsightedly blinking through his long eyelashes, he stands perfectly still, his breath rattling in his chest.

Come with me, please, is the message.

A small committee of elder yaks, mixed bulls and cows, is waiting for us at a more even spot on the mountainside, out of the wind. Two of them, one a bull, a bit younger and very black, and the other a greyish-brown cow, are strangers to me; they seem like specialists, called in from another herd, for a consultation. Regarding me.

The old bull stands off from the rest, staring with weary majesty into the valley.

So, he says in effect, you've been dabbling in black magic, have you?

By remaining still, I reject the assertion that I've performed any magic.

The old bull blinks slowly and turns his head, meaning, You have had at least one exchange with the Figure.

I remain still, not denying that I encountered the Figure, but only that there was an exchange.

The old bull looks to the black specialist and snuffles.

The black yak, who has been eyeing me appraisingly since I came among this group, raises his head and extends his snout in my direction, then rotates his head and turns it, so as to look strangely askance down his cheek at me. He addresses the group.

There is a great mass of magic actions which show a similar motivation, but the foremost, which has always played a great role among yak herds, is the art of attracting cows by magic. Cows are attracted by imitating sex acts and perhaps also by imitating cows themselves. "Playing cow," we call it.

The black yak waggles his horns, flutters his eyes and nods, shifts his weight on his forelegs from one to the other, and finally urinates in two jets that each inscribe a sloppy crescent in the dust beneath him. This means:

The earliest magical operation intended to attract cows is, of course, a series of indications with the horns directed to suggestively-contoured gaps in the clouds, but in a later phase of cultural development, instead of these more or less direct magical conjurations of cows, the young bull makes a ritual ascent to appease the spirits of the heights so they will send him cows. But all this is simply a wishful misunderstanding, which puts psychological laws in place of natural ones.

I lower my head and inspect a clod of earth between my front hoofs, which means that I maintain I have made no magical operations intended to attract cows.

A matronly yak from our herd, whose relations with the old bull are strained even though, or perhaps because, they've had several calves together, is the next to address me. She opens her jaws slightly and heaves a long creaking sigh, closes her eyes and turns her snout into the wind.

No one is looking to restrict your personal freedom, she is telling me. I am sure we will all agree that none of us wishes to interfere with your spiritual practices. We are concerned, however, because we -- all of us -- have seen young bulls like yourself go completely insane after encountering the Figure, sometimes even after only one encounter.

The old bull farts, and inhales in two quick gasps, as if he were short of breath. This means, You could hurt others or yourself if you go insane.

By remaining still, I thank them for their concern, and express a desire to avoid going insane or causing trouble in the herd.

The black yak nudges the grey-brown cow by his side, and she takes a step in my direction. Her smell washes over me in a delirious wave; in a few weeks, perhaps, such a wave will induce an intolerable frenzy of arousal. At present, however, it only confuses me. This gesture of hers means that the black yak is inviting me to further conversations with him.

I don't really object, but it seems to me that if I agree quickly, I'll seem like I'm only saying yes to weasel out of it. So I allow my stomach gurgling to become more audible, to show I'm actually considering my answer.

The grey-brown cow turns to look behind her, meaning that I should not worry, that no one is accusing me of anything.

By remaining still, I agree to meet with the black yak again tomorrow.

Until then, is his answer.

... The other yaks watch me as I walk back down the slope. The flies have returned, flinging themselves at my face, but I barely notice.

Something is cracking and collapsing like a rock face inside me. I don't care anymore -- I just -- suddenly I'm full of shame for listening to them -- the way they talk that shit -- agreeing to talk more about it tomorrow -- all the weight vanishes from in my chest -- I run back -- I don't look -- I just run, and feel the ground go up -- crying and running --

The ground drops away -- I stop at the edge -- no I don't want to jump down and die -- if I'm going to be damned either way, whether I see the Figure again, or submissively reduce myself down below, then I might as well see the Figure some more.

... There's no windbreak up here, and the wind hits the tears all over my big nose, and it feels sliced. I can't let them scoff at my heart so I might as well, I might as well. I'll see the Figure if I fucking want. ... I'm wrung out.

... I turn around empty to face the Figure, who isn't waiting, any more than a tree or a stone would be, but always ready, the way stones and trees are, and I'm ready.

⊏▭⊐

Tertiary Credit Furnisher Stephanie Debnebdld 25 leaves California Fedality a little after 4 PM. She stops at a red light a few blocks away and glances into her rear-view mirror. The driver of the nondescript black car behind her sits so low in the seat that she can only make out the top of his head -- what appears to be a very short person, dark skinand close-cropped hair with a dramatic widow's peak. Something else is also strange, but the traffic is moving.

... Then, at the market, less than ten minutes later, as she turns into the frozen food aisle, she glimpses again the top of the head. It is just visible above the pushbar of a shopping cart. She is distracted now, unable to interrupt the momentum of doing her shopping, checking and rechecking her phone, loading her car, leaving the lot. She remembers the cart was in motion when she saw it, but there were no hands on the pushbar. The cart may have been empty. There may have been someone else, a regular sort of person, pulling the cart from the front end. So the small dark person might not have been pushing the cart, but only following it, very close behind.

... But what was particularly strange about it, she now realizes, as her house on Park Drive wheels into view, was the greyness of its blackness, and the way it shone. Oily skin gleams, but this skin glinted.

... Now that she thinks about it, having pulled her car into the tree-shaded carport, the brow was narrowly furrowed, as if whoever it was had winched their eyebrows up all the way.

... It is now about 5:45.

... She stows her groceries, changes her clothes, checks and rechecks her phone, and goes out again at quarter to seven. A dinner date with an old friend, Paralegal Associate Steffi Grnobkgln 25, at 1850 Bistro on Industrial Street.

... Stephanie arrives first. The maitre d' has a shaved head, dark skin. That's what I meant, she thought. Gleaming, where that other head had been glassy. She is seated in a red vinyl booth. One menu for her, and another in the place opposite. Steffi sends word that she will be delayed. Stephanie orders a Negroni even though she doesn't like them. Taking a sip right away helps her to overcome her distaste for the drink.

... When she looks up, her gaze falls of its own accord into the sizeable mirror on the wall in front of her, and there in the second booth behind her she sees the very top of the same head, facing away from her, glinting in the muted light of the restaurant, the very close-cropped hair forming a sort of pattern radiating from the crown.

... Nonplussed, she dithers with her drink, keeping her eyes fixed on the head, which is motionless. As still as a sculpture. Without fully realizing it, she is hoping it will become indistinct and lapse somehow. She very much wants it to stop being conspicuous. Embarrassed, she hurries to the women's bathroom.

... There, over the top of the stall behind her as she washes her hands ... and no feet below the door of the stall. The head is right up against the top of the door and there are no feet at the bottom. Stephanie turns and leaves, almost forgetting her phone, not bothering to dry her hands, nearly colliding with another woman coming in.

... Walking out onto Industrial Street, over to her car, mechanically getting inside, then whipping around in sudden panic at the thought that she might now see that head in her rear view mirror again, this time inside -- in the back seat.

Her car is empty.

"I'm in a horror movie. I'm hallucinating."

... She texts Steffi, explaining that she is currently experiencing hallucinations of a disembodied head. There's a sharp knock on the driver's side window an inch from her ear, and Stephanie flinches, recoils, drops the phone, looks up into Steffi's confused, rather stern face through the glass.

Steffi's confusion only deepens as her friend, having rolled her window down, jabbers apologies and half-intelligible excuses before driving away.

... Stephanie drives home with her window down and air buffeting her face, rushes to the front door, flings it open, and confronts a gargantuan face of lustrous, supple black lead. It's Messerschmitt's "A Strong Man," floating in a void of its own that dwarfs the house ... dwarfs her.

... Later that evening, Steffi, having received the texts about hallucinations, is contacting people, trying to get a handle on what's going on. She receives a fresh text from Stephanie.

"Right now, in my left ear, is the hottest record of the summer."

... That was the first "spell."

Somehow, at the next gathering, Anthony Motion is the only one who turns up. Grant catches sight of him silhouetted under the arbor by the fountain. The breeze dies down; in the still air, Grant puts on his veil and sits in his usual spot. Through the white film he can see Anthony rise smoothly and step out into the sun. He was introduced to Grant at another session a few weeks ago, and since then he's kept on cropping up. He was always alone, and always appeared somehow as if he were centered in a picture frame. When he sat down anywhere, he always was perfectly still in every part except one; maybe one hand's fingers would be evenly drumming, or one foot would be vibrating in the air, crossed over his knee, while the rest of him was as still as a picture.

"This is Anthony."

Grant glanced up and locked eyes with him. Anthony had steady, fashionably compassionate, pale brown eyes that were very large in a smiling face framed in cherubic blonde curls. He nodded once, unhastily and deeply, his eyes closing as his face descended and opening as he lifted it again.

Now Anthony glides up to take a seat directly in front of Grant, lowering himself deliberately into position. He folds his hands in his lap and rocks them up and down. There's never anything really nervous about his fidgeting. Grant notices the stillness about Anthony, that is only punctuated by these tremors that seem intended to amplify the statuesque unwaveringess of the rest of his stationary body.

Becalmed in the golden afternoon, the college is quiet. There is no breath of wind, and the beams of sunlight are static. The gobbling noise the fountain normally makes is muted and intermittent. The whir of traffic around the campus is as muffled as if it were coming from beneath the ground. The whole unexpectedly subterranean day is buried beneath heavy blue and gold strata of light and sky, an oppressive glory that dazes like sunstroke, although the day is not too warm.

Grant's hands rise and fall. His smothered voice is chanting from an adjacent space. The pupils of Anthony's round eyes are so black. They anchor him against the world in an intolerable way, and intimately, like dark pins drilled back through his head and into space. The movements he makes are shackled to still points that hold their positions like a sardonic reverence for the blastings of the world, as if to say that it's all nothing, and what's more, a nothing that can never be mastered, that only reflects an inner blankness, a horrifying, perfectly smooth and powerful and beguilingly useful blankness. The blankness of Jim Jones' sunglasses.

What matters, those two pupils are saying, is the grand curl of emptiness inside the wave, that's what you surf on.

What matters in the chant is the silence it sheds around itself like a sacred precinct in sound, and the gestures do the same in space.

The void power is a smooth and even horror; and, motionless, it travels everywhere in silence. The blank is the vampiric slumber of the magic black and white of mirrors, that reflect the specious reality of whatever comes before them, while draining off for themselves the latent empty power of what they show.

Grant knows that Anthony will still be gazing at him with unappeased expectancy after the chanting is over, and that they will walk together then.

... And later on, when Chalo comes to pick Grant up at the hospital, it's Anthony who has just quit his side. Anthony was already in the ambulance when it came to retrieve Grant, and he sat beside him, staring with his compassionate eyes down on Grant, as the EMTs drove him through the night, drumming his fingers regularly on his knee. Anthony was with Grant when Grant had his terrible attack.

... I can handle this, Grant thinks, straining for breath. He has something I can use. This isn't about me, this is about Catalina and building the Annex, remember that.

Grant's chest is rigid as steel, refusing to open up for air.

The Annex is greater than I am. If I go down, I go down, but I'm not going down – Grant feels as if his diaphragm is right in the back of his throat – slammed shut, no breath, no breath – I can manage him – no breath, panic, dying, dying – I can manage him –

Grant feels his lungs beginning to soften again, and, knowing he will come through, finds Anthony's steady, compassionate, unblinking eyes, and it's like looking up to know you're not alone and finding only the bare white expanse of the ceiling. A ceiling that goes on and on, never meeting a wall, unsupported, and drawing down.

I can get through it, Grant thinks. If I can get my breath back, I can get through it.

Breath falls reluctantly into him again.

There.

See?

I only need enough – think positive – it will never fail.

... And when they are sitting outside in the gloom, Grant waits for Chalo – he refused Anthony's offer of a ride – one day when he's stronger, but tonight no.

... Now, Anthony sits with his long legs crossed. His ankle swings up and down. His face is turned toward Grant, motionless. The air, motionless.

"How are you feeling, now?" Anthony asks.

His lips barely move when he talks, but his jaw compensates with exaggerated action.

His facial expression is always the same, warm, compassionate, understanding, tranquil. When he's finished speaking, it's as if he'd said nothing.

"It was like someone stuffed my chest full of wool."

Grant looks up and recognizes Chalo's shitty hatchback pulling up. Anthony whisks away into the dark at the same moment. It's as if he were yanked into the shadows on a line.

... With an effort, Grant pushes down on his *dantian* and draws a reasonably full and refreshing draft of night air into himself. It's as though he'd been unwilling to exhale all the way out while Anthony was still there. Grant stands as Chalo heaves out of the driver's seat.

... Grant meets AC at the usual spot, a table on the sidewalk; she hands him the next swatch of translation and he passes her a cash envelope through a plume of pu-erh steam. He pages through her work while she clutches the arms of her chair impatiently, waiting for him to give her something new.

The Narthex and the Nave stand suspended thirteen feet off the ground on an invisible pavement, gazing down at them. Other vague figures, fellow book people, revolutionaries, pass to and fro on this glass sidewalk, attending to their victims. The Narthex kneels down for a closer look, his black mouth snarled around a thin green cigar.

Grant puts AC's translation into his drooping undyed linen messenger bag and pulls out another sheaf of the *Complutensian Polyglot Terma*, which he hands to her in a roll, like a newspaper.

"Whaet's in that one?" the Narthex asks.

The Nave lowers her head like a boa constrictor checking out the forest floor from a tree branch.

"*Thaet's* aebout anti-tulpas. I wonder why."

"If he knew whaet thaet waes aebout, why would he need it traenslated?"

"He doesn't know. *Someone* knows."

"Hmm," the Narthex grates.

He stares at AC.

"I'm going to give thaet girl her pick me up," he says.

He reaches into his shoulder holster and draws his 1911. All the parts are made entirely of amber. It's heavily ornamented but transparent, so the decorations are inscrutable. The Nave backs up and places her fingers in her ears as the Narthex chambers a dazzling spark that gutters and dribbles tiny blue spuming's through the gun as if it weren't there. He aims down his extended arm, his head thrown imperiously back. AC's head slides easily into the center of the sight, and the Narthex immediately lowers the gun, crouches down, and peers into the depths of her mind. She's reviewing the anti-tulpa text on the outside, while on the inside there is a sleeve of helical caves turning around a transit.

"You're not going to shoot?"

Clear pistils of sound, like fat parentheses, glide out of the caves and brush AC's bright red brain. The Narthex can see her astral form gritting its teeth and snarling in pain. The pistils are painting AC's red brain clear with tiny Tibetan characters that flip like dominos, becoming Roman letters in English words, while her whole nervous system shudders with rage and loathing instantly converted into pain.

"She doesn't need it ..." the Narthex says, surprised.

Scintillant points uncoil from his eyes and fall in loops around her, as if there was a disco ball spinning just above her head. The colored points strafe around AC, caging her in moving light. The Narthex drills his gaze through his own sealed eyelids and inside her red brain, where he sees a vast, open earthquake landscape shaking under a green-black sky with a tornado just starting to form. The rocking ground is consumed by what at first seems like lightless flames; it takes the Narthex a moment to realize the flames are thousands of shadowy human forms tangled in mortal combat. The Narthex struts through them, brushing the soft bodies aside with the muzzle of his gun, until he finds AC.

Most souls have a subroutine, a characteristic gesture or action they're usually doing. Some people's souls are always lecturing at a podium. Other people's souls are always eating. Still others are always sleeping. AC's soul is straddling a prone form, someone whose hands are on her face, trying to shove her away, and AC is rearing back, the fury of her expression made even more frightening by the way those hands are distorting her features. She is driving an enormous blade into the body beneath her, which is so dense that she can barely force the point into the flesh, and she has to push with all her might, steadily, not giving up, pushing and pushing while hands scrabble at her face, bending her back, the flesh of the body pushing the blade out, and while a scream comes over the horizon rushing in this direction to join with its body like a hurtling storm wind.

"Thaet one's got staemina," the Nave says over his shoulder with a little sniff.

The Narthex jumps.

"You're alwaeys creeping!"

AC scowls at the Tibetan writing in her hand. Grant sips his tea, reviewing her translation. The Narthex can see an unsettling rhombus of nothing glowing around that dzi bead. No visible brain, no soul. Instead, Grant is suffused with a deferral so smooth and easy that it threatens to draw him out into an infinity of blankness. But there is something familiar there ...

Switch back to AC.

"I think I can get a freeze off this one," the Narthex says.

Bending forward slinkily, he passes his face and head through the clear pavement and keeps moving until he's standing upside down on the reverse side, his face inches from the crown of AC's head. With the ember of his cigar he sets fire to a trembling plume of angry spirit chi that whirls out of her top chakra and inhales it in savage gulps, snapping his black teeth. Breath bursts from his nose with a whistle, and his nostrils are coated in frost. He teakettles onto his back and flips straight up onto the top of the pavement again, then hops up and down in front of the Nave with his head flung back, jouncing like a pogo stick, bliss strangled in his throat.

The Nave's face crinkles in a knowing leer of appreciation. Her features are daubed with roving patches of shapeless sunlight, as if she were always in the dappled late afternoon shade of summer trees. From her vantage point above the crowd, she watches Chalo amble up to the table and sit down next to AC.

He greets them both, says something to Grant, and then turns his attention back to her. The Nave detects an intense and fruitless mental effort to come up with an icebreaker.

"Poor fellow!" she chuckles, spit dripping from her teeth.

He manages to come up with something he doesn't think is toxically lame and says it. The Nave watches Chalo reach inside his own head and pull out a colorful cellophane pinwheel on a stick and hand it to AC, who doesn't notice him.

"Slow down turkey, she's not for you," the Nave giggles.

The pinwheel starts melting into grey smoke that blows away to nothing, and Chalo's spirit partially deflates, generating a tempting chocolatey gloom.

"Who would you saey she's for, old son?" the Nave asks, glancing at the Narthex. When she looks at Chalo again, her eyes sparkle like dirty water in the sun.

"I want a whiff of *him*."

Now she oozes face-first through the pavement and her long tongue laps at Chalo's heart. Chalo flinches, clears his throat, fumbles with a napkin. Now he stands, driving the iron chair away with the backs of his knees, and excuses himself, clearing his throat, pawing at his neck, heading for the bathroom, sweating.

"Sensitive," the Narthex says, and purses his lips.

The Nave coils and uncoils, rolling in a circle.

"He really feels it," the Nave says.

She begins giggling inanely, lifting her head up and slobbering through bared teeth. She looks at the Narthex and flicks her eyes at AC.

"You like her," she says.

The Narthex gives her a withering look with his flat, painted eyes.

"Kind of but not sort of," he says.

He thrusts his right arm out ahead of him and they're driving the long opalescent Catalina Grand Prix, the Narthex has the wheel, and the Nave sits beside him, her head draped along the open window and the wind in her stringy hair. The wheels hum on transparent pavement above the freeway; it's still daylight below, but up here it's always night time, the attic of the world.

From up here, the city is a glowing lake in a shadowy landscape, and the city lights percolate up through shadow air that fizzes like black champagne. From time to time, the baleful lamps of an oncoming daemon car streak by on the opposite side of the divider, which is inscribed with occult characters of inconstant meaning. Beside them, a rocking carriage, streaked with moonlit fog. Frantic-eyed horses kicking sparks in silence. The invisible highway splits around a massive metal head with downcast eyes, brooding forever over lanes of glass.

⸺

... When I see the Figure is ready, everything I'm aware of concaves in on it. All threads bind right there in a Figure sitting on the ground and against the sky, who begins to describe to me what their education was like. All from behind a black lead mask with a broad toothy grin and a weird hat. In one move, indistinct words from the other side of the wall pass me into a dream landscape of mountains without valleys, the staggering ascent up trails barely wider than your foot and those rickety Chinese plank walkways maybe two feet wide bolted to sheer rock faces, mouth breathing and cold sweat prickling out of your palms, a sick dizziness in your arms and legs as you glue yourself to the stone, as the wind plucks and tears at you like a teasing monster.

... There's no relief when you arrive on the other side and the teachers descend on you like vultures. You can't see them, because they smear your vision, but you have the idea they are like nine-foot-tall mummies with convulsively flailing jaws and squawking voices. They bring a cloud of vocal racket with them, but if you listen carefully you can usually find some fragment of intelligible speech in it, and if you concentrate on that fragment with all your might, you can usually locate some sense.

They are expressions of Gilshrakes. They are recognized by the Predikanten. They are your Gorgons. They will teach you Zaman Wislin. They will inscribe you in Dub Tables.

"The Narthex's got ae girlfriend," the Nave croons to the Apse.

"GO FOR IT TIGER," the Transept says from the back seat.

"Yeah, well thaet's more thaen you've got," the Narthex says back, and snaps his fingers at the Nave.

The Nave snaps back. The Narthex overrules with another snap and the Nave countersnaps. The Narthex and the Nave both start snapping faster and faster in a spontaneous snap race to see who can outsnap whom.

("Quit thaet snaepping!") the Apse says sharply.

They quit.

("Snaepping HIC aet eaech other! Whaet's *next?*") she says in disgust.

Grant finishes waxing his board and scans the water. The sun is still below the horizon and the ocean and sky together are like rainbow sherbet.

AC stares out the bus window at streets filled with Nazis dressed in casual contemporary attire goose-stepping with their right arms outstretched. She breaks the window with her elbow and starts tossing grenades into the street. They go off with regular thumps, flashing in the tinted bus windows all around her like a dance floor and the more she shovels grenades out the window the more it becomes a party of leaping revelers and cries of delight.

... You have to memorize every detail of this mountain side with a mummy barking at you, starting over and starting over, never to be done. Destiny never misses a thing. At last do you see where you are? At the heart of the book, there is always a little aperture to the passages, the wind, the uncanniness of these mountains where destiny is made by workers who are masters of their craftless art and slaves to the destiny they make. These corpses, absolutely desiccated, lining the stone galleries, meditating in inaccessible creches beneath the peaks, your teachers, who know destiny and who show you how to make it, are masters of destiny because they are its victims. What they know is destiny itself. They speak to you in the wind that blows through their chapless jaws, their language is a sobbing howl, out of their control, inscribed in hidden vintage termas written not by conscious minds, but by destiny. All this is only as it is. Why do you love it?

The Narthex lights another cigar.

("Oh Narthex, the turn-off is up there,") the Apse says.

The Narthex takes the end in his teeth, closes the hellbrand in its pearl box and sets it carefully back in his jacket pocket.

("Well, I wonder whaet you're thinking being this far over if you waent to maeke thaet turn.")

"I'm getting over."

("Is there some other exit you're thinking aebout, Narthex?")

"I'm doing it, Mama!"

The Figure turns to show me the mask -- a gleaming, black, expertly-molded human face, smiling, showing its teeth, and wearing a black knit hat. The Figure shows me mountain slopes as steep as flames. The slopes are covered with chimneys, disciples pounding anvils, disciples on peaks swinging censers of heavy iron on mile-long chains, wreathing the slopes below in glowing blue smoke. Lightning bursts between the mountains. The mountains are armored with titanic iron plates welded to their sides, scored with fulgurant lightning scars and flaky with rust. There are no valleys below, only plummeting crevasses of inky nothingness.

The scene is now an island of light in a vast round stone chamber of living rock, deep in those mountains. The flames of numberless butter lamps are motionless as stars and the stone is eternally quiet, but the air is churning with the relayed force of a hurricane tearing at the mountains above. The Figure is brought in like a captive between two mummies as elongated as Giacometti sculptures, wearing the type of cheap suits people get buried in. Then the Figure strides up to a rickety wooden platform, all interconnected with a webbing of knotted cables, performs a ritual hand gesture, then seizes and drinks off a saucer of clear liquid. The Figure's hands reach spasmodically for its throat, and with a visible effort those hands are returned to where they had been. The Figure lifts, the chest heaves, and is seized again and driven with strictly regular steps toward the center of the island of light.

A cube of dull steel, thirteen feet on a side, rolls a bit out of shadow, facing the Figure; it might be resting on something, but from here the cube seems to have nothing but a few feet of air beneath it, and there is a half-circle window cut into the thick metal about six feet up the front. The poisoned and trembling Figure is lifted into the air, high enough to see the two dim eyes through that half-circle, shining like two eclipsed moons well back inside. The Figure is brought directly up to the opening and the gaze from within presses itself into the Figure's eyes with a sickening heat. Now the Figure can just make out the two hands clawing the air only inches from the opening, as if the one inside were bound in place and were, with a straining reach, trying to catch and maul and drag in. They claw and claw without stopping, trembling with effort.

A shriek erupts from the interior of the box. It splits the air and stuns the Figure. It's as if the metal were speaking. The words are lacerations in the shrilling. These are instructions.

The Figure is planted on the feet, and the next instant someone comes up from behind and snaps a tight rubber collar around the Figure's throat, but cutting off the breath. Weights are clamped around the Figure's ankles, and now the Figure is driven forward, and must not stop tracing the straight line of destiny out into the storm.

The Figure is engulfed in a blast that forces air into the lungs, despite the constriction of the neck. The Figure's abdomen heaves with the effort to vomit air back out, and must not stop driving down the line against the wind, slowed by the weights. Delirious with the poison, the Figure sees the stern peaks of the mountains swing, sink, and lift through veils of icy tears; deafened by the roar of the wind the Figure hears the scream of the metal, and feels the narrow end of a poisoned whip slash open the upper arm. The wound burns like brine and the poison eats into the meat of the bicep. Lashes fall on the Figure's arms and back; the Figure staggers and drops to its knees suffocating, wracked with poison and the agony of countless envenomed wounds behind that smiling black mask.

The Figure pushes all the air out of the lungs with a supreme effort and feels the collar clamp the windpipe shut. The Figure does not claw at the collar, but folds the hands submissively as the whip descends across the back with such savagery that blood sprays like the tail of a comet, a spark floats out of the Figure's head and becomes a bolt of lightning, launching the line off the stone ground and into the sky. The pink and blue light blazes and disappears, and the thunderclap slams and the Figure stands upright and sees where the white blade of electricity cuts the storm, exposing the bluewhite hellparadise of azure sky and dazzling white clouds beyond, and either very far away huge or right before the eyes small the Figure sees the dragon. Even with eyes closed, the Figure can see and even feel the dragon twist and flex in a purple halo. Falling back, swooning, being dragged roughly out of the wind, the collar smartly cut loose, the deep drafts of inbreath, the lip of a rough stone cup banging against the teeth, the cloyingly sweet antidote ...

... The cavern darkens, and the sardonic wailing of carrion birds is heard. Stinking flies swarm in the air and shadowy forms lift themselves from a hinterland of your graves. They stand out from asylums and prison cells, all in the shadows like people drifting among desert rocks, but not hiding. Their mingled voices are heard from hidden burials, bricked-up alcoves, from beneath foundations, from between scantlings, from back alleys and the tall grass of vacant lots, blended in a chuckle that's steady and low and that seems to swing like an evil spirit among desert rocks. By ones and twos, the teachers, the masters of destiny emerge into the constant light of the butter lamps, wasted, mad, staring, glassy-eyed, hollow-cheeked, sunken-chested.

Here is Rath Torturelle the Rhetoric Instructor, a corpse, with hair like a bird's nest, her shoulders twitching with suppressed mirth. Her whole face is pinched together with the effort of suppressing her laughter. Her mouth opens, casually vomiting toward her feet.

Here is Rath Taskin the Grammar Instructor, a corpse, swollen-bellied and laughing raucously, his whole head one continuous felt of stubble seething with tears, wobbly on his emaciated legs, holding himself with emaciated arms.

Here is Rath Craplin the Logic Instructor, a corpse, with scarlet blood trickling incessantly from his nostrils, a snarling mouth always in elocutional motion, a lividly pale, bent and peruked man leaning on a tree branch.

Still hidden in the shadows, the master of arithmetic, a corpse, extends a bony glove into the light, showing an artificial snail shell made of coarse feathers.

Still hidden in the shadows, the master of astronomy, a corpse, extends a bony glove into the light, showing a wing made of dense wood.

Still hidden in the shadows, the master of geometry, a corpse, extends a bony glove into the light, showing a pair of eyeglasses made of orange flames.

Still hidden in the shadows, the master of music, a corpse, extends a bony glove into the light, showing a brush made of green stone.

These are your instructors. Your classroom will be an avalanche.

-- There's a shaft of light shining down from somewhere up there, and a shadow twists in the column, like a worm dimpling a patch of water. I know it's the dragon that crawls at the center of the universe, but as it turns, it's also the Grand Caliginous in its coiling bouquet of fire, stamping bare feet on heaped up cadavers in slow motion, with ropes of severed heads around the thick neck and waist, decelerated bellowing coming from between the tusks and far away, forming words with a voice that is the whole planet complete with its sky, space, and time, and holding out in one of six hands a tulip-shaped ladies' compact. The compact opens and I can see AC inside, sitting at a desk, taking down some of what the voice is saying: the shaking words zig-zag out of the air and into her brain. She leans over the page holding the pencil in her fist, practically ripping the words onto the paper, but somehow the paper is flat and neat and the writing is even.

I see it clearly -- teeth gnashing and eyes flaring, she's really trying to shred the paper, and it's like the harder she tries, the more smugly neat and tidy the writing is. The more she tries to lie and bullshit, the more implacably true the words become; through her ... despite her ... the *Complutensian Polyglot Terma*, which is nothing but nonsense, is becoming a genuine holy book. She has absolutely no idea she's a terton -- a transmitter of hidden knowledge -- and the harder she tries to hoodwink Grant the more exactly she reaches through the text, which is kind of baloney itself too -- kind of, but not sort of -- and it was itself only pretending to be. Thinking she is beyond powerless, and the whole time she's got the power. Thinking she's faking it, when she's actually getting it right.

The Grand Caliginous snaps the compact shut, whirls around swinging decapitated heads, and jangling the heavy gold baubles around wrists and ankles; a hand holds out a bronze teapot now. Daintily, the lid is plucked off. Inside, I can see AC storming and raging in a mountainous landscape. Like a cartoon character, she reaches out to someplace and retrieves a bundle of lit dynamite. Shouting with anger she throws the bundle. Her movement is strange; it's like she has to shove the bundle through semi-solid air, but at the point of release it snaps away a dozen feet and jumps through space before bursting against the side of the mountain. The rock face coughs white dust and fractures. Rocks tumble down. AC hurls dynamite bundles at mountains and monasteries and the explosions are somehow building them up instead of tearing them down, tripling her fury so that she raves and froths. Her faculty of anger is bottomless. The dynamite shatters the Grand Caliginous to pieces. Each piece is turning into a new Figure, all different.

On the slope of the mountain I see an expression in the Figure's blank metal eyes that is so different from the look in Grant's eyes that it makes me think of him, as if I were recognized. Something important has just happened in my past. A change, that came through the Figure from wherever the Figure came from, and went into my past through my yak present, and did something there, something that will affect my yak life too.

AC translates:

Up, breath,
    into ritual shoulders!
    In, moment, in!
    The the-six the,
    and stun thirteen shadows,
    a face
    might halo eyes.
    Air like laughter tracing its metal
    in the the Now-line
    with air
    stone-bent motion --
    It's suppressing across forces --
    Eyes small,
    launching Rhetoric of prison --
    whip stand were submissively beneath
    banging the like in webbing
    with clamped the the the
    the collar floats in knotted shadows
    writhing's cut the brought, dragged Figure up the dazzling out-
artificial interconnected Figure's Figure
    the hinterland light

vibrating evil "to" lists
in between
like The in speaking,
The and That of mirth.
Among the air
sweet trembling hands nothing it,
tearing back in
and pushes on legs, with The That speaking salt around her
he me
others, other deity in invisits
reach higher whites
proffers devil's eye -- close he he -- walk in in.
A man perhaps parking outside has sorrow,
like individual A all over whites
together power salt
appalls white man.
Something comes again equal to support temptation
can white man smell
I I between it, envious light.
Joy into the would
and he not even universal
yet joy tragic assaulted
the while the he the hero the You
any box
like joy the course the white tragic outside.
Is it looking?
Call for looking.
Hear again,
Birds and sky
open Grammar Figures.
Stars inside lightning
be to upon-be
the the --
A,
a whole A,
the about A,
the's are instructions.

Do A, the says.
The is of where up its to.
They the is a the they.
The the on the -- in shadows, light.
Supreme folds out of the the the the.

I don't know how, but this is what Grant needs -- kill the bank, get the loan, build the Annex on the island, be there when the Special Guest arrives, do ... what he's going to do. But when you make arrangements with revolutionaries -- this is what the Figure is showing me -- when you make arrangements with book people, something always gets away from you.

I remember that cube of living flesh and bone that I saw just after the sex cathedral turned into the Narthex, the Nave, the Apse, the jacking-off one, the creepy standstill one, the little twerpy ones. That cube was another -- not one of them, but some other, that kind of slid through opportunistically into this life. That life, I mean, my human life. Seeing that cube again in my mind's eye, I realize who it is: the Pulpit -- Anthony Motion. He's not like the others, who all have these really distinct personalities. He's from a place where he's so unbearably alive that he's paralyzed, like someone who all they can do is come, so he has to come over into this space because he can't stand there. Here, he's correspondingly dead, but still talking, still walking around, making gestures.

He wasn't personally summoned, so you can't manage him. He wants to stay on this side, but the only way he can do it is by keeping to just within life; the deeper he goes into life, the harder it is for him to stay on this side. I don't know why the two sides are divided or by what. The Figure isn't showing that. There's always some other side, basically. But the two sides are always sides in something bigger that keeps them affecting each other. Anthony Motion has to stay liminal, and to do that he has to keep life neutral around him. He latches on to Grant because Grant is surfing major life forces, martialing them now to try to burst the mains and spread the vibrations.

The Grand Caliginous One picks up fire and tosses the flames overhead like a wig. The flames flop down over the snarling face, and go tumbling down the broad back. With two hands it plucks apart the flames and lifts them, showing me the demons.

The Narthex veers toward the exit, but somehow the offramp is still further to the left. He swerves toward their one getaway point, and watches nervelessly as it recedes from them.

Grant sits down cross-legged on the grass. From his pocket he pulls out a huge white veil. Deftly he tosses it over himself so that he looks a little like a translucent pyramid. The slope is dotted with aromatic desert scrub, sagebrush, wild thyme. He sits at the apex of a gnarly isosceles triangle outlined in live oaks, and chants with his lips barely parted in an inscrutable smile and moves his hands and arms in a series of distinct gestures, each in its own place in the air. The sky is quick-moving overcast with a single rent in it, from which comes a slanting beam of sunlight. The patch of light travels over the ground until it reaches Grant. Then it stops.

The exit is gone. The highway is gone. The car is gone. The daemons are suddenly sitting all together in a groove below the slope. Grant sits above them.

"Shit," the Nave says.

Each of them begins helplessly copying Grant's gestures, against their will. All the colors of the landscape and sky deepen. The whole scene is becoming saturated with telluric power, so that the ground, the plants and trees, the stones, the clouds, the wind, even the light are coiling like muscles. Nature is becoming treacherously supple and aroused.

The Nave shrieks, holding up her hands in front of her face, horrified. Her pale, snaky hands are now firm, square, tanned, in white linen sleeves. There's a dzi bead at her throat. Long and flowing hair, equally black and grey, falls silkenly about her face. All the daemons are howling; they're all turning into Grant. The Narthex is yanking at his hair. The Transept claws at his linen pants but he can't get them open. The Triforium have already become little Grants and are sitting in the lotus position. With a screech of horror, the Apse leaps up onto the surfboard her chaise lounge has become, standing in perfect surfing posture.

The ground shudders beneath their feet, then begins to sway

with a distant, all-pervading rumble. A pane of sunlight shears away from the rest like a calving iceberg and collapses into the valley behind them.

All this glory, all this wildness, this panoply, but who am I? What am I? I am an animal, a man, is there a difference? Does any of this touch me? Does any of it change my heart?

A moment later, the lightslide rampages down the slope and sweeps the book people through chorusing, pagan landscapes shimmering with phantasmal gold, down to the Pacific. Grant placidly conducts the scene with unhurried, masterful gestures. Washed down to the beach, the daemons are left writhing and snarling on the diamond sand, talking backwards, groaning, belching up mercury. In desperation, they call on the Crossing -- but it doesn't come. The Nave alone has the presence of mind to see what diverts the Crossing along a tangent, away from them. From here, the Crossing looks like a sizzled spider, or a piece of withered fungus, crumpled up on itself and rolling away along a trough of nothing that cuts it off from them. Who's doing it? It's *that other one*, the Pulpit, holding the trough open with his wooden hands. The trough is dark, but the Figure is illuminated by it and shadowed by the sunlight, an animated JC Penney catalog manikin with an unconvincing mop of golden curls on its head.

Grant completes another series of gestures and an overpowering will puts an immediate end to daemon antics. Lifted to their feet, each of them is possessed by something coming through a Figure that is coming through Grant. Grant is like a cavern in a bluff of sunlight, and there is a vividly grey Figure inside that cave coming through from the heart of the bluewhite hellparadise to override their individual mischievousness for the purposes of a whole other order of mischief. The book people walk up to the water's edge in a line, the Narthex's swagger, the Nave's fawning creep, the Transept's jagged jerkoff, the Triforium's tumbling gambol, the Apse's supercilious glide, all gone: now, they walk like Grant, with the smooth, lightly-windblown poise of a male model in summer wear. As one they reach down, pluck up the lacy fringe of the water in their hands like a quilt, and whip it, as one, chanting --

"ONE, ONEONEONEONE, ONEONEONEONE..."

With each plunge of their arms, they send greater and greater ripples heaving back out to sea. The full moon barrels down the clouds toward them, streaming with semen and milk. Ten-foot waves, then twelve, then fifteen, working the ocean harder and harder until the spell breaks. Exhausted, the daemons collapse like heaps of books, mercury streaming from their smoking faces. They moan and toss on the sand as the full moon steamrolls over them. Grant lifts his right hand above his head making the "OK" sign, while his left hand hovers before his navel doing "hang ten."

That Grand Caliginous One drops the flame curtains back down and goes backflipping away from me. Somehow this is all pointed at me through the Figure, and I can't move, I can't feel my body, I'm looking out at the mountains from the valley -- the wheel-chair is whipped around by a Grand Caliginous One that thrusts its maniacal face into mine. I kick out my back hooves and throw my horns up. I roll around on the ground in a cloud of dust, the wheel-chair on top of me, grinding its arms into my ribs. There's a circular hole in the patio just big enough for my eye and the interior is lined with gold flakes. I think there's a many-armed thing, silhouetted by its own fluttering garment of fire, sort of rock-and-rolling down in there, and I press the nearest available yak eye to the opening to see better.

I see Steve Browlshweer and Steven Brairbershn down in there, sitting around a table at an exclusive interview with a mortgage loan analyst named Stephan Dblawbdm. Steve Browlshweer is having brioche ailloli, Steven Brairbershn is trying to finish his Koshihikari charcoal-grilled-animal chorizo squid and seared Catalina seawater, and Stephan Dblawbdm is having blistered goat Bouquerrones topped with caramelized garlic snake, golden goat cremosas, and trout supplement. They've put away a bottle of $300 wine apiece and are getting ready to go to the even more exclusive bar. Stephan Dblawbdm has just received a text from his colleague, Stevynne Hwehheh, about some foreclosures, and they all toast the dregs before heading out. Steven Brairbershn, who is perspiring lightly, asks Stephan Dblawbdm what Stevynne's middle name is.

"Arkwright, I think."

"Nice."

"Part of my job is sexualizing Winnipeg," a woman is telling someone as they pass through the tables to the exit.

"Have you seen *Labhoragni* yet?"

At the exclusive bar, surrounded by more expensive cheapness, fake people pay a lot of money for authentic cocktails. Well, who isn't a fake? What's real here is my confusion -- no, it's all real, but there's a lot of real lying going on.

The street opens up beneath your feet -- the hole is real, the falling is real, your fright is real. The one who realizes the illusion is able to change it, sure, that's Grant I guess, and yeah, the Grand Caliginous One is really right here, to tell me that the new illusion is still an illusion, but that's not what confuses me anymore, because I have an exciting new confusion about what's next, because I think I see what Grant is driving at, which is that reality is a skill -- and for a moment Steve Browlshweer and Steven Brairbershn wince and squint at stunning California sunlight that pounces on their eyes through the tinted glass windows of the bar. It punctures the tinting and brings the street inside. Steve Browlshweer throws up one hand to shield his eyes, but the sunlight turns his hand into a pink glass mitten and presses a fierce, palpable glare on his retinas, while Steven Brairbershn stumbles to the bathroom, vomiting again. He almost makes it. Sashimi on his shoes this time. Bending over the toilet he feels the churning in his guts transmitted through the floor, and in the midst of his wild disorientation he recognizes the onrush of an earthquake.

Not much he can do about that.

The whole building trembles with the clattering of glasses and plates, cellphones smack the floor, people rear up startled, bemused, others still obliviously conversing away, and then the fluttering underfoot starts to roll with a growling mumble from down below and out abroad.

Everybody turns to the person on their right and imperiously orders them to keep calm. The bartender and servers evaporate; Steve Browlshweer is walking with his hand still upraised against California sun, moving sideways like you do when you try to avoid a rip current. Without seeing where he's going, he somehow exits the bar and encounters a vision of Grant. He knows Grant's not there, but Grant is there, fully illuminated by sun in the middle of the night, riding the ground waves of the earthquake, remaining uncannily still, just steadycammed there in the center of Steve Browlshweer's field of vision, so that no amount of drunken sway shifts the image. The scene vanishes, leaving a vacuum that jerks the air from his. He erupts in a fit of coughing, and barely avoids barfing. A stink of rancid fish gushes from the alley.

On the beach, the daemons are still woozy. The ocean is rolling heavy tides back out to sea, away from the shore.

("Come on,") the Apse says, a note of renewed vigor creeping back into her voice. ("Come on now.")

"ONE ... ONE-ONE ..." the Transept roars.

("Stop thaet, Transept. HIC! Nave? Where did you go?")

"I'm *here!*" the Nave whines, at the end of her rope.

("HIC -- Narthex?")

"Yeaeh yeaeh."

("Come on now, whew!") the Apse says, climbing back onto her chaise lounge. ("Come on, let's do whistles. ... Come on, now!")

Stiffly, the battered daemons gather around the bedraggled Apse, whose hair is plastered to her face with dewy sweat. They lay their arms across each others' shoulders and begin to whistle together.

The two bankers are kind of reeling around the set, looking for each other.

"Chmag?"

"Brab? Is that you?"

No harm done, right?

Can't say the same about what they get up to the following day, which is business as usual where business can only do harm -- but then it happens again. Steven Brairbershn is trying to explain the intricacies of a new scam to Stevynne Hwehheh when the sun looms in at the window like King Kong.

"I can't see the fucking screen!" he snarls, sending it spinning.

Steve Browlshweer comes in a moment later.

"Brab," he says ominously. "Can I talk to you for a minute?"

They step into Steve Browlshweer's office.

"From the Director," he says, pointing to his screen.

Hey guys! the screen says. **Hey Steve Browlshweer and Hey Steven Brairbershn, you're going up to San Jose! Your car will be here in ten minutes! Your car will take you directly to your meeting! In San Jose! Peaccce!**

The two bankers look at each other like human beings. In other words, with misgivings.

Their phones both go off in unison with texts from the Director that say

Hey! Your car is here right now! TTYL!

Steve Browlshweer and Steven Brairbershn are zooming north in a self-driving, convertible made entirely out of glass. Everything in it is a screen. With a dread that mounts quickly to near panic they imagine the straight shot up the Pacific Coast Highway, the sun lowering at them above the terrifying expanse of the ocean. As they veer toward the inland route instead, construction brings them up short. They don't recognize me in my orange vest and construction hat, holding up the detour sign. GPS reroutes them.

GPS being General Pandaemonium Services.

That inland path to salvation shines just out of reach as they pass one blocked turn-off after another. The Narthex watches them from a police cruiser parked by a taped-off onramp. The Nave leers after them from beneath an overturned tractor trailer that's closed off all the exit lanes. Pumping wildly at his groin, the Transept deftly swings a bus into position, right out of nowhere, cutting them off and forcing the glass car to swerve away from the interchange. The Apse raises her martini, hiccups, the computers glitch, somehow mistaking one number for another, and now they are speeding along the coast, right up against the mountains' unbroken rampart, full in the California sun.

Steve Browlshweer is in what once was the driver's seat. Steven Brairbershn glances over at him, and beyond, catches sight of the wave, like a huge bar of green shadow sinking into the ocean, its line massing to face the north, not the shore. Now they both see it -- the chipped flint edge of a wave lifting straight up, as if a gargantuan magnet in the sky were pulling the water up to it. The wave stretches out to sea as far as the eye can reach, and it rolls gigantically, looming toward the north.

On the left side, the edges of the highway rise up into a berm, and heaped-up blonde rocks form an improvised crenelation along the right side that strobes their view of the wave. After each interruption the wave appears to have very drastically narrowed the gap between them -- the air vibrates with its breath and the highway whirs beneath them. The air is growing humid, the wave, with unbelievably slow velocity, is drawing up its mass.

OK Steven Brairbershn has just noticed *a tiny human figure* surfing on that wave, etching a barely-detectable hairline on its curling face, just below the soaring peak. The surfer is barely moving, holding steady to the water. Even at this distance, Steven Brairbershn can tell that the surfer's hair is perfect.

"He's following us!"

Steve Browlshweer presses the accelerator to the floor. The car ignores him. The pedal offers no resistance, no feeling. The highway ahead of them is uncharacteristically empty -- in fact, that lone surfer is the only other human being they see. A moment later they flash into a tunnel. The noise of the car rebounds from the walls at them, but even so, they can feel the musty humidity of the onrushing wave, its rumble, thundering right through the mountain. The tunnel mouth spits them out into dazzling sunshine, and the wave is right there, chasing them, already level with the highway and still unfurling, still climbing. They can smell it -- it hisses and sizzles at them, the sunlight reflecting from its broad convexity is broken up by its facets into chaotic warpaint.

The two bankers yelp with fright, whip out cell phones and tablets, swipe at screens, one rips open the glove compartment and flails through its contents wildly, while the other is dabbing and punching at buttons all over the wheel and the dashboard like a cartoon switchboard operator, as an inexorable shadow engulfs the car. The rim of the wave looms eighty feet over their heads, and the two panicking bankers can discern the tip of a surfboard jutting out plumb at the midpoint. Steve Browlshweer flails out wildly, inverts in the driver's seat with his legs whipping around in the air like a breakdancer while Steven Brairbershn somersaults in place, whirring like a top, throwing off little spurts of litter, old receipts, gum wrappers, expired condoms, cracked and dingy cell phone

Receipt

Paperback Book: Standard x
1

£0.50

Total   £0.50

| Cash Tendered: | £0.50 |
| Change due: | £0.00 |

Thank You!

AM   1749466264817

cases. Then they feel the spatulate foot of the wave shove itself under the back wheels -- the car pivots above them and then flips forward, back over front like a pancake, landing upside-down in the water. Steve Browlshweer and Steven Brairbershn are borne down by the car and swept instantly away from the coast. They tumble out to sea, clawing and strangling in one hundred and sixty feet of water.

The surface is a choppily radiant screen that curls massively into the air, carrying them with it on a rip current Grant is riding all the way out to Catalina. In the sunset, one side of the wave is blood red and the other is midnight blue, with Grant like a snowy pennant flickering just on the blue side of the dividing line, cruising with a fractured glass convertible and two bankers up to their chins in water, twirling round and round like lathes in Grant's wake.

The island is iridescent purple in a red ocean, sloping up out of the water. Grant stands up straight on his board and, gibbering bankers in tow, glides down to the shore while the wave passes to one side of the island and flies out toward the sun, to vanish in the greater vastness of the Pacific.

I'm somewhere on the 134 when I get a call from Grant.

"Well, Chalo," he says merrily, "we *have* the loan, dude!"

How high is the water, mama?
Thirty feet high and risin'
How high is the water, papa?
She said it's thirty-three feet and risin' ...

Dr. Achittampong smokes by the open window of his office. He has a view of a bare cinderblock wall and a little paved walkway. The narrow stripe of sky he can make out from here is dusted with plumes of black smoke, and from over the wall come the noises of countless emergencies.

He fantasizes about making great strides in the study of the syndrome, even as the nicotine in his blood struggles in vain to get him to notice an article in one of the medical journals lying open randomly before him. The authors of this article, being unfamiliar with Messerschmitt's work -- and ignorant of art history in general -- used the name "Phantom Head Psychosis" (PHP) to refer to a bizarrely selective disorder that broke out suddenly among bankers, financiers, and people in managerial positions in business or adjacent to business. Every individual affected by this disorder believes they are being stalked by a disembodied, sculpted head. In each case, the heads have certain curious features -- they are always male heads, wearing fixed grimaces, and they are never quite natural in color. If they are white, they are uniformly white, gleaming, cracked, and yellowing, like old ivory or meerschaum. If they are black, they are uniformly black, gleaming, and really more dark grey than black. If they are brown, they are uniformly brown, gleaming, and unnaturally purplish in color. Each patient seems to see a different head, although this difference is not always so obvious, but each patient will see only that particular head. Without exception, patients also report seeing a small quantity of smoke emerge from the left ear of the head that follows them. The appearance of the head seems invariably to accompany the onset of the psychosis.

PHP's chief symptom is manic hyperactivity of a catatonic variety. Patients lose all sense of their surroundings and become engrossed in repetitive motor activity, typically sitting in one place and agitatedly poking, swiping, or scrolling at the air around them. Patients fixate on electronics, screens, panes of glass, reflective surfaces. It is not uncommon for patients to poke and swipe at their own reflected features, behavior referred to by Dr. M. Yutondo (Kyushu University) as "facial emendation." Patients who do not remain silent babble a word salad of business jargon.

Since patients with this disorder will perform managerial, financial, or other professional functions more diligently and efficiently than the unafflicted, initially there was abundant corporate funding for further research into the disorder, albeit entirely oriented toward determining -- and reproducing -- its cause. However, when researchers determined that those suffering from PHP are incapable of spending their own money, and that, without some form of constant care, they tend to die as a consequence of exhaustion, hunger, and thirst, this funding naturally dried up.

The nicotine in Dr. Achittampong's brain is trying to get him to notice the clue that would, given a moderate amount of research, reveal all manner of striking affinities between "Phantom Head Psychosis" and "Catalina Syndrome" -- namely, that the fixed expressions on the faces of those afflicted by the syndrome come in 47 varieties, all of which match minutely-detailed descriptions of the fixed expressions on the phantom heads. If Dr. Achittampong or any of his associates were at all familiar with the Messerschmitt heads, they would have made an even more startling discovery.

Dr. Achittampong stubs his cigarette out in the cheap tin ashtray he keeps hidden in his filing cabinet, on top of a heap of unread medical journals. He sees a distorted, quasi-silhouette of his own face reflected in the shrinkwrap that still envelops the edition on the top of the heap.

Slam!

<hr/>

"What's smoking?"

"It's the halal."

"It's so smokey!"

"It's halal!"

"Smokey and the Bandit!"

I guess I'm observing this. There's a halal food cart on the corner with so much smoke flying out of it it's barely visible. Two women going by. I'm waiting on my golf cart. My golf cart isn't ready yet, so now I'm waiting. There are cars on the island, but everything here is just a bit smaller than it is on the mainland, including the streets, so most people on Catalina leave their cars behind and hum around on golf carts instead.

Avalon is a heap of white, yellow, and blue boxes, pale green doors, a cat's cradle of wires and cables and ropes strung everywhere, many of them decked with colored flags. It's quiet, almost silent. The people are all dressed up for summer fun, but they just walk slowly around looking at things and not talking to each other.

I'm seeing old people everywhere, sitting in doorways, leaning out of windows, wondering why they're here. The constant sea breeze blows up from the water, the sky is overcast.

White-trunked eucalyptus trees grow out of pale, sandy soil in the lot opposite me, and through their drooping, blade-shaped leaves I can see the refractory jumble of houses climbing up the slopes below the towers. I'm sitting on a bench about a dozen yards up from a massive church of black stone, huge and narrow, like a gothic railroad car. Me and benches. My utopia is just benches. Benches and shade.

I glance over to my left and nearly jump when I notice I'm not alone. A chapfallen old black man sits right on the corner of the bench, one skinny calf draped over his knee, looking steadily at me.

"How's it going, Chalo?"

His voice is reedy ... but it makes the bench vibrate.

"Going good," I say weirdly.

He nods, still eyeing me.

"Can't complain," I say.

Still eyeing.

"How about you?"

"You don't recognize me, do you?"

"No."

He blows air, drops his head and shakes it, then looks back at me.

"I'm Wilson," he says, spreading his hands a little. "Wilson CO."

The sea wind rustles in the eucalyptus and a bus groans one street over. The overcast gloom of the day deepens.

"What the fuck happened to *you?*"

Wilson was a friend of mine I lost track of right out of college, and he was my age. This man looks about sixty.

"Well," he says, dropping his eyes to his feet. "After graduation, what had happened was, I had too much debt, you know, and I was irresponsible. I let drinking get, kind of out of hand, you know, and I paid the price. But now, I'm clean. Seven months."

I can't bring myself to believe that this is the man I knew. But, if he isn't, how does he know my name, the college connection?

It occurs to me this man might be looking for the whereabouts of a bag of money from off a Brinks truck. A chill passes over me.

-- but, if this man is some kind of informer, how does he know about Wilson CO? CO meaning "see the cypher" in the supreme alphabet? He never explained that anywhere, not in writing, not anywhere where anyone who wasn't there would have found out about it.

But -- but -- what if he isn't Wilson CO, and he hasn't been put up to talking to me for some reason, either. Then he'd have to be a stranger.

What did Grant say about strangers? Is he one of *those* strangers?

"You're looking to hire some people to do some building for you," he says, looking me straight in the eye.

I'm sitting on a public bench, in a plain white t-shirt, with a pizza stain right over my heart, and he thinks I'm hiring.

Another male is coming toward me. At intervals he stops and turns, watching me.

-- -- -- I don't believe it, the little fucker's charging me!

I roll with him.

We grind scalps, and then he pulls back a bit.

Neither of us budges. We turn our heads, watching each other closely. He starts walking along the slope, puts on a little speed -- I bound up the slope and keep alongside him but above him. He wavers a little, so I come down on top of him.

He stops me with his brow and I drive against him, but some way he gets his head around me into the sweet spot behind my ear and drives me back up the slope. After a moment I pull my head away, get brow to brow, and use my horn to lever his head up. He tries to roll me off, but I've got him -- I've got the fucker now -- my horn is under his and my brow is in his neck and I drive him around a little rise so I'm above him --

OK, what happened? I had him!

We somehow are brow to brow again, swinging our heads together, and he pushes me back down -- I don't know how he did it.

My eyes roll and strain, trying to see past my nose.

We separate.

Now we're just looking at each other.

-- -- -- That stain is small, by the way. It's not big. I just ate, too, it's not like I'm just throwing on a stained shirt in the morning like "fuck it, a shirt's a shirt."

Wilson CO leans over and bats my left forearm with a limp hand.

"You asleep? I know who you should talk to."

"I don't know you."

"I'm Wilson. Wilson CO," he says firmly. "We were in college together. We both lived in Bruder. We hung out with Kevin White and that weird Asian guy, Josh or whatever."

None of this is bringing him into focus, even though it's all true.

"You need workers. You're here to scope out the land for Grant and break ground on the Annex."

He presses the tips of his long left fingers to his chest.

"I can introduce you to the 'migrants'."

I want to stand up and splutter and leave, but what do I know about this stuff? That might be worse. And we do need hands. The realization lowers itself onto me. I'm like a toilet for this realization.

Dusk is starting, doubling the enchantment of the overcast light, and Wilson's shirt seems to glow, like fluorescent chalk. A hood of fading gloom is closing down conspiratorially about us, and the colluding wind slides over him to me carrying a faint smell of cigarettes.

So, when he gets up without a word and begins to walk rapidly away, I follow him along the narrow, winding streets of Avalon.

Small men with scarves and hands tucked into threadbare wool jackets, leonine women in day-glo bikinis, skateboarders in what looks like medieval peasant garb -- hoods and hose -- pass me in the opposite direction, and I'm a bit concerned -- no one is going this way but me and Wilson. The streetlights are little better than candles and they shine leprous blue. Overhead, the sky is a canal of mottled backlit blue and grey, swiftly flowing. The clouds are going with us. I don't know if that's good or not.

We cross an open space where a number of roads cross without apparently meaning to, since there's no planter or circle or anything marking the intersection. Wilson is heading for a white adobe wall with an arched entrance. There's more blue light pent up inside. A little girl with one arm in a blue sling is scooting around in front of the archway on a tricycle, not pedalling, just scooting with her feet. Wilson goes right by her, I catch her eye. She very slightly compresses her lips and watches me. I can feel her eyes on me as I duck beneath the narrow arch.

Inside the wall, there's almost a jungle, big plants I can barely see; wide, glossy leaves, feathery fronds. The path bends to the right and as I round the bend I see an adobe house with a low plank porch, no lights anywhere. Almost imperceptibly glowing, Wilson tramps up onto the porch and goes inside, waving me through the screen door. He sinks into the gloom of the interior like a wan stone sinking in shadowy water.

I walk in on some kind of elaborate card game, about a dozen people seated at a big round table. There's a beer in my hand before I know it, in a chilled glass, and I've got a man in front of me who shakes my hand with one firm pump. How I manage with the beer I don't know, and I didn't see him come around to me; it's like he just walked right through the table to reach me.

"Hey Gorgio," Wilson says, fading into the deep shadow around the table. "This is Chalo."

"Hello," Gorgio says. "Nice to meet you."

The others have stopped playing and they all look at me pleasantly.

"Hi," I say, abashed.

Gorgio introduces me around. Ernesto, Elena, Clavo, Ixcuiname, Zeferino, Yolanda, Arginaldo, Hedilberto, Jesus, Pablo. The big girl with braids who sits at the upright piano in one corner, gently picking out little melodies and chords, is Malinche. The beer is refreshing but insubstantial, like angel beer. Gorgio, I notice, has one eye brown and the other pale blue, and pale blue, pale yellow, pale pink are the colors they wear. I don't know why the thick white walls are so dark, because they still are visible, like slabs of moonlight all around, and covered in intricate wrought-iron screens.

"I hear you have some building to do," Gorgio says.

He seems to be in his fifties, hair all white, receding a bit, neat white moustache, even brown complexion, not tall, but completely solid, like a Turkish wrestler. His bulky wristwatch blazes like a little piece of platinum armor.

"A whole campus, yes," I say.

"*We*," he says, reaching out his hand and touching my chest lightly with the ends of his hard fingers. "... will build it for you."

"Fine by me. But you haven't heard how much."

Gorgio waves his hand benignly.

"No problem."

He takes me by the arm. I feel like he could casually flip me up in the air.

"Let me introduce you to Bakarne."

The game resumes as I am led around the table, past Malinche who smiles at me, down a hall and many rooms wide open to the outside, through the windows of which I can see a blazing peach ribbon burning in the sky beneath a livid blue ceiling of clouds. There are old family photographs and pictures of outer space on the walls. Together, we pass a far greater number of rooms than I would have thought the house could hold.

"We built this house, you know," Gorgio says, his voice booming in the narrow hall.

He leads me into a small parlor in a back corner, where a woman is sitting in front of a shuttered window, facing the one door. There's a book in her hand, so she must be reading by the trivial light that shines in through the shutter, which is closed. Fresh flowers in a water glass on the table next to her fill the room with their scent. Having heard us coming, she is folding the book into her lap as I enter.

"Bakarne," Gorgio says gently, "this is Chalo. He would like to hire us to build the Annex for Grant, his friend."

Does she line up the words on the page with the strips of light from the shutters, I wonder inanely. The light falling over her from behind makes her hair seem grey, but it might not be. I think she's blonde. Ash blonde. Even though her face is hidden in the shadows, I know she isn't looking at me. She speaks like someone whose attention is riveted on something else, and I know her eyes are on whatever that is, too.

"Hello, Chalo."

She holds the book out to me, in both hands, allowing it to fall open at random.

"Take this. Read the first thing you see."

"... what I reach out to is that you ..."

"Ah!"

She claps her hands over her ears.

I can't see Gorgio anymore; that thump or shuffle behind me might be him, going away.

"That's enough. Give me back the book."

I turn the book slightly, to get a look at the title.

"Don't look! Just give it back to me."

I give it back to her.

"Gorgio?"

"Yes?"

"Tu puedes pedir los otros que si quieren tomar este trabajo."

"Si."

A hand on my shoulderblade steers me quickly from the room. I have the feeling that she needed to get me out of there in a hurry, that something was about to happen that no one should see.

"Nice to meet you," I say.

She pauses, having taken up the book again, without any evidence of haste or impatience.

"Y tu tambien," she replies, then resumes her reading.

The card game is visible at the end of the hall for a long time. When we come back into the room, Gorgio gestures to the wrought-iron screens.

"You see this? We made all of it."

I step up for a closer look. The wrought iron is all narrow ribbons, beautifully worked into curlicues and little medallions with skulls and bats and iguanas and what look like egrets. It's easy to visualize Gorgio working the iron tape on an anvil or something.

There's a seat for me at the table. They deal me in. Malinche is still picking away at the piano in a disjointed, twelve-tone kind of thing, like a kind of a Berg bagatelle. I'm sitting between Clavo Horcasitas and Zeferino Jojobal, who both explain the game to me. It's called "Garceta Negra" and it involves maintaining two hands, one of seven cards and the other of six, playing them against each other and then trying to match results with someone else, in order to create a pair of "alas grandes" which have a sort of run-off with other "alas grandes" and so on.

Clavo has a broad face with an arrow-shaped nose and his hair is slicked back in blades. Zeferino is tall and skinny, with a wildly happy expression in his wet eyes and around his wet mouth. He keeps his arms up in front of him as if he were always typing on a keyboard about level with his prominent Adam's apple.

I pick up my drink, but it's just a cube of solid glass. Everyone laughs when I raise it to my lips. I guess the cube is part of the game? Everyone else has one -- no, some have iron pyramids, and others have wooden cylinders. The laughter is friendly, strangely relaxing. A woman sitting next to Zeferino lights a cigarette -- that's Yolanda Espantoso. I learn that Bakarne's last name is Bigotes, that Gorgio's last name is Huidameros.

After a few hands in this interminable game whose purpose only seems to be to keep going, Gorgio comes around and sets down in front of me a brightly-colored document, the size of a playing card. It says:

Estimate:

I, _____, am offering to pay
the "migrants" _____
per hour, or a sum of _____
no later than _____
in exchange for _____

Gorgio smartly click-clicks his ballpoint and puts it down next to me. Grant laid down all the details in advance, so I am able to fill out the card without hesitation and hand it to Gorgio. He examines it, poker faced. Then he passes it to Zeferino. The card travels around the table, to Ernesto Huesca, to Elena Hurtado, to Ixcuiname Monje, to Yolanda Espantoso who transfers her cigarette to her lips in order to hold the card in both hands and squint at it, to Arginaldo Caldito, to Hedilberto Vago, handed off to Malinche Azazul at the

piano, then back to the circle and Jesus Chapulin, to Pablo Huitztlacatl with his Santana bandana, to Clavo Horcasitas and then back to
Gorgio. All of them poker faced.

"We'll discuss this among ourselves, and give you an answer
tomorrow. Where can we reach you?"

I give Gorgio my number and leave a little while later, the
atmosphere of grace and hospitality sort of cushioning me still as I
come out onto the street.

It must have rained while I was in there. Everything is panting
and sweating, but the air is clear and the sun is out. I thought we
were near sundown. I guess the day was not as far along as I thought
it was.

"That's interesting -- I didn't know I was there."

AC storming through the fascism on the way to campus, and on
campus, seeing phalanxes out the bus window; everyone in lockstep,
everyone on television, everyone in lockstep, everyone on television.
Everyone in lockstep. Everyone on television. Gary Oldman roaring
everyone. She wishes she could punch sharply in the face everyone
around her with barely an eyeblink separating each distinct punch,
just like thinking. Bam bam bam bam.

Now she is standing in front of her tutor's door, which is closed,
when she realizes that the bus must have gotten in bizarrely early.
Her tutor isn't even on campus yet.

So, now she has to wait.

She leaves the building and goes around to the back, where
there's a little patio beneath a neglected, raggedy arbor. It's one of
several abandoned spots she's located on campus. One bench has a
bit more shade than the rest.

Once seated, AC is unable to drum up any interest at all in
doing anything. Her vigilance has tired her out. Eyes on the ground
about ten feet in front of her, she does nothing. When she stirs at
last to look at the time, she senses someone sitting quietly next to
her, freezes, then turns her head slightly. A young Asian woman
wearing big pink headphones sits right beside AC. How she

managed this without alerting AC is a mystery -- it's like she was just there. Looking straight ahead with her mouth wide open, she is sticking her tongue all the way out over and over again, sort of speculatively, as if to see how far she could stick it. AC is flustered and startled. She hates suddenly finding out that she hasn't really been alone.

... Something is touching the inside of her right arm.

Looking down, she sees a cigarette pack, open, in the woman's hand, extended to her, touching her arm. AC looks at the woman's face. The woman is looking at her. She has a cigarette dangling unlit between her lips. AC looks at the cigarette pack. She looks at the woman's face. She looks at the cigarette pack. She looks at the woman's face. She looks at the cigarette pack. She looks at the woman's face. She looks at her own fingers sliding a cigarette out of the pack. She looks at the woman's face as she flicks a white disposable lighter to her own cigarette, then to the one AC has just put to her lips.

Snap.

Orange flame.

Away goes the lighter. The woman looks forward again, sort of grooving, and blows a long, flat cone of smoke out. AC takes a drag and does the same; this is not the first time she's ever smoked, but it nearly is.

The two sit and smoke.

The other woman smokes coolly. AC draws fiercely on her cigarette, puffing vehemently, in order to destroy it as quickly as possible. Then she flicks the butt into the trash, still lit.

"Thanks."

"Sure," the woman says, with a swoop of her head. She has long hair and a long neck, and she is wearing a long flowing skirt, with a long white t-shirt.

"Are you here for Professor Wilson?" the woman asks.

"No."

An unfamiliar pressure of speech makes AC elaborate, which is not like her.

" ... I'm waiting for Mr. Sonam."

"What's he teach?"

"Tibetan."

"Hm."

Wind, birds.

"Today's nice," the woman says.

"If you say so," AC says.

"I'm Rachel."

She offers AC another cigarette and lights it for her.

"You smoke pretty hard."

"... Yes."

"What's *your* name?"

"AC."

"It makes me think of air conditioning. That makes it a *cool name*. Nicotine is good for the brain. Nornicotine is created when the body breaks nicotine down, and it impedes the development of Alzheimer's, which is had by my grandmother, who stopped smoking. Are you going to live in Tibet?"

"Maybe."

"I'm going into pharmacology so I can get drugs on a discount. My grandmother has so many prescriptions we're going broke."

"Why don't you just steal them?"

"Oooh, robbery!" the woman smiles and looks away.

"If you want to steal drugs, I'll help you."

AC looks morosely down at the ground.

"I want to fuck up *something*."

Rachel doesn't answer, but she suddenly plucks up AC's Tibetan textbook from the bench beside her and opens it at random.

"Tell me what these are," she says, indicating a page full of illustrations.

"Those are the eight auspicious symbols of Tibetan Buddhism."

"A flower, two fish smooching, and what's this one?"

"The medicine urn."

"An urn full of medicine?"

AC nods.

"That's a good sign!"

AC looks up at Rachel, who seems to incline humanly out toward her from a seamless backdrop of Nazi insanity. Is she making *a friend?*

⊏══⊐

Kids are doing wheelies by the pier. Rachel watches through the window of the Beachcomber while AC heads into the Seaside Drugs.

The sun is setting.

The whole world is like a vast empty room lit only by a distant fireplace.

Seaside Drugs is clearly a converted seafood restaurant; it's still painted an anemic blue and there's a statue of a man in a diving suit standing on the roof, a scuba ghoul backlit now by the rainswept mercury and pink ember clouds. The drugstore lights are blue-green and the whole building, which stands alone with its tiny parking lot, looks like an aquarium. From here you can still see the rain falling on Catalina, out there.

It's Rachel's job to warn AC at the first sign of police.

The pharmacist is alone behind the counter, the music is off, the store is empty. Nearly closing time. A moment ago, a young woman with pink headphones was talking to him, now she's vanished.

Suddenly there are three things for him to be aware of at once.

On the counter to his left, there is an orange and cream tote bag, empty.

In the center of his back, a point of concentrated pressure, round, and hard.

On the counter to his right, there is a notepad with these words gouged into it:

It's a gun.

Stand still.

Hands in the air.

Flip this page with your right hand when I tap you in the back two times.

Nod your head two times when this has been read and understood.

. . .

Total silence. A minute passes, and then another. The pressure in the small of the back is unwavering. The man is panting.

He suddenly collapses to the floor, pissing and shitting.

AC stares down at him. She notices his medical bracelet.

Scowling fiercely she pockets her gun, takes the pad and the bag and begins searching for drugs, tossing in anything with a familiar name.

When the man moans, she turns and points the gun at him.

He doesn't get up. He's just making noises, like a bull having a bad dream. Then he moans again, so loud -- again and again, he fills and empties his lungs, and the sound rises through the roof, and into the air, and scatters toward the horizon in all directions, like the bellowing of reality.

AC gets out of there.

They regroup beneath the awning of an empty storefront with a sign that still reads Surf Antiques. Before stuffing it in her backpack, Rachel looks inside the bag of drug packaging and smiles at AC.

She says: "Thieeeevvves ..."

"ThieeeFFFF," AC says, pointing to herself.

Rachel unchains her bicycle and insists on walking it with AC to the bus stop, and as they hurry in the weird mingling light and darkness of the sunset, the rising air seems to carry them along. Rachel throws back her head and starts to crow like a rooster.

Engulfed in unaccountable happiness, AC strides buoyantly alongside her, dwarfed by her big backpack, their reflections flashing like blades in the thin radiance, and embedded in a storefront window where the Grand Caliginous One dances, twirling ribbons and cleavers slowly wildly.

⊏⊐

I'm held up talking with lawyers and bankers, wondering where Grant is and putting them off in his name, so I don't reach the site until dusk. The sheer amount of emptiness involved in these conversations leaves me mentally numb. There came a point when I straight up told them they were talking to me about nothing at all, that they already had all the information they needed and had had it all within about the first six minutes, and the other six hundred and sixty were all more or less repetitions and reconfigurations of the same four or five facts, as if forcing me to reword what had already been said sixteen times would somehow precipitate Grant into the conversation, and change reality. This so-called conversation only ended when I realized it had no way of stopping on its own, and hung up, and ignored the immediate callbacks.

Much of the canyon floor has already been cleared of brush, although the trees have not been touched. For a few moments I stand in the darkness that hovers close to the ground here, looking up at a sky that the light hasn't fully left yet. Blue up there, and brown down here. It's cool, quiet without being serene exactly, tranquil listening, some birds, bugs, the resinous fragrance of the cut brush. Sage and sweet grass. I begin to walk around the site, and turning around I see something long and level glowing blue-white in the twilight. It turns out to be an adobe longhouse. Was that always here?

Gorgio steps out from behind the building and hails me.

"I'm just looking at this thing. I don't know how I missed it."

"You didn't miss it," Gorgio says with a quick shake of the head. "We built it."

"You built it in the time since --?"

He nods at me smiling, his eyes and teeth and his gold necklace gleaming.

"Can I see inside?"

As we head to the front door I say -- "So quick! It's like magic."

"No magic. Just work."

His eyes shift, and before I can turn to see what he's looking at, Grant's cool linen arm slides inside my elbow and he steers me back out toward the site.

"Hello, Chalo."

I'm so surprised I stumble and turn to my left, away from Grant. I catch sight of the car that must have brought him here, parked next to a big rock. Someone is sitting in the driver's seat, in the dark.

Whoever it is sits so still they don't seem alive. The silhouette has a mop of curls on its head, and a sharp, skinny shoulder, like a mannikin's. Two long, pale hands rest on the steering wheel, rigid, slightly curled, not gripping. Like mannikin hands laid on the wheel by somebody. The sight of that person in the driver's seat welds me to the ground like an electric shock. I want to beg Grant -- don't get back in the car with *that*. But he is already steering me out into the basin. I turn to him.

OK now Grant has never looked quite like this, before. There's something frightening about him now -- he's radiating, he's like a cartoon drawn against the sky.

"You ... uh ... How are you?"

"Me? I'm great!"

We walk on.

"... Twilight is lasting a long time tonight."

"We should take advantage of the light while it lasts."

As we go over the site, I begin explaining to Grant in more specific terms what should go where. I'm laying out the particular problems this site is going to pose for us, what he calls "challenges." It's going to be expensive and slow, getting all the materials here from the mainland and over these shitty back roads. The annex is going to have to generate all the electricity it uses, handle all its own waste, its own fire response; it's going to have to have its own infirmary, arrange its own food supply. Grant listens carefully, asks questions, makes some astute suggestions, but some part of him just isn't there. He barely makes eye contact with me, as if he were distracted.

I wonder if he's thinking of the one sitting behind the wheel of that car, waiting for him, motionless in the gloom back there.

"But the *biggest* problem of all," I say, holding this point for last, "is going to be *water*. You got no mains out here, no reservoir, nothing. The other stuff is tough, but without water ..."

I shake my head.

Grant is still looking fixedly toward the end of the canyon. Suddenly, he beams. He steps past me.

"Come on, Chalo. Let's have a look down there."

The twilight is still not turning into night. It's like the day is deliberately hanging on, so we can check the site. As we pass important spots for development in my plan, I try to talk to Grant, but he seems to be in a hurry.

"We can look at that later. I want to show you something."

"Well, what is it?"

Grant keeps walking, a bit ahead of me.

"What is --"

"I want to show you something," he says dreamily.

The canyon fills with brown light as the twilight finally begins to leave the sky. The brown light seeps up from the ground, or whispers itself from the scrub and the shadows of the trees, rising around us, engulfing us. It's a kind of nostalgia. For nature, I guess.

Grant is moving quickly, financially charged and faintly glowing like a white linen spectre, but I can keep up with him. This brown light agrees with me. It's like a sign that gravity is easing a little.

I follow Grant along a narrow dirt pathway through a kind of tall grass that has these seeds that corkscrew their way into your pant legs and socks until they begin to poke into your skin. We head into a defile that forms a corner on a shallow incline, occupied by a handful of mummified trees that sprout from a heap of boulders. Abruptly, Grant stops and holds up one hand to stop me.

"Huh?"

"It's ... It's not far ..."

"What is?"

"It's --"

A shout. An inhuman shout bursts from the back of the canyon.

That pounding -- my heart, a heart attack?

Three distinct words were shouted.

The ground thuds. The words echo. My feet sway under me. A rumble grows around me. I stagger -- there's crashing. I look to Grant. He rises and falls easily with the ground, joy on his face, his eyes sparkling in the brown gloom. The valley floor lurches, and I end up fastened onto a tree like a sailor clutching the mast in a storm.

The tumbling inside me outlasts the earthquake. I cling to the tree with my cheek pressed against it. The words *what's happening in my life* appear in my mind on their own, printed directly on the morass of my consciousness.

When Grant puts a steadying hand on my shoulder, it feels as if he were balancing the inner stability of that crystal-clear thought with the outward stability of his own uncannily smug hippie balance. I hear a human voice as I pull away from the tree -- it sounds like Malinche, calling out in excitement.

"Let's go have a look," Grant says, smiling. His eyes are sparkling, talking to me but looking away, toward the source of the voice.

The earthquake dislodged some big stones at one end of the canyon.

Grant glides along a bit ahead of me, zeroing in on Malinche.

Now I can see her, standing on top of a huge boulder, waving her arm in the air. Some of the "migrants" have already gathered near the base of the rock, looking down at something.

I hear it and smell it before I see it -- water, gushing up out of a crevice the quake cracked open and collecting in a natural cistern.

Gorgio comes up to me, beaming, all worked up. He claps me on the shoulder.

"It's fresh! Come taste it!"

I let myself be hustled over to a spot nearly on top of the jet of water. I scoop some up in my hand and taste it.

"Spring water!"

I look across to Grant. He's leaning a bit to his left, craning his ear to listen to someone I can't see, a tree is in the way. Grant is nodding, looking down, his face is wrong -- it's too blank for someone who was almost jumping for joy a minute ago. If it was a minute. Perhaps it's been longer. It's not even as if he was getting bad news, it's like he's a different person.

I want to ask Gorgio if he heard that voice, but I can't get his attention. He and the others are all studying the spring, pointing with their hands and sculpting shapes in the air.

If this is a real spring, and not just a pocket of groundwater ruptured by the quake, then our water problem just solved itself.

Where's Grant?

Here comes the car ... dark, rolling up to us slowly, in silence, through the trees.

◁———▷

Whistles reach for each other across the tenuous suburban scene. A high, clear note, interrupted by hiccups, repeats like a homing beacon. It shivers through the suburb's flimsy veil. If you had second hearing, you would hear it, and see how it troubles the apparently solid world of neat houses, square lawns, orderly streets, domestic units, work and play. If you had second sight you would see how frail it all is, how subject it is to stir at the slightest breeze, how ghostly and unknown.

There is one reply slithering up street gutters, a warbling, loping sound. Another reply: a terse bleat, like a car horn coming right down the middle of the street. There's a throbbing bass flute bouncing from swimming pools. There's a plaited bundle of whistles that turn around each other, coming from the playground of the park over there. An almost noiseless, creepily low whistle from deep within the house.

The sun is about to rise. The black east is turning blue.

("Well? Have you HIC haendled it?")

"HAENDLED," the Transept says.

"It was a lovely daey todaey," the Nave croons. "The sea, the sky, the sunlight glimmering on the shaeme ..."

"Aell haendled,") the Narthex says complacently.

("How? HIC.")

"Aen upbuilding exercise ..." the Nave says.

The Narthex seats himself grandly in a big armchair, an empty highball glass tinkling in his hand, and a cigar in his inky lips.

"We sent Wilson in," he says around the cigar, "... Wilson took him to meet the 'migrants,' aend the 'migrants' aegreed to do the job."

"FAIET AECCOMPLI," the Transept says.

("Well! HIC. Whaet will we do with aell our free time?")

The Nave rolls over to the Apse, whose silvery face registers mixed feelings. The Apse takes a sip of her mirror martini and lowers her head, gazing steadily at nothing, as she always does when she's turning something over in her mind.

"Aere you caerefully considering aebout something?" the Nave asks.

("I'm wondering ... whaet do the HIC 'migrants' get out of this?")

"Who caeres?" the Narthex says in a jet of smoke. "Aenything beaets working."

"THE MORE THEY BUILD IT THE MORE IT'S THEIRS,"
the Transept says, oiling himself with his free hand.

("I think you're right aebout thaet, Transept, HIC! Now, who
caen tell me aebout that earthquaeke?")

"Thaet waes the Pulpit's," the Nave says.

("So he reaelly haes taeken Grant HIC on?")

The Nave nods vigorously, eyes rolling.

"Vituperaetively!"

("Well, thaet's HIC something. How aere our 'spells' working
out?")

The Nave laughs fiendishly. The Narthex chuckles deep in his
throat. The Transept wheezes loudly. The Triforium giggle mind-
lessly. A dry rustling comes from the Close.

("Now thaet's more like it.")

The Apse turns her attention back to the Narthex, who's rolling
his glass to and fro between his palms.

("You look like the caet thaet aete the canaery. Whaet haeve you
been HIC up to?")

He turns his face to her and the glass stops.

"A little side project."

("You mean thaet girl?")

The Narthex grins, taps the tip of his nose with his index finger.

"Just so."

("You're HIC taeking her on?")

"It depends on her. I sent her ae friend, too."

("Aend?")

"They robbed ae drugstore together --" he spreads his hands, "--
no violence, but it's still eaerly daeys yet."

("Haeve you figured out whether Chalo died aend haes been
reincarnaeted aes a yaek, or if he's on-HIC! ... only dreaeming of
being a yaek while he's comaetose?") the Apse asks the Nave.

"It's shaeping up to be a fine night tonight," the Nave says
turning away abruptly and paddling over to the window. "Good and
daerk."

("Hm,") the Apse says with displeasure. ("HIC!")

———

... I had my head down, my eyes glazed, and my mind nowhere, and the wind was blowing her scent away from me, so I didn't know she was there until she was virtually on top of me.

Now I snort, and stagger, taking a couple of involuntary bounds away from her.

"What? What? What do you --?"

What's she doing, approaching me?

"Would you warn me? W-what is it? What do you want?"

... She's staring at me. A white cow. She looks a little crazy.

"What did the Figure tell you?" she demands.

I'm too much ambushed. I don't answer.

She takes a step closer.

"What did it say?"

What did it say?

I sidle awkwardly away from her, up the slope a bit. She stays where she is, still staring. A kind of collapse is taking place down in my cavernous interior. The sight of her is suddenly preposterous to me.

The sound of a clogged drain, a big one, starts gurgling. I seem to be laughing.

"What did it say?" she repeats.

Dizziness washes over me. My laughter won't quit, won't stop growing. My legs fold under me and I settle clumsily onto the turf, my sides heaving, mortified. A little spurt of green vomit flashes from my mouth and trickles away into the grass.

"Hm!" the cow says, bitterly.

Without hurrying, she makes her way up to me.

"Stop staring at me," I say, miserably, heaving, laughing.

"Tell me what it said."

"... Buzz off!"

"Tell me what it said."

I lunge wildly, trying to get to my feet, but I'm laughing too hard. She doesn't budge. I'm dizzy and massive and convulsed with laughter I don't understand. I think I'm just going to lie here for a while.

"Tell me what it said."

... I'll get up in a minute. I can see myself doing it.

I'll get up and walk away, maybe eat something.

The rest of the day is pretty well mapped out. I'll eat, and get some water, and I'll look for a likely place to sleep, close enough to the bulls so I can keep an eye on them, I'm not sure for what reason, but not so close that they'll want to hassle me.

"Hey!"

"... I'm resting."

"What did it tell you?"

"I don't know."

"You don't remember?"

"I don't remember."

She makes a sound that, among us yaks, means "psshhhh."

At last, I haul myself to my feet, pushing up through my queasy instability.

"Tell me a little bit, at least."

"Haven't I told you I *don't know*?"

"I dragged myself all the way out here, I spent all day looking for you."

"Well you shouldn't have. That-that's your problem."

Apparently I'm dealing with some occult kind of yak.

"You're not an expression of Gilshrakes," I mutter, not knowing what I'm saying. "You're not recognized by the Predikanten. Your name isn't in Dub Tables. You don't have Gorgons. You are not Zaman Wislin."

Huge vulture wings are spreading out from me and throwing their shadow over her, the wind carrying from them to her the stink of carrion that terrifies us yaks. The Figure appears on the ridge above us, stepping into view from among the rocks.

"There," I say, tossing my head toward it. "Go ask for yourself."

She does. She rushes up the hill toward the Figure at once. The Figure retreats a bit, holding up one hand in a small gesture that could be an invitation to approach, or a warning. Looking up at the Figure, I catch a glimpse of black feathers just behind my head ...

There really is a vulture perched on my back! It hops down onto a big rock and looks at me steadily -- it isn't a vulture, it's a condor. What's a condor doing in the Himalayas?

The condor gives me a slow, sly wink. Then it hops up into the air and begins to swoop around me in a circle, pivoting and teetering on the uneven wind. It slides down and then lunges back up, moving like a roller coaster. I can hear its dry, evil voice, folded in the smell of decay like the dried blossom of a poisonous flower as the layers of crepe paper are peeled. All of a sudden I have an avid desire for arduous climbing, struggle, exhaustion.

"Thinking of running up there? I wouldn't, if I were you ..." the condor rasps. It glides by me and I see its elder head and gimlet eye.

"The power of a secret is in its getting. A secret is better for being inveigled or stolen."

Do I have a secret? I just thought I was confused.

Was what the Figure showed me supposed to be a secret? What did it show me, anyway?

"A stolen secret is better. It's better when your secret belongs to someone else."

The secret of someone else's secret: a secret secret?

The swooping continues circling around me and the wings are shrinking. A black egret, shedding gelatinous cold of outer space.

I look up and see a planet in the blackening sky, and when I look for the egret after that I can't find it --or any bird -- but all around me the ground has sprouted delicate blue flowers.

Can I actually see that color, with my yak eyes? Or do I only remember it?

The flood warning came when the preparation of the grounds was nearly half complete. The ocean was coming for us, no one could make sense of how, but a run up the ridge and you could see it, boiling in a crease in the ground like a rampaging brown snake.

The "migrants" quickly scan out where the water will enter the site -- if it gets in here, weeks of work will be ruined. More weeks will be needed to re-prep the ground, if that will even be possible. Bakarne Bigotes has emerged from the long house and perched on top of a lifeguard seat, shielded from the sun by her bright yellow parasol, and she directs the "migrants" by playing her trumpet, with Gorgio Huidameros as lieutenant. The bulldozer digs a run-off trench with the displaced dirt shoved up into a berm, and every-body's tamping and stamping it together, to make a rampart against the water. Meanwhile I end up wasting a lot of time looking for a way to stop the flood by blocking its way through the hills, with fantasies of blasting down an avalanche and cutting it off at the pass, but there were about seventy fucking passes so the trench option turns out to have been the better one all along.

I can already hear the water rumbling down the gullies. The bulldozer stands ready to drive back the wave, and the rest of the crew already has massive wooden rams -- posts attached to pallets. With two or three on each ram, the "migrants" charge the water, battering it back. The water bulges and splatters over the rampart and dashes over the bulldozer's scoop; Pablo Huitztlacatl is working furiously at the controls, pivoting the bulldozer to keep the water down without damaging the earthwork rim. The waves rebound from the rams in frothy bursts.

The flood tide is like a writhing monster silverfish smashed back along its flanks by those rams. It recoils and foams, hisses, gushes forward again in renewed surges, balked again and turned, forced charges aside into the run-off trench. The water snuffles and lowers and rallies and pours back, driving against us.

Steam boils over the tops of the rams onto the fighters, who stagger against the force of the water. I see Zeferino Jojobal stumble to the side rubbing wildly at his face. Gorgio rushes in to replace him.

Bakarne's trumpet seems to be at their backs, prompting them -- then a heavy bolus of water, like a clenched fist, comes tumbling down on top of a ram below me and nearly knocks it back, but the thrusting of the "migrants" confounds and shivers the bulb of water, it dissipates in bursts of foam and mist. The spray scatters them as though it were scalding hot; they drop the pole and fall away, I'm not sure why. It's as if their morale had been overcome despite their success. Bakarne's trumpet peals out a warning, more loudly right behind me -- but very far away -- I hear a kind of guttural mountain belch reverberating through space -- I flash on the image of a bull yak charging.

Next thing I know I'm in agony, scorched all over and my arms feeling broken and my palms raw and bleeding and there are hands on every part of me, jostling me, holding me up and half-carrying me. I'm surrounded by terrifying faces all shouting and zealous.

... Here's what happened – evidently I let out a such a sound that people thought an airplane had come down on us, then I ran to the abandoned ram, grabbed the post and drove it into the water all by myself.

"You were roaring like a lion!"

"I feel like roaring like a fucking dying lion."

I'm raw everywhere. The skin on my face is blistered, my hands are ripped up, and all my muscles are beaten to dogmeat. And my throat hurts. Elena Hurtado, who's been to a year of medical school, is dabbing stuff on my face now.

"How's the site?"

Gorgio turns with his fists on his hips and surveys the scene with his lower lip stuck out, nodding a little. He turns back to me.

"Mas o menos. A little wet."

"How many days did we lose?"

He makes a little face and shakes his head quickly.

"No *days*. Maybe a few ... maybe half a day, maybe."

"Half a day? That's good! You're heroes."

Gorgio tosses his head a little, as if to say "of course we're heroes."

⊏⊐

Rachel and AC have become menaces and they groove around town casually preparing their latest caper, easing along as if the blows of life were a kind of dance, a kind of glide, a kind of boogie and letting things ride. AC is dogged and now usually half bent over under a heavy backpack full of loot; Rachel is wispy and gauzelike as ever. AC is a chainsmoker now, and her paranoid dread of Nazis has turned into intrepid vigilance. Rachel always seems to be doing something a bit unsightly with her mouth, is always interested, always grooving, swivelling her head on her long neck and making little vocalizations of elan every one and a while.

Grandma is fresh out of medicine. The delivery man is just

turning to go into the pharmacy when he feels something hard just below the small of his back, and a little brown hand thrust up past his shoulder clutches a neatly-printed note.

This is a gun.
   Don't move.
   Nod your head when you have finished reading this.

The word "Fatso!" has been scrawled at the bottom in different handwriting.
   The delivery man nods, frozen. The little brown hand deftly rotates the note to expose the other side.

Put the drugs on the ground slowly and get into the back of your van.

The pressure in the small of the back does not vary at all as the delivery man sets his box down on the blacktop of the parking lot. It remains steady as he climbs into the back of the van. It is withdrawn abruptly and the doors slam shut behind him. At first he flattens himself a bit uncertainly on the floor, and brings his hands up to clasp behind his head, then, hearing rapid footsteps outside, he thinks to clamber forward toward the driver's seat with a vague idea of getting out that end. By chance he happens to see the two thieves vanishing behind the liquor store that L's out from the line of shops. Long black hair, one tall, a small one with a backpack nearly as big as she is.
   ... The early evening finds AC and Rachel down by the beach sampling pills. AC stares slackjawed at the gathering wafer of dimness between the sand and the blue air, then smiles showing all her teeth, while Rachel floats around her on rollerskates, headphones on. There's a box of shrinkwrapped medication, two and a half cigarette cartons, and a loaded gun in that big pack on AC's

back. The cigarette drops to the ground as her hands loosen and she sits grinning at the powdery eye of darkness condensing like reversed smoke, dissolving the air and the daylight, digesting and burning it, turning it into dancing motes of soot. The Nave squeaks invisibly in circles above them, carrying her pitcher of daylight, wringing the fabric of space out into it, while the Narthex sprawls in his armchair directly above AC, thoughtfully rubbing his chin. Flakes of cigar ash rub off and float down through the top of AC's skull, landing directly on her brain with tiny sizzles, like snowflakes falling on a hot griddle.

The Narthex pulls a whole box of cigars out of the inside pocket of his maroon jacket and judiciously selects one. He peels off the band and snips the cap with his glistening black teeth. Then he leans down, lightly resting the tip of one leather disco boot on AC's shoulder. A plume of colorless fire whirs up from the fissures in AC's brain, and the Narthex expertly toasts, then lights his cigar by it.

"Coming aelong nicely," he says to the Nave.

"Given a chaence," the Nave says, without taking her eyes from her own paddling left hand, pitcher uplifted in her right. "We don't haeve her yet."

"It's aes good aes," the Narthex says.

Elena Hurtado leads me into the barracks they've named "Rancho Otro" and puts me to bed. The pain of my burns is getting worse, and I'm just starting to realize the weird voices I'm hearing are coming out of me. Elena dabs my arm with alcohol and slides a needle in.

-- A moment after she straightens up again --

... That wan smear is the window, ghostly in its white curtains. Grant is coming into view on the tawny hillside beyond it, walking with Bakarne --

... A cool hand is pressing my forehead -- Grant's hand. He stands over me, his face in shadow, hair hanging down. I want to ask him if he's faith-healing me, but all I can do is mouth at him. He smiles his old smile. I know he's smiling. I know he's smiling, because I can see his teeth glint in the shadow. His smile hangs there after he's gone. It's still there after my eyes have closed again. It's weird, I can feel his hand there, but not my own body.

... Erotic dreams -- everything sharply outlined in thick rails of a viscous light that spreads like glue injected through the separations between things. My voice lingers in the corners of the room when I start upright in the dark.

... It's night. Is it the night of that day, or some later day?

... Through the window I see the "migrants" moving around in the brush out there. Their heads rise up out of the bushes and then drop down again as they criss-cross the slope, like a menacing pod of killer whales. All without a sound. Silent, intent, still working, somehow, on something.

I get up and stagger to the bathroom on numb, inert legs, leaning on the walls for support. When I pass the common area, I am only just aware that everybody's in there, sitting quietly in the dark.

... Switch on the light. The bathroom is like a paper lantern lost in the night, a porcelain elevator with me neatly inside it, pissing noisily. When I'm done, I snap the light off again, sit down and wait for my eyes to adjust before I head back to bed.

... The darkness is like fresh water, offering no impediment to the bone-dry moonlight streaking the tile floors. They even had time to lay tile.

... My legs are tingling, a bit more responsive. They hurt more, but they are also more free to move. I can pause by the common area now and look into it. The "migrants" are sitting in the dark, with the front door and all the shutters open. Some I can see sitting outside in chairs, looking like blue watercolors. Soft bursts of yellow light, produced by hovering insects, pull the living faces briefly out of the darkness. It's as if they were bobbing to the surface of a black lake, then sinking again, always in the same places. The space of the room is greater. The bugs aren't fireflies, are they? We don't have those out here, not fireflies, so did they bring them?

None of them look at me -- they all seem to be staring at the ceiling.

No wonder -- Bakarne is up there, sitting in the rafters with her legs crossed and her head thrown back. She is gazing into a reflective spot, like a pool of clear, motionless water, upside-down on the ceiling. She has hands pressed to either side of it.

... Tensely deliberate peacefulness. A vigil.

I'm done taking all this in, ready to put my weighty head down on the pillow -- but what's that sound, coming toward us from so far off? It's like the noise of an earthenware lid grating against an earthenware lip, steadily but with varying pressure, fading and swelling, like remote music on a windy day.

... So now what appears to be happening is, I'm receiving a series of visits from different "migrants," punctuated by periods of unconsciousness throughout what might be one or more than one night. I wake up and Zeferino Jojobal is sitting in a chair in the corner, no lights on, and he notices the moment I come to. He's skin and bones, but he doesn't strike me as unhealthy. He's just too strange for eating, or he can't maybe eat regular food. His jawbones jut out on his skinny neck, and he keeps his wrists against his chest. Grinning so that all his wet teeth show in his damp mouth, eyes all lit up, he starts saying

"Pasaportes-documentos, documentos-pasaportes, pasaportes-documentos, documentos-pasaportes."

"What time is it?"

Zeferino snorts. Then he swallows noisily, turning his head as if he were trying to locate my voice, and a clock on the wall. There's no clock in the room. He looks at me and says

"Night time."

He giggles nervously.

When I next wake up, Pablo Huitzlacatl is sitting where Zeferino was, leaning back in the chair with his hands on the wicker armrests, and I think I see Malinche Azazul peek in for a second, but I'm not really sure she did. Pablo has mystic vibrations. He has one earring that's something white and dangling I've never gotten close enough to see. He wears a bandanna and a denim jacket covered in buttons and patches. One button in particular is either Haile Selassi or Lee Scratch Perry waving at me, I can see the hand moving. Now all his buttons are pulsing colors and little striated black wavelets, like visualized sound beams. There's a lot of junk around his wrists and neck and he's one of those guys who can function with about twenty rings on.

"You OK?" he asks abruptly.

I shrug.

"Mind if I smoke?"

"Fire it up."

He lights up a stick of something that smells like incense.

"White lighters are bad luck."

A viscous cloud of ectoplasm slithers out of Pablo's mouth, luminous in the dark. He bats it apart with a wave of his hand.

"Not for me. I was born on the thirteenth. Bad luck is good luck for me."

He takes another drag, narrowing his eyes through the smoke at me.

"You know your man is working with daemons?" he asks, leaning forward with his elbows on his knees and talking smoke.

I nod.

"You're not freaked out by that?"

I shrug. A spasm of pain shoots through my burned face and arms, making my whole body contract like a scorched spider. Why did it hurt this time and not the last time?

"Hey, you alright? Should I get Helena?"

The pain subsides and I slump back.

"No, I'm OK. Just a ... little episode."

He sits back down and smokes for a bit.

"You sure you're not freaked out?"

I think that over. Then I let my hands rise and drop again.

"I've been freaked out by everything so long, what's one more thing?"

"So you're already at maximum freak."

I nod.

"Maximum freak."

"You've transcended freaking out."

I let that one sink in.

"No ... nope!"

This answer pleases Pablo and he smiles, nodding. The wind

rustles the brush outside like a wave hissing on a beach, joining its sound to the undulating whir of crickets.

An owl hoots abruptly, very close by, and Pablo reacts, turning his head and grasping the arms of the chair. He listens, as if someone were shouting some important information to him. Then he slowly turns his silhouetted head back to me.

"Did you ever see them?"

"You mean ...?"

"Yeah."

"I saw them. I saw them take shape."

"What did they look like?"

"One is a big bruiser who dresses like Tom Jones ... there's a weaselly one who has a wheel instead of legs ... there's one who looks like a sixty-year-old who's always jerking off ... and one who looks like Myrna Loy on a divan with a martini and little horns."

... Dreams of hammering, lumber, piping, water jets, pumps. Shovels chopping. I'm on a boat that goes up onto the island, up the steep slope to a high plateau and splashes into a blue lake, not onto the surface but down beneath it, driving like a submersible truck along the bottom of the lake, and I'm seeing blue angular rock faces forming a bright trench with the fluctuating silver and blue lake surface sixty feet above us. I have to get through the lake to get to the island. But I'm already on the island, right? So, an island on an island?

... Now it's Ixcuiname Monje in the chair, with a sort of pinkish, pre-pre dawn vapor clinging to her wan face.

"... so if you make it real one way there's nothing left for reality to do."

... I think that's what she's saying. I'm still waking up. How long has she been talking?

"Then it never happens."

"What?"

She raises her eyes to me and smiles ruefully, exhaling through her nose.

"Nothing. How are you feeling?"

"I don't know."

"Need anything?"

I shake my head.

She nods and lets her eyes drop back to the floor again.

"How are *you* feeling?"

Eyes back up to my face again. She sighs again. Eyes back down again.

I nod and my eyes drop too.

"Did you really see the daemons?"

"Yes. I know how it sounds. I don't really care if I'm crazy. ... I saw them, somehow."

"Can you describe them?"

I give her the best description my wastedness allows.

She listens without moving, her head hanging forward and her hands knitted on her stomach. I don't so much finish as fall silent, and she sits in silence for a while after. I find myself wondering if all the "migrants" are going to file in here one after the other to hear my description of the daemons to see if the absurdity of my description finally dawns on me after I've repeated it a dozen times, and I have a therapeutic breakthrough, abandon the whole thing.

Her eyes lift to look at me yet again.

"And you're not afraid?"

"Oh, I don't know. I guess not knowing means I don't -- I mean, I'm not. I should be. I guess."

She keeps looking.

"They don't seem to pay any attention to me."

Still looking.

"I haven't been threatened."

This time I wait out her looking.

"Daemons want to take your soul."

"... I don't think anything's been done to my soul. What do they do with it if they get it?"

"They dissolve it, and it's gone."

"So why do it? Do they get off on that or what?"

"... I think they want everything to be falling all the time, like them."

"*You* ever see one?"

"Yes."

That wasn't an inviting yes.

"Your friend is spending too much time with that one with the blonde hair. -- Don't say his name! Never say that one's name."

"If you say so."

"I say so."

She points to herself, bobbing her head a little as she speaks.

"I know what I'm talking about."

Her voice sounds scorched and her gaze is all clawed up and ragged.

"What happened?"

She sits back in the seat and looks away for a moment, pursing her lips.

"I don't want to talk about it," she says finally, shaking her head so that her earrings swing.

"It's better not to."

A moment later she gets up.

"I'll get you some water," she says, and walks out.

... I don't know if she comes back, because the lead hood of sleep drops over me again.

It's daylight when I wake up, alone. What day is it?

... I throw my legs out of bed and sit there with the sun strobing down different colors on my poor shellacked head. I let my eyes wander over the floor. Freshly swept, it looks like.

... When I see a bare white foot on the floor I jump back onto the bed like I saw a rattlesnake -- someone white is sitting in the wicker chair, someone with no eyes is looking at me, talking reversed words at me. I flatten against the wall. My throat won't open. I can't call for help or move. Gaze pours from black pits above an intermittent mouth creaking backwards. Paralysis sinks into me -- disgust, revulsion. Language shitted right into my head I can't protect myself from. I pound the wall with my fist and I hear feet clatter up to my door. It flies open and Gorgio Huidameros hurries up to me.

"What is it?"

I look up and see her sitting in her chair by the window, light falling across her like milk. The apartment we shared together in Costa Mesa with the purple drapes -- her eyes that I turned into shame lasers burning me -- her disappointment in me, lodged in me like a ball of sour white phosphorous ... the steady watchful way she gazed at me without moving, without speaking, without changing her expression ... almost without blinking, until I felt welded in place, a failure, not able to so much as reach out to her from the ceaseless unfolding of my shortcomings. Turned into a stinking, mute yak I stand there. She sits by the window with her careworn face turned to me, with nothing left to say to me, not even "get out," or the first insult from her, which might have saved me. Nothing. Never an unjust word from her. Every word was only too just and even too merciful. She was always right. If she had been more merciful she would have insulted me. Her mercilessness mercy was all too just in giving me nothing, not an inch or a second. Part of my life now. That is, part of the malignant cosmic conspiracy to deny me any ground for complaint by making sure that whatever pain comes to me comes as a result of my own failure.

Do her eyes see a yak, dull-eyed and smelly, or a dull, plodding human man? How could I ever touch her again, knowing what she saw reaching out to her? All I want to do is to reach out to her. I'm not a yak or a man, not Chalo, not one or another of these things but all of them in the dark -- not on Catalina or in the Himalayas -- in the *dark* where I've always been with my arms reaching out not to anyone anything anytime anyplace but reaching out sobbing come back, all all all come back, come back. Don't leave me. Don't leave. All of me is only just the begging for that.

-- It's broken now. It's broken.

-- I'm staring at nothing and Gorgio is staring at me.

"Chalo!"

He grips my shoulders and shakes me sternly.

"Wake up! You're dreaming!"

... I laugh in his face.

Tears are spurting from my eyes, and a gale of laughter gushes from my stinking throat like vomit.

Gorgio rivets his eyes on mine. Two blazing, almost colorless slots in his dark face.

"You are dreaming," he says very deliberately and particularly. "It's time to wake up."

It doesn't work. He looks preposterous. Laughter is playing the devil with my insides, leaping and churning in me like the gushings of a black indigestion through my dead tripes.

Gorgio is as solid as a statue.

"If you won't wake up," he says inflexibly, "then go to sleep *again*."

-- That does the trick. I shut down, and slump back onto the pillows, damp with sweat, his hands still firm on my shoulders. When I'm lying down, he straightens and marches right out the door, closing it without another look in my direction, leaving me to the plaster whiteness. The colors lose their forms and reach out for me. I want to pass out. I can't take any more. The colors are all telling me "I am you!"

The daemons got me, there is nobody here, but there's been a mistake, because someone is still in the room, someone feeling pain and terror. Being pain and terror, a cubist asterisk of anguished faces whirred together and impossible to save, not even by descriptions, just unbearable self-consciousness without a self, without a wisp but a slight, agonizing deviation of nothing, unable not to notice itself, and flooded with memories out of order. Full of strangers, acted by strangers like actors playing roles with no originals or models, on sets supposed to be places that never existed, where even the daylight is false to no original, nothing is anything but violence against a victim who is a victim of not being, where the victimlessness is the crime, listening and being lost, reaching out, possess me daemon so I can be somebody and slow this plummet, shrinking into the dark. I put my hands out to the daylight to grope for it. I could throw it over myself like a sheet and go out into it and be seen and heard, an empty sheet.

The rut hits.

It engulfs me out of a cloudless day like a dart of infernal fire. It gets us all. Vibrating, eyes rolling, electrified, watchful, blind, jumpy. I glance up at, flinch, look away from the females grazing with feigned indifference on the upper slope. The sight of a cow, even at this distance, whips up my madness. They're watching us, with hatred. They want to see us kill each other. I look at the bulls and feel no emotion, just an impersonal desire for straining and exhaustion that belongs to my body alone. Glancing up at the cows is like slamming into a rock wall, with a repercussion that rattles me to the heart, and shakes loose a daze of unaccountable sadness. I want to lower my head onto the nearest bull's shoulder and burst out sobbing convulsively, I don't know what I want to do, I want to eat black flowers and run upside down on the sky cutting grooves in the ground with my horns and feel the buried rocks crack. I want to be buried asleep in winter snow.

I remember there was one place in particular she loved to be touched, so I would touch her there, like the piano string is beginninglessly touched by the felt hammer. Her breath always smelled like milk.

... I look up at the white furnaces of the clouds, and down in the valley at dry streambeds like twined skeins of white silt, tearbeds really, passing in and out of inksplotch cloud shadows, like the sooty footprints of the cloud furnaces, where voices are hammered out of something like metal, kneaded by the cauliflower hands of the clouds, and flung like javelins, harpooning the world.

"You have to know how to follow directions to be you know good at life," someone somewhere is yelling into his phone.

The clouds and the landscape mix freely with the geoelectric volcanic eruptions going on inside my body, passing in and out of me. Like blobs of painfully intense stimulation, and the shadows like the troughs of the roller coasters, plying me with gloom. Like long liquor drinks, so that my eyes are plated with violence, half-blinded by the steam off my own organs.

Put it all together and it spells the word AGAIN.

                                                 ⬚

Having ground through another lustreless afternoon violin lesson, Rachel wafts out of the Skinner Building and heads home. Swinging around the corner and turning down the block she clips a parked police car with her violin case. A police officer bursts from the car and comes after her, drawing his club. She starts to run without looking where's she's going and collides with a trash can. The police officer is nearly on top of her, his face blank, club raised high above his head for a heavy blow. In her sudden fear, which still seems barely real, she runs back inside the Skinner Building, up the stairs. The police officer is pounding right behind her. The whole stairwell reverberates with breathing, and the boom and clap of footsteps.

She's nearly to the top floor landing when she feels his club graze the back of her knee. She is thrown against the wall. The police officer comes down on her, and then out of nowhere AC -- she shoves him back, snarling curses at him. Half his size, she shoves in close to him. They grapple clumsily and he punches her in the face. The blow doesn't quite land, but AC has to lunge back to avoid it. He whips out at her with his club, his face slack. AC ducks. Then she seizes hold again.

The Narthex embraces AC from behind. Grinning ear to ear, he slides his arms along her arms and his hands over her hands. Rachel can't see him, and watches in amazement as AC smoothly lifts the police officer over her head. She pivots and flings him through a closed window, CRASH, and out into forty feet of air.

Rachel is one step toward the window when she feels AC's hard little hand snatch at her arm.

"Don't show yourself!"

She points upward.

"Let's go to the roof!"

Cries of horror and alarm rise from down below. The rooftops up here do all connect, as Rachel suspected, and most of them have projecting doorways -- locked, locked, locked -- sirens now rise and fall, helicopters coming, coming down the many streets toward them. AC waves Rachel over to a fire escape. Down they go, then scramble over a folded chain link fence and into a weedy alley. They hurry to the next block and then slow down, walking normally and inconspicuously.

The pupils of the Narthex's painted eyes are burning balefully.

"Did you see thaet?"

He throws back his head and puts his fists on his hips.

("Aell right," the Apse says. "Very nice, Narthex.")

They all go limp, and spin together like leaves twisting in a flirt of autumn wind.

AC and Rachel get away, but there are shitty drawings and faded, stretched-out mosaic images of them in circulation now. It seems the officer landed on his head. AC thrusts her hand out at the Pacific.

"Let's go to Catalina."

"Are you nuts? We'd be trapped."

"We can stay at the work site. Nobody would look for us there. Grant's invited me."

"We should go to Mexico or something."

"What are we going to do in Mexico? You know Spanish?"

Rachel shakes her head.

"I know Latin."

"Catalina," AC says.

Rachel swings her arms, head lowered.

"OK," she says.

Above them the Narthex revels in the night sky, doing ecstatic obeisance in front of a vast ectogram of AC's face, crushing one of her soulpomegranates against his mouth, sucking the nectar of what was not supposed to happen.

⊏⊐

... I've been up and around since yyyesterday I think, or maybe the day before that. A group of people are setting up a campsite right beside the earthquake spring. Grant called me earlier today, and I think he spoke to Bakarne too, to tell us all that his "Rheterostylites" are undergoing some kind of linguistic reconditioning that requires them to avoid ordinary language for the time being, so it would be better if none of us approached them or spoke to them.

So there they are, all dressed in grey. There's a blonde older sunburned woman, a smooth pair of baby boomers, and a lean, hard-looking younger man. They sit on low stools facing Grant in his white veil, copying his gestures.

"Do you know how many more are coming of those Rhetero-consuelos?"

"Not consuelos, stylightees."

Later on Grant stops by to say hello and have some more of his pu erh. He pushes a sheaf of curling graph paper toward me.

"That's the latest terma."

He points at it once I have it in my hand.

"I'd like to know what you think of it."

I flip the pages, groaning at the sight of several charts.

"I won't talk too long."

Here we go. Here we go again. He's either going to say something stupid, I'll lose respect for him, the wild impossibleness of this project will break upon me at last and I'll have to go find something else to do, or he's going to convince me again and leave me wondering if I'm not an idiot or what is the world or being just more crazy. What I should do is get up and say I have to go to the bathroom or something and then find a non-offensive pretext not to come back, but he's already telling me and it's too late.

"You don't like the termas?"

"I don't know what they have to do with anything. They're just weird poetry to me. When I was young ..."

I hear the wistfullness in my voice and uncertainly stop.

"-- Just seems silly."

"The termas don't work in any obvious way, but they *do work*. To carry out a ritual -- and to make it an effective ritual -- it isn't necessary, to understand it. In fact, it's impossible to understand, a ritual, until you do it. And even then, you won't understand it right away. Even if everything is done perfectly. It must be completely over and done with, and you must be somewhere else entirely, doing something totally different, before you will even be able, to begin reflecting on it. Just like anything else in life ...

"People believe that rituals express ideas. That's where they go wrong. The description of the ritual is like the record of some event in history. Like the Lincoln assassination. Was that an expression of an idea? With a ritual, you start with nothing."

"Yeah, but -- that's not possible."

"That's the real ritual. ... Because, if it's done right, then, you will have started from nothing, by the end. And once you've done it, and reflected on it, then you will learn what it has to teach you. It's not like being told something, or memorizing something, or being taught something. It's an experience, that changes you, in ways that you come to understand. You have to intend, to perform the ritual before, you begin, but by the time you're done, you never intended it."

"Is that why your rhododendrons aren't allowed to talk? So they won't know what they're doing? Not too soon?"

Grant smiles.

"Rheterostylites."

"Yes. Is it?"

"What we're doing?"

"Yes."

"Once the Rheterostylites are done with tertogestation then, we'll work together, as primitive machines, to produce, original gestures."

"What?"

"The Rheterostylites are each preparing, a soul, for themselves, to act as an unconscious regulator, for articulated conscious thoughts and actions, which we can then, do, and record, and decipher. They will all become tertons."

"What are you trying to decipher?"

He smiles.

"Paradise."

Everything's normal, so why are my teeth gritting? Why am I suddenly rigid in my seat with the feeling you get when you know your car is about to hit something?

I can't see Grant's face, just the hair sloping down to the shoulders, and suddenly he seems like a corpse propped up in the chair. His voice sounds like a television in another room.

"AC will be joining us here soon."

It's all so conversational, so why am I wrestling with panic?

"AC called you?"

I can't see his face.

"You're smiling that smile again, aren't you?"

"She called."

How is it I'm the one isolated in this landscape while he is part of the murmuring trees and lights and darks, and all the soft pastoral intensities vibrant with death out there beyond the window, surrounding the house ...

Grant sets his tea down on the table and heads for the door.

"I had better get back out there. I'll see you."

Grant stops on his way across the room, pausing for a moment. Then he crosses instead to the bureau very austerely set against the wall, opens the top drawer, pulls out a pair of work gloves, closes the drawer, places the gloves on the nightstand next to me, then leaves. I stare at the gloves.

As he is going out one side, Gorgio comes in the other side with plans in his hands and tosses his head back at me. I get up, we meet halfway as some of the other "migrants" are coming back inside, wearily banging their dusty hands together and batting at themselves with their hats.

"It looks like there's a subsidence problem starting to happen here."

Gorgio shows me a spot on the plans with his finger.

I glimpse Anthony Motion in the doorway and the ground sways under me like a trapeze. I'm suddenly terrified of death. Why does the emanation of death, welling out like invisible water from the dark reliefs of the landscape, turn me into ancient music?

With eerie clarity I see exactly what Gorgio is talking about, but my mind is at a total standstill. I know I can solve this problem, but the answer is in another place and I can't leave here, the place I stand in.

"You OK?"

Gorgio claps me on the shoulder.

I can see he's looking around for someone to call -- Helena, probably. Something in me is rejecting that help.

"Let me go outside. ... I want to go outside."

I don't sound too plausible.

Gorgio is coming with me, concerned, and the others are noticing as well. Why didn't I want Helena's help?

Or any? Who said "no" inside me? Just because I hear a voice coming from inside me doesn't mean that it's my voice. And just because a voice is coming from outside me doesn't mean that it isn't my voice.

I get outside and I see Grant and Anthony over together by Anthony's car, and Anthony is introducing Grant to a big man in a hoodie. They shake hands. The big man's face is vague in the gloom, all smiles. He has a tic; every now and then he sort of clenches his head and left shoulder toward each other in a rolling motion that seems to lose all urgency the moment it begins.

"Let me," I say, holding out my hand for the plans. "Let me see that."

For some reason I feel more firm in my outlines now. I notice I'm still holding the new curly terma, bundled with the work gloves. I roll them up sloppily and shove them into the cavernous back pocket of my pants.

OK so there's a problem building on ground with clay in it because the weight of the building squeezes water from smectite clay and the ground sinks. My idea was to build on pilings sunk beneath the smectite layer, and section the foundation while distributing some of the weight of the base out sideways so it wouldn't rise or fall and crack up everything attached to it. Now it looks like there's going to be more drop over by one corner than I allowed for. If that happens, the foundation could crack, the building could list, and so on.

"I can show you, if you want," Gorgio says.

I follow him to the corner and he shows me where the foundation line is already sagging under the berm. From her lifeguard tower, Bakarne Bigotes shines her flashlight on the subsidence points as Gorgio shows them to me, first one, then the other.

"We can add concrete, but it would be better to wait 'til it's done sinking and then build."

"Shore it up first thing," I say, and my emotions, my voice, startle me. I feel defiant.

Looking at those little slippages, I feel like someone who's just found smudges on my cherished cut-crystal glasses. I hate those little slippages. I want to pull the imp of damage out of each one and throttle it to death while it squeaks and flails in my grip like a living puppet.

Gorgio shrugs and goes off to tell Pablo to get the cement mixer ready for tomorrow.

... Now I'm lying in bed, checking out the new terma.

Oh Son of a Noble Family
The Pure Land exists in its destruction.
Above your head visualize the collapsing heap of fungus,
dissolve it in eclipsed darkness and disperse it.
Unspeak the dead syllable of the name of Gilshrakes
and scatter fungus with Dub Tables.
Stab yourself with the wish-fulfilling venom
thrice beneath the ground
thrice while falling down the slope of the transparent mountain
thrice while the enemy beheads you.
Become a dead carrion bird and learn ten hundred languages

This terma folds in on itself to form tangent bundles. It looks like a crown of shredded straw.

... AGAIN, it says. Rut surfs. My thoughts scatter in montage scarves when I look up at the cows. Can they hear them? No? No. To get to their bodies I must first fall on the bodies of the bulls. I turn my heavy head and my glazed, wall-eyed stare, and see the bulls all staring, mouths open, staggered like they've just gotten the tap from the humane killer, how would I know about that? I was a human that's why, remember? Yaks have human-shaped gods and monstrous gods that are yaks with human heads, all their power concentrated in the obscene line along the throat where the utterly human head becomes part of the ... the yak body.

... I look at the other rut-battered bulls without animosity. They are stomach breathing, carrying their heads as if their horns were too heavy and tipping. I just want to run them all down, it's not personal. We're not persons. We all feel it. We're all rivers boring through the landscape the rut makes us helpless masters of, toward crashing into each other, like the sex tumbling down the Himalayas through the bare bones of our ancestors and into us.

... I'm coughing so hard my throat is tearing, trying to form words with this uncouth voice that's good for nothing but wheezing, as if that would matter. A divine hand meshed in the tuft on top of my head, hoists imperiously at it and my upper lip, my eyes rolling. Sky strobing day and night. The ground bouncing like a drumhead. Memory asteroids of past events and feeling shatter on the earth, drive the bulls together, straining and jostling, growling --

"Give! Just give!"

Fucked up.

Fucked *up.*

"It's cracking!"

People streak by the windows, toward the site. I charge out after them and it's like the crack, already visible in the concrete wall shoring up the subsiding corner, reaches out and seizes me, pulling me to it. I sprint down to the wall, and as I go I am hauling on those work gloves Grant pulled out for me. I grab a long support beam off a pile of lumber and carry it like a pole-vault pole. I don't know what I'm doing, that comes later, maybe, maybe it does, I run up to the base of the wall -- the crack is nearly an inch wide in places, and there's another fucking crack too, starting in the second fucking subsidence spot.

I hoist my post and ram it into the upper portion of the wall, wedging the other end into the ground. Already there are others running up with posts to help me. The wall groans and I can feel the shaking through the timber in my hands -- I don't dare let go, but if the wall comes down, it comes down on me.

-- Well then the foundation isn't *going* to come down.

-- You hear that?

-- This foundation is *founded.* It isn't moving, gravity.

... There are about a half dozen props against the wall now, but the feeling through the wood is like some giant grinding, twisting monster raging on the other side. The gloves give me traction. Arginaldo Caldito darts past me and, with Gorgio's help, mounts a foundation jack of his own design at the base of the wall; the two of them start cranking wildly and after a moment I can feel the strain on the timber is dwindling. Then my post cracks.

The splinters fly into my left eye and I nearly let go. In a moment I feel what I think is Helena Hurtado swiping wood chips away from my eye. Meanwhile Ernesto Huesca has clamped a big vice around the crack in the post and is deftly screwing it shut. I can feel the flex in the post straightening out again. It pulls me slightly more erect with it.

I thank them both over and over again, tight-chested, stomach breathing. Looking around it's like each of the "migrants" is in two or three places at once, there's so much going on. They're charging up like lancers with their posts, and Gorgio and Arginaldo are both pushing on the crank handles, eye whites blazing like incandescent phosphorous in the shadow of the wall, inching the handles forward as the subsidence force is driven back, gurgling and churning in the watery soil on the far side with a noise like berserk intestines.

Bakarne's trumpet blares and we all look up.

This signal means that the wall is perpendicular again. Cautiously, two by two, the "migrants" begin to separate themselves from their posts and stand back. Arginaldo locks the jack and comes skipping back out from the wallshadow, batting his thighs with his hands and spitting dust. My arms are hugging my post so fiercely I can't get them to let go; I have to force them apart to get myself clear.

"We gotta fill the cracks," I say. "And we have to brace the wall laterally to the rock."

Gorgio comes up to me, breathing hard, the little gold chain around his neck rising and falling.

"It might be better to pull it down and firm the ground up again," he says.

"We're not doing that. We don't have time or money for that."

"Yes but gravity is not going away, Chalo."

"I've fought gravity my whole life. I'm a *fat* man. I've always been a fat man -- I was a fat kid, now I'm a fat man -- fat *and clumsy*, and I've fought *gravity* my whole *life!*"

"Fuck you! Fuck you!" I shout at gravity, down in the ground. "My building stays up!"

They're all looking at how weird I am but I don't care.

I point to the annex and I'm choking up.

"That's my *dream!*"

I'm at the window, listening. It's brown Rembrandt night time out there. And, pouring into here. Music is coming from the tents, where Grant's students are. One person is playing isolated notes on a piano, and at least two others are playing tanpuras. The peacefulness of the music washes over me. So, why does it make my teeth snap shut and clench? Why does it make me clutch the windowsill until the wood creaks? Why are my eyes popping, and why is cold sweat bursting out, painfully, all over my body? Why does it feel like my spine is trying to straighten my skull up through my scalp?

A high, thin sound from nowhere ... like another voice joined to theirs ... a voice from outside ... from history the way it ought to have been instead ... the way things should have been ... might never have been ... might not have been able, ever to have been, ever to be ... I'm straining to hear it ... when there's a startling knock at my door, and Grant comes in.

"Just passing by. I thought I'd drop in and see you."

My throat clears.

"... I was listening to the rhodomontades."

"Rheterostylites."

"Gorgio is supposed to come by later and tell me how bad the damage is from the subsidence. We're probably going to extend the construction period by maybe a week to shore up the base. Can we do that?"

He nods, standing in the door like a figure in a portrait frame.

"I mean, if your heterotirades --"

"Rheterostylites."

"-- are waiting for the campus to be built, you'll need to plan on, you know, whatever they need, a week more of whatever they need."

I can hear some kind of activity elsewhere in the house. There's a low murmur of voices and the faint tremor of footsteps. I'm guessing that means Gorgio is making his way to me, and so I get up. The one who enters the room, stepping past Grant, is the man in the hoodie I'd seen earlier, and he says "yeah."

He walks into my room the way people walk down busy sidewalks, and stops only a few feet from me. With his hands plunged into his sweatshirt pockets, his hood is pulled down tight over his skull, which waggles a little to one side.

"Gorgio" -- he pronounces it 'Jorjo' -- "... says they're going to have to take up part of the foundation and pour it over again. He says you're going to need concrete, more concrete."

He smiles at me.

"Have we met?"

He smiles and shakes his head vigorously.

"I'm Ban."

"Chalo I'm Chalo."

"I know."

"Are you one of the Rhodeislandites?"

"Rheterostylites," Grant says, with the same tranquil smile as ever.

Ban smiles drunkenly and shakes his head.

I realize, though, just now, only just now, Grant's wearing sunglasses. That's the one California thing he never does, and now he's doing it. What does that mean? It means there's something less about his smile now.

... Now it's tomorrow. I'm on the boat back to the mainland, and I'm catching sight of myself reflected in the window wearing my habitual expression: stunned.

Got to get the concrete.

"I said those exact words to you and now you say no!" a woman shouts into her phone. She's been pacing up and down, and now she stops while her anger battles to overcome her self-consciousness, and the divotted blue water goes pulsing by outside, and the green and tan coast inches nearer with a steady roar of engines, zapping my fillings with vibrations.

Why am I so tired all the time?

I'm going back as is, in my t-shirt and jeans, with nothing. Car keys. I know where to buy concrete but a magical fairy in my mind is telling me not to bother. No one is going to want to ship the amount of concrete we need at the price we can afford. Not with the subsidence. This whole thing is so up in the air, it's making me light-headed. It's like dreaming about being badly sleep-deprived in the dream.

The air is so soft it's harsh, and the light is so bright I can't see anything. The sea air makes my head swim and my body sink. I want to stuff my head into a bucket of warm sand and die quietly for a while, maybe roll downhill into some situation that doesn't depend on me to do anything. Poetry. In my mind. No different than a headache. Less meaningful, in fact. A kind of game I play with the world. The only one. Guess who wins? I always have to guess.

... The phone jolts me awake. On the other end of the line, a remote voice, half-buried in music, identifies itself as an old friend from college days and he's having a party and I should come out. He texts me the address. I barely manage to speak to him, fumbling to form even the sentences I leave unsaid. I wonder if there's something the matter with me neurologically.

"You stoned this morning, Chalo?" the voice asks wryly.

... Now I'm back on the mainland, with terra earthquake beneath my feet. There's so much to do that I can't do anything. I stand in the parking lot, staring at cars like a time traveller from the Stone Age, trying to realize that one of these things is supposed to belong to me, because the keys I'm holding go to it. What about that phone call? It felt like a dream, but the text is there.

A hand on my shoulder. It's Wilson.

"Hey man," he says.

The sun hits this one spot in his left eye, illuminating the brown iris like a dead leaf in a little pool of rainwater, and sun right after the rain, and the clouds warming and cooling the light by turns.

"You should go home. ... You feeling a little blank?"

"Yeah, a bit."

"Well, I'm real!" he says, raising his eyebrows, smiling. He lifts his hands and pulls his elbows back to sort of expose himself as himself, standing there.

"I'm right here! You're not crazy!"

He leans in.

"I mean, you are crazy, but you're not just seeing me!"

"How did I know you was how did I know -- how did I know -- how did *you* know I was going to be here?"

"I was on the boat too, man, that's how! I'm coming over to see my cousins!"

"I thought you were adopted."

"I was! Adopted people have cousins! Listen -- you OK to drive, man? I mean, no offense, but you look kind of out of it."

"Compared to what?"

"The chips and dip were so expensive!" a woman is telling someone behind me. "The *chips*, the *dip* ... so *expensive!*"

"Are you good to drive, though?"

"I can drive, man, thanks."

"Can you give me a ride?"

... Wilson and I, together in my car, and he's smoking with his hand dangling out from the window. Blazing supersunlight stands up straight off of everything and we whir through the town in my shitty hatchback.

"You can drop me at that 7-11."

He slips nimbly from the car. Wilson has spiffed up since I saw him last. He seems to have improved noticeably since he got into the car, like the ride did him good. He flashes me a cryptic smile, waves, and trots into the store. He's already greeting a big man just by the front door as I pull out and something about it doesn't sit right.

The car floats along weightlessly and the light illuminates everything I see like an illustration, shining on a uniform surface of reality without penetrating it at all. When I'm in the intersection I realize what it was that hadn't sat right exactly.

The big man was me.

Or close enough.

... I pull over. I park, and sit, and nothing more. The light makes collecting my thoughts difficult; that light just wants me to release the edge and let the current pull me along to my house, but I should go back, right? And find out.

Find what out?

Either that I made a simple mistake, and after all, only a glance, only an impression. But if I'm right? It's as if there were a huge iron cube between me and the idea I know is there, involving me and another me. I can't move it out of the way, because I put it there myself and I'm keeping it there. Its shadow falls over the whole landscape of my day, like unwavering holy light.

If I put the car back in gear and drive home now, the way I want to do, the way I want suspiciously much to do, then that is going to count and be recorded somewhere as an official decision. A final decision not to inquire about Wilson and that other man, which means I will have to forget them. Somehow legally. Which I can't. Which will be itself a transgression, somehow, against. Against what? Just against.

A feeling of inspiration. An intellectual halo. A voice that I am very graciously permitted to take credit for -- since it happens to be in my head, unlike the chips and dip lady -- is bestowing scientific revelation on me: the cosmos is bound together with knots of forgetting, trauma is illicit laceration of the present by an intransigent past, and forgetting is the scar on the knitted bone, a noble thing higher than memory, and the mother of invention. So to remember is a transgression against holy forgetting. We can't have that. It isn't done. I know I'm crazy and it's fine, it's fine.

... When I get back to my apartment, there's a woman standing in the middle of my living room, spreading little dabs of butter on a toasted bagel with small surgical gestures. My toilet flushes, and a moment later an older man, like an aging hippie, comes in from the bathroom, rubbing his still-dripping hands.

"Hope you don't mind," he says, without looking at me. He crosses to my chair, the one in the corner, closest to the window, and drapes himself in it wearily.

"Hi," I say. "This is my apartment. How did you get in here?"

"Front door," the woman says, still buttering.

"I assumed as much," I say. "How about where did you get the key?"

"You hadn't locked it," the man says. He's taking his bare feet out of his shapeless, paper thin loafers.

The woman shoves the bagel in her teeth and pulls a card from her breast pocket.

CALIFORNIA CRETAN CONCRETE COMPANY
the future of concrete
Tarti and Carhart, REPS.

"Wilson sent you," I say.

The woman makes a sound around her bagel while she wipes her buttery hands on a wet nap.

"Sorry about the butter," she says eventually. In the time it takes her to get ready to say that I notice how underwatery my apartment looks, and how the familiarity of my surroundings only adds to the feeling that I'm not here, because I'm already here.

"Which of you is which?"

"I'm Tarti," the man says. He has a rich voice, like a retired theater actor.

"Word is you're looking for some concrete!" Carhart presumptive says.

"Yeah," I groan, sitting on my least comfortable chair. It's an old kitchen chair made of steel tubing.

"How much?"

"Six tons," I say, with what is meant to be a hand gesture.

"Mmm," Tarti says.

"Mmm," Carhart says, beginning before he ends, and almost an octave lower. "When by?"

"Yesterday. As soon as possible."

"When *at the latest?*" Carhart snaps irritably. I look up at her. Her eyes are on the wall behind me. I think she's looking at my shadow. She's sturdy, with little hands and feet; a redhead, with all her hair coiled up tight in two braided buns.

Before I can answer, a sort of weak rolling spasm goes through me. It hurts, like a hard bubble forcing its way up through my gelatinous interior. Indigestion? I wince, and wait for it to fade.

... "Well ... maybe three days. Our schedule --"

They sigh with relief, the two sounds at the same harmonic interval as before, and she interrupts me.

"That's fine, that's fine."

"We can't bid that high."

"We won't ask much," she says.

"It's an experimental product," he says.

"Wouldn't that make it more expensive?" she asks him over her shoulder.

"Probably," he says with equanimity, sliding down further into the seat until his head is forced forward onto his chest. His long grey hair is touched by a dim glow of fading red, and his face is pale to the lips.

"So we're selling it for less than we should?"

He tosses his hands and lets them fall back onto his stomach.

"How we going to get it out there?"

"What do you mean by experimental?" I ask.

Carhart turns, still without looking at me, her eyes fixed on future radiancies, her little hands forming rosettes, and somehow she makes my imagination show me a vortex of their outlines in gold, fanning out into infinity.

"We make it live!"

"Here we go," Tarti says under his breath. "Here we go again."

"Concrete is alive. Did you know that?"

"... Well, I --" peter out sighing.

"-- Did you know that, *engineer?*" she interrupts, trying to drill her eyes into me and missing. Can she actually see me, or is she just pretending to?

"WELL if you mean," I raise my voice, "do I know about microbial concrete, then yeah."

"*All* concrete!"

Tarti is quietly gurgling a blue bong. He must have had it inside in his denim vest.

"Tell me how anything stays alive in granulated blast furnace slag," I say.

"No no, the concrete itself is alive once we make it into concrete. It's not microbes. It breathes, it gives off heat, it's composed mainly of water, but the way we make it --"

-- and here she glances back at Tarti, who seems barely awake --

"-- it lives. We use polyvinylidene fluoride instead of cheaper polymers, and metakaolin extracted from paper sludge. Our secret process causes piezoelectric fibers to form concrete nerve bundles. These link together nodules of metakaolin, which react to the current by forming functioning organelles in piezoelectric circulatory orbits. The current respirates in response to pressure fluctuations as the concrete warms and cools with the climate."

"You said *all* concrete when you meant *our* concrete," Tarti says.

"Wow, all this is making me tired," I say.

"You need *fixing!*" she barks over her shoulder at Tarti.

"Watch your blood pressure," he replies coolly. The red contortion drops from her faceand she swivels back in my direction.

"You're not even going to offer me any?" I ask Tarti.

"Oh!" he says, lifting his chin. He seems completely dark just now, but he doesn't look at me. "So sorry!"

He holds the bong out at me, at arm's length.

"You don't get it -- I'm talking about *self-healing concrete*," Carhart says.

"OK," I say. "It's a good idea, if it works."

Carhart whips out a small metal case. She clicks it open crisply, withdraws a ball of concrete, and holds it up between her thumb and index finger for me to inspect. She turns it this way and that, then tosses it. I catch it clumsily and nearly drop it. It's warm.

"It's a warm biosphere, all right," I say, holding it up.

"Hand it back," she says. She takes it from me and whacks it with abrupt violence against the floor.

"That left a mark!" I say approvingly.

She shows me the crack she's just put in the ball, then she spits on it.

"Sorry," she says. "But now watch."

She sets it back down on the floor, puts her foot on top of it, and stands on the ball with as much of her weight as she can. Time passes. She's staring at her digital watch.

And here's me, like a cartoon from the thirties, all those throbbing colorless hearts bobbing in place, this is *normal!* I'm sitting here on my bottom with my feet on the ground, yes sir! *That's* the way we human beings sit! And *I'm* a human being! Two arms, two legs, that's me! My head up top and my ass down below! I sit upright! My eyes face forward and my hands make gestures! My mouth and jaw work together to produce sound, arduously, for communication! I'm having *a conversation!* A normal conversation!

Carhart gets off the ball, snatches it up and shows it to me, without bothering to examine it herself first. The crack isn't gone, but it's much smaller than it was, or I think it's much smaller.

"I think it's much smaller," I say.

The concrete has a strange, fresh smell to it, like a fruit with unpierced skin.

"Now, she'll tell you about earthquakes," Tarti says wearily.

Carhart enumerates points with her fingers, starting with her thumb.

"Pressure from earth tremors generates additional current, the concrete reacts by absorbing more water, elasticity increases, concrete becomes less brittle ... *less damage when the earthquake hits.* What's *more* --"

She leans in now.

"When current drops abruptly, as in the event of a subsidence or collapse, the concrete responds by instantaneously decoupling polymer links and granulating, so structures fall in smaller, less dangerous pieces. Want to use it?"

"Yes!" my voice shouts. "Yes! I want it!"

The two of them smile one smile.

⊏⊐

Another interminable phone call with the bank. I speak to roughly a dozen different people. By 'speak to' I mean 'speak at,' because I don't believe they heard a word I said. It's like I was butt dialed by the bank, and only eavesdropped on an incessant, nervous murmur of bankspeak -- but the voices kept saying my name, prompting me to input numbers and redirecting and redirecting and redirecting me. Music and jabber, terms of art, voices fading in and out, I listened-in on the dream of a bank. I felt the delirium taking hold of me too. I heard the words "automated underwriting" and "no claim bonus" and "ciphertext." I heard them in the car with me, because I spoke them. That's when I shut the phone off completely. I meditated chucking it out the window. In my mind's eye I saw them, all the financiers, rocking back and forth in their chairs, eyes riveted to screens, numbly swiping and prodding at the dancing lights, mumbling jargon to nobody.

⊏⊐

... Party time.

The invitation wasn't weird, I was weird. Even if I haven't seen him in a long time, it's not weird that he would think of me. Back when I knew him, Omar was a high-strung character, lightly built, light brown and tense, always looking over his shoulder and keen. His tall girlfriend Ernestine opens the door for me and smiles. It's a warm smile.

"Hey, come on in! I'm so glad you could make it! It's nice to finally meet you ...!"

Aw gee whiz shucks gosh, something like that from me. I step in out of the fog. I lumber through the door like an ambulatory piece of furniture, a wardrobe.

Omar comes right up to me and hugs me.

"Hey, Chalo, all right man!"

He's mellowed; his movements are easy and he doesn't have that hunted look anymore. Whatever he's done for himself is working. There's a flash of concern there as he reacquaints himself with my face; I guess he's reading me the way I'm reading him, and the outlook is perhaps somewhat less benign in my case.

"Everything good?"

"Yeah," I say half-heartedly. "I'm hanging in there."

There are five or six other people here, music. It's a regular party. The lights are the usual colors, the people smile and laugh and chat with me, and there's no uneasiness. I settle into the corner of the sofa over by the sliding glass door. I drink beer and my brain gets cozy. Music plays and so on. A man sits next to me.

"Gordon Achittampong," he says, holding out his hand to me.

I tell him my name with the soft pang of disbelief I always feel, and that I can't account for; he goes back to his conversation with the woman sitting on his far side. I am reminiscing with Omar, whose armchair is now scooted up alongside the sofa. He gets up to change the music from time to time, leaving me to myself. There seem to be more people here now.

The night outside the sliding glass balcony doors is black down in the valley, glowing corpuscle traffic is slithering among the stationary lights, all fog-blurred and muted. This is all normal. So why don't I feel *here*? I am a hollow outline around a windswept, empty park; the camera on an empty park bench, empty where I sit. This is no dream. In minor moments of incapacity related to food and drink I begin to think that I don't usually notice that life is a nightmare because I'm incessantly, and unconsciously, fending that realization off, and sometimes I begin to slip, and all the noise and the soundtrack, the heat and the smells, my own body surge in to smother me. Then blink -- all gone. Normal, inert, fashionable. Only one inkling remains of an entire emotional life walled up in the next room.

I heave myself up and go to the bathroom. Shut in with unfamiliar soap smells, I check myself in the mirror. No insight there. Same stunned look as always. I wash my hands and go back to my place, still cratered into the sofa. Omar brings me another beer and breaks off to greet a new arrival. The surface around me isn't breaking, though, because, and I'm just now seeing it in its embedded starkness, Grant's Catalina caper has already led me so far out that I can barely -- I'm a ghost, here, basically, or maybe all but. I should be dramatically out on the balcony, fog in my hair, melting into indistinctness, but crammed into a couch corner is going to have to do for this epiphany. How weird am I? Not enough?

... I *could* not go back. I could. I could forget about the whole thing. I don't even have a contract. I could go on, do some other thing, and I'd probably never hear anything more about Catalina. Catalina itself might vanish, and I'd never know, and never care.

I have to go back because the Annex is the biggest thing, the one chance. The phrases sound uncertain now though. From here, who knows? If Omar had enough free time to get around to asking me what I'm doing with myself, and if I told him, I'd get to watch an expression of appalled incredulity spread over his face as he began unconsciously recoiling from me, because the truth is crazy.

What bigger thing do I have? That's my dream; I said it.

"You're a dream machine," is the lyric right now, and I feel myself slipping. Exhaustion I didn't even know I had is caving me in.

Was I any less real back there, listening to records in stale and sequestered little bedrooms with Omar and my other weird friends? There's a film between me and everyone else in this room. I want to break it, urgently, but I'm too tired to do more than paw at it a little. Nobody can say anything to anyone that isn't shorthand for something anybody can recognize instantly. There's nothing I can say to anyone here, because nothing in my life makes any sense. It isn't that they're all too normal and I'm too interesting deep and strange; it's that I would have to take someone aside, out of the party, sit them down and talk for hours to answer a question like "how are you"?

I imagine going back to the island, and an icy spur of fear gouges me, a mantle of doom settles over me. I see myself back with those funhouse phantoms and I want to stop. It's too weird. I don't know what I'm doing. I know even less than I normally do about what I'm doing. The dream is dreaming me now and it's more than I can handle.

So stop, break the film, reach out. Tell everybody. They'll all think I'm crazy, but they'll be good to me, they'll give me advice -- they might convince that it's all just some kind of mistake, and I'll be able to find my way out.

I see a vivid sunset: the sun is icy and clear, an orange dome bisected by a horizon black as outer space, and the people around me are transparent to it like pale cream-colored flames. Death. What about it? Where? What is ending?

Now the flamelike people around me are frightening. They are starker and starker, more and more weird.

Their weird and mine are different, and if I stay, forgetting all about Grant and Catalina, then I am going to have to come to peace with their weird. Because I will have tossed mine.

The mantle of doom and the arctic claw aren't nice, but they appeal to me. That's why they're here. I keep them here. I fear them but I know them, like family. They are all part of something bigger, my own life.

Taking unusually long strides behind the partygoers, strobing among them, Wilson crosses the room and comes over to me, appears between me and the window, pantomiming a surprise that's not even remotely plausible, his lanky body draped in a quadruple extra-large t-shirt that reads "Surfer's Paradise."

"Hey Chalo!" he says, holding out his hand to me. I shake it. Then he locks his pale, drooping eyes on me.

"You OK?"

"I'm good."

The eyes don't release me.

"I'm *good*, man!"

He drops his gaze.

"I guess you are. Anyway, I'm supposed to tell you that they need you back at Catalina right away."

"Like tonight, right away?"

Wilson lowers his head and drops his gaze again.

"Come on man, come on," he says sheepishly.

I stand up.

"Just roll with it, man."

"I'm just going to go over there right now, OK?"

I point to another corner of the room, where Omar is chatting with someone. His eyes are filled with warmth; he's got his arms crossed, hugging himself, nodding, listening to a woman I kind of know, Barbara, very animatedly telling him some kind of story. A smile is playing around his mouth, and someone else I don't know is there, too, a short bald man.

"OK, OK," Wilson says softly, still not looking, holding his hands up and nodding.

"Don't follow me."

"OK, OK."

He sounds sad, as if I were renouncing something important, or abandoning him personally.

I tell Omar I have to go. He's understanding.

"Call me," he says, giving me one of those human looks.

I step out into the dark and the air that always gives me so much life. Like wind in a willow. There's a patio out here, overhung with bladelike fronds that are black underneath and gleaming on top. Wilson emerges from them, his imploring eyes steady on me.

I watch as my hand snakes out, grabs a fistfull of his shirt, and drags him right up to me so I'm peering directly into his startled eyes.

"I'm *tired*."

"OK OK, you're tired!"

I let him go with a little shove.

"Don't get mad," he says, almost to himself. "Don't get mad at me, I'm just the messenger."

"Everybody I meet is 'just a messenger.' That doesn't mean ... you aren't all fucking with me. ... It doesn't mean you're not fucking with me."

"Nobody's fucking with you."

"I'm not carved out of solid patience, man."

Wilson rubs his face with his left hand.

"Are you fucking with me?"

Wilson widens his eyes.

"I'm not, man! I'm not fucking with you!"

"Don't you get mad at me. You don't get to get mad at me."

"I'm *not* fucking with you."

I just look at him.

"I'm not *fucking* with you. I need a ride. I'm not going to fuck with you. I need a ride."

"You need a *ride?*"

"I need a ride, yeah!"

"I hope you get it," I turn away.

"Aw, don't be like that!"

"I hope you get it," I say over my shoulder.

I walk away along a path that leads to the street, with a lawn on my left, a wall of lacey cinderblocks on my right, and a blue pool glowing on the other side of the wall. Three women in matching white jumpsuits are cleaning the pool with long-handled nets and they all watch me go by, stirring the water a little, as if they were doing something private. But they smile at me, all three of them. Slow and graceful as sirens. The hammer again.

"Did you knock?" the second one asks.

"No," I say. "Did someone knock?"

She just smiles at me and goes back to cleaning the pool.

I wish I felt that I'm doing what I'm doing because I want to, because I'm dynamically striving, but that hammer always comes down to make me think I'm a sucker mistaking a downhill roll for a surge of my own will. I drive to a pier where I know there will be a boat waiting for me complete with passengers and perhaps even nearly overflowing with them even though it's the middle of the night.

⊏――⊐

... Crazy I can feel the crazy look on my own face. My eyes are bugging out, my mouth is hanging open, my head is thrust right back into my shoulders. Little flirts and blips of wind are dosing me with cow smell and every time it hits I stagger and stomach breathe and tilt my horns as if I were shifting a weight of sand from one to the other. I see the calves creeping behind their mothers in the green grass beneath the crystalline sky and the sun flashes off the air like water and my mind shatters. Life carefully gathered and stored all year long now must explode and be completely consumed; that's rutting.

All the bulls are floating. We drift toward each other and recede. Now and then there's the odor of newly-scored earth and I know somewhere the fighting has already started. A large bull has been sizing me up for a while now. I've got my eye on him -- so I don't see the other one coming until he's on top of me. I turn my head and end up turning with him; he keeps going, corkscrewing me around, not letting me loose, but he's not getting me to expose my neck. Then my footing slips, my head swings out, away from my shoulder -- fuck, fuck, there's a horn under my chin, I'm going to get stabbed, I'm going to get stabbed, I have to break it break the clinch --

I jump straight back and bring my head down, retreating, and he comes on, but breathing hard. I veer at him, trying to get him to move, expose himself, but no, he just brings down his brow and charges. He hits me obliquely, so I can roll him off, and my horn grazes his shoulder so that he jerks back.

Now we are watching each other crazy-eyed and wheezing.

A spurt of wind flaps his mane down over half his face; without thought, I lunge. He senses me and frisks away giving ground, then sets his feet and pulls himself together but I do it quicker and come down on him. We grapple heads and he shoves back against me hard, and something in me refuses to roll -- even though it's stupid I seize up like a rock. He blindly pushes at me but I stand without budging, all my muscles locked and straining, determined not to give an inch. We're both panting raggedly. Spasms fire up all over him. Now he's worried because I'm not moving, because I'm trying so hard, I'm not getting tired fast enough for him. He ducks his head suddenly and tries a desperate slicing move with his horn against my side.

I can't believe it. I just resisted effectively. There's a gap between us and I didn't give ground. So it was him. Must have been him.

I advance. He drops his head. I bear down on him. Inside I've got something that's neither tranquility nor exhaustion. He could probably knock me back, or even down, my legs feel so watery.

That doesn't matter, though. Somehow, I've won. There's a burst of absolute silence when he turns away.

At the heart of my exhaustion there is a patch of sterile calm. The silence fills with wind. The wind tosses the silence and gets into it the way it tosses in my pelt. I am vaguely anticipating something. My opponent has shuffled off to graze meekly by a big stone. It seems to me he's forgotten already.

... Forgotten what? -- That I bested him. There's no need to remember that; the moment the fight is over it becomes a fact like sunshine wind grass turd patties, all that glamour. But if I'm breathless now, it isn't because I'm out of breath. Something catches my breath. Heavy waves rise up from my success and wash over me. What is this it's like sexual excitement without energy, like an arousing fatigue, and it brings my whole life back to me in the weary elation of a sustained gush of presence.

... I pant and sway, my head weaves and my mouth lolls open, my vision smears. There are other lives. There are unfamiliar voices. There are other languages. There are flashes from other scenes. They billow and flip past my gargantuan head. I feel the exhausting scope and scale of living. A cloud covers the sun. Daylight contracts, then expands when the cloud slides away and the sun is naked again.

... I seem to have wandered off ... I am being filled with majesty. Raising my head, I see the higher ground, where the cows are.

I go berserk. I spin around on the bulls as if I'd been cracked in the head with a hammer.

Who's next?

Which of you fuckers is next?

My hindquarters are jumping up and down like a separate person, snot bursts from my nose, my eyes start from my head. I trot up to the bewildered bulls, all deliriously cantering about each other with wild, blank minds on a dance floor of vibrating green light.

It's daylight when I wake up. Did the boat take the long way around, or stop or something? I stare at the ferry's empty lunch counter in front of me for a long time. Then I make my way to the window. There's the island. We're nearly there.

I can see almost nothing but the island. I know that it's a mountain top, emerging from the water. I also know that I am never leaving this island again. I know I'm going to die here -- or do I? For a bunch of buildings, for a footnote prophet. The deck is going to buckle beneath my feet, but nothing in the world is going to prevent me from getting onto that island. That's the world's decision, not mine, anyway. I don't seem to exist anymore. There's just things that happen.

Then I look back toward the vanished mainland and a wave of emotion comes down heavily on top of me. I'm not going back there, because there isn't anything back there; there's just a green line that vanishes as you approach the shore of California, and then buildings that fall past you without a sound, people who drift past you without a word, a cloud of pains and colored lights and shames and forms, bubbles of fiction.

The island must be more of the same, but it's not. It's a real dream. Abandoned, and so, an erased page, for Grant to write on. Or an untouched site for my buildings, my legend.

I wonder if the boat has made the trip more than once. I don't know what day it is, and although the clocks tell me the time, I don't know what to make of the time. Nine AM. Nine oh seven. I should be ravenously hungry, but instead I'm nauseous.

Back on the streets of Avalon, I pick a corner to stand on, trying to get my sluggish brain to think practically about transportation to the site. Right on cue, I see Wilson loping through an adobe archway, lazily beckoning me to follow him with one oarlike hand. The archway leads into a little walled patio overstuffed with potted plants. Always plants around him, it seems. Wilson slouches there, smoking. He draws a breath and pulls the cigarette from his lips. I know he's about to tell me something about a ride. I haven't stopped walking and I don't -- I walk right up to him and shove him. He stumbles back.

"Don't tell me anything" I say, my voice muffled.

Wilson just spreads his hands. I brandish a slack, nerveless fist at him and he collapses as if I'd hit him, dropping down on his knees, his head down nearly touching the ground, his arms lying in front of him, palms up.

"Easy man," he says to the ground. "Go easy."

I turn and leave him there, determined to get to the site on my own. I think I'm going to try to walk there. I have a fever, chills, weakness. Cold sweat pours down my face as I climb the steep street in what I guess is the right direction. Nothing more than a few feet away has any reality for me. A few minutes more, and I'm here, stepping down from the ridge top into the canyon. Refreshed. The fever, broken.

The canyon is suffused with brown light. White rocks and trees, saturated pale blue, and shadow, clotted with density and the suspense you feel listening to the steady even breathing of someone deeply asleep. The air rising from the canyon floor lifts the fragrances of wild herbs and grass, mixing with air off the Pacific as it coils over the ridges. Making my way down, wading out into the valley. The brown light closes over my head, and the sounds beyond the valley all stop.

The orange of the sunset rests on top of the brown, without mixing. Meanwhile, the shadows of the plants and rocks are inhaling and gathering substance, twinning everything in the canyon with a dark companion. Warmth seeps up languidly from the ground, everything is intimate and holy, like a painting. Crickets make the sound of the light. There's dreamy activity down on the canyon floor; there is stately promenading, a Victorian garden party. The invocation of the overrated engineer.

Grant's randosublighties sit together practicing the gestures of "village elders" listening to petitioners. As a group, they frown, they shake their heads slightly, wave their uplifted fingers indicating no, they make sagacious parcelling motions, then mime dividing a little heap, then lean forward widening their eyes under their brows quizzically, like Socrates.

Then, I see.

My knees give way beneath me, my mouth falls open and tears start from my eyes.

A platform of serrated white stone connects what will be the high plaza with the large meeting hall, resting on big broad columns, all asymmetric, their surfaces slightly wavering as if they were sleeved in water. Two slender white arches span the platform in a single bound, like bridge supports. From these, two other arches fold inward to form the roof. The walls are thick sheets of water, which fall into acoustically dead troughs below the serrations, making no sound. The gallery is framed in water like living glass, and at the tops of the arches there are small ornamental fountains that lift up little bulbous cones of water which do not wobble, but spin in a constant shape, without a sound. I never thought those would work.

My water architecture. There in front of me. Water walls. Water ornaments. Silent and steady as glass. Permeable, like bubbles. Refreshing the air, cooling the light.

I'm looking at the grand gallery, exactly as I envisioned it -- exactly. It has been built in my absence as surely as it was built in my dream.

That's my dream, in concrete, for all to see, right there.

Grant is standing over me smiling, wearing sunglasses.

"Super job, Chalo. Just -- super."

Anthony Motion is standing right behind him smiling blandly at me.

They sweep away grandly before I know how to feel about it. I get off my knees, and stare. AC is shooing a bunch of Grant's Rodeosodalities away from the big slouching man in the hoodie, Ban, who is smiling back at her patiently. She yells at Yolanda

Espantoso too, who immediately flips her off. I turn the other direction and I see Bakarne Bigotes and Gorgio talking to Concrete
Carhart. There's Tarti sitting on the ground with his back against a
big tree. I wipe my face on my shirt and head over to them.

"Hey, Chalo!" Gorgio says, shaking my hand. "You OK?"

"How did you get it done so fast?"

Carhart tilts her head.

"Living concrete!"

"Just *ideal* conditions here," Tarti chimes in.

Why was AC wearing a white lace dress? She doesn't wear that.

"It looks complete!"

"It was finished today," Gorgio says.

"In record time," Tarti says.

"It's -- " I wave my hands.

"What do you think we should do next?" Gorgio asks.

"Well, the hall should go up next."

"You see?" Bakarne says.

You could tell AC was wearing the dress over her regular
clothes. She had jeans on under the skirt.

"You can work on the hall!" Carhart says a bit shrilly. "We're not
saying you can't! We're saying it would be better to work on the
plaza now, wait for the shipment, *then* work on the hall."

She turns to me.

"Then it will go up faster."

"Shipment of what? More concrete?"

"Food for the concrete," Tarti says.

"Growing the hall will be more efficient than building it,"
Carhart says.

"And you could get the plaza working sooner, our way," Tarti
says.

"Well, what does it eat?"

"Semen, *ideally*," Carhart drags the word out, "but it *can* manage
with seawater."

"How much seawater?"

"That's the problem," Gorgio says. "Too much!"

"Standing seawater around here, after all the shit we went
through to firm up the ground?"

"All absorbed by our concrete," Carhart says.

"Forget it," I say. "You can paint the concrete with cum if you want but no seawater."

AC in a white lace dress. Like a soft kick in the stomach. Like a soft kick in the stomach.

━━

... I'm back in Avalon, leaning over the pier railing, staring out at the water. White froth bows and straightens, lettering the rolling black page, streaked with harbor lights. I can feel those little, multicolored lights come loose and dance out toward me in long, lazy vaultings behind my back where I can't see them. Colored lights run down the tall slopes behind me where I can't see them. Like a row of skiers carrying different colored paper lanterns, streaking down the slopes on no snow. Flaring streaks of color, rainbow perspiration streaming down the flanks of the island. The light soaks into the black water. Death swallows the reflections faster than I can find them, and holds me where I am, so I can't turn and see even the ordinary town and the bare slopes. AC in white. Her vicious eyes over her dark glasses slip down her nose as she barks orders. That dark eye over lace. An eye of rage in the lace. The -- sight? Memory? The shining image eating into me like acid.

... I'm back in my little room in the labor barracks. The place has changed overnight. Tarti and Carhart have their own matching campers right next door, and two ribbons of weed smoke wriggle up into the early night. Crickets, an owl. The murmur of people and some kind of ritual music. Me sitting by the window waiting like an impaled person to see if AC happens by, maybe somehow still in white lace.

... I don't see them, or realize they're there, but those daemons cathedral are all standing on a thick pane of glass just above me. They see right through to the hopelessly real desire stuck in me like a spear. Their gloating faces, their attention, drive me down further and further toward the floor, doubling me up in my chair. I'm leaning forward with my head between my shoulders. In a moment, I'll have to put my hands flat on the floor to hold myself up.

... I need to see Grant. Ever since I "grew up" I've been trying to live in the so-called real world of disappointment and abdication. Grant has given me the chance to realize a dream here. I've systematically relegated every desire into fantasy. For a while I thought of Grant as something like the magic man who would let me enter the world of my fantasies, but now I see that he's getting *at* the world. The magic doorway would be the one that leads from the world of disappointment and abdication to the world, but you can't get there from here. So you need a halfway house: Catalina Island, a monastery. Here you can make the fantasy real, because here it isn't about your individual masturbation anymore. The only trouble is in keeping the other people you involve on the same page with you, and that's what worries me. To do that, Grant has to become a blank, like a no-man's land himself, for the passage. I think he knows that, and he's letting it happen. If he doesn't let it happen, then all this becomes just another little world. There's a little world, like her own little world, that world, AC's world, which to me is a fantasy but is not a fantasy to her. And she discovered, not that people are actually good and not Nazis, but through her connection to Rachel she found a way to broaden her little world and to found it on actions, a change that happened like all changes, i.e., without her noticing, an insouciant little change -- so she finds that she can live her fantasy of killing Nazis. She doesn't have my problem, because she doesn't think of her fantasies as fantasies; she thinks of them as things to do someday. I tried to see the best in the "let's try" approach, and I got fucked.

I'm outside. I'm walking up to AC who is, incredibly, wearing a white lace dress over her jeans and her sweatshirt. Rachel orbits her on roller skates, and the man in the hoodie, Ban, is standing nearby with his arms folded, and the two bankers sit nearby, rocking to and fro, poking and swiping at the surface of a water feature -- I can barely recognize them. They are shaggy, bearded, all decked out in clattering hippie beads the size of ping-pong balls. AC has sunglasses pushed up onto the crown of her head, and she's working on some Tibetan stuff clipped to a clipboard.

"I need to see Grant."

"He's having his treatment right now."

"What's the matter with him?"

"It's for exhaustion."

I go directly into Grant's house, through arched doorways in many dim, large rooms with Spanish high rafters. I hear Grant chanting. Then I see him. Anthony is bending above him. Grant's eyes are glassy, sweat pours down his face. He's drawn, haggard, nothing like himself, twitching, struggling to hold himself upright. The color drains out of his face and hair, while Anthony Motion becomes clearer and clearer.

"What are you doing?"

Anthony's head swivels smoothly on his motionless neck, on his motionless body, and he looks at me with unblinking, painted eyes.

Blind, I wade into the gloom, pawing the air. My hands close on big leaves, the wind in my hair, I can see the moon -- I'm outside. Grant is sitting by a nearly colorless fire in the dark, floating in a black zone, and behind him I can see one of the "migrants" clearing brush with a shovel. He swings the shovel in broad arcs, slashing thick stalks and sage trunks. Once again I can hear remote chanting and the music of Grant's people, somewhere toward the constellation of lights beneath hillsides of dark blue and fluorescent ash.

The tossing radiance of the flames throws a limpid darkness out beyond the ring of light. Grant sits in the dark. His empty eyes on the fire stir and glance up as I come over. He pants a few times before he manages to speak.

"Don't worry about it," he says vaguely.

I sit down on a cold rock a few feet away from him.

"Really, it's OK, Chalo."

Grant tries to smile.

"What are you doing? What was that?"

"It's something I have to do. I'm still too much a person to be the future."

"Who says you have to be the future?"

"I do."

"Why?"

"Someone has to."

"Why you?"

"Because too many people are doing it wrong."

"I can't disagree with that. But it looks to me like you're killing yourself."

"In a way I am."

The words hang there. I'm not thinking about them. I'm just aware of them.

"You're going to stop being a person?"

He nods, and bites his lip. His face is drawn with suffering.

"You're *trying* to be a figurehead?"

Grant nods, sighing raggedly.

"I thought you said you weren't a killer ... When we met, you said that religion was killing and dying. That this wasn't going to be a religion."

"Well ... I guess I ... overestimated myself."

"I think this is a bad idea."

My words vanish into the lustrous blackness tossing just above the flames. Grant is staring into them as if he were watching his soul float away forever.

"I think you're overdoing it."

"I have to overdo it. It has to be all the way."

"Yeah, but --"

"Think about it," he says, interrupting me and emphasizing his words by punching the air with his chin, "the banks, and all the bullshit massed against there being any future at all for anybody."

He shakes his head in wide swings.

"You don't go up against that with half of what you've got."

"Instead you ... do this?"

"Make an opening. Keep it open. You don't think about it. You don't clog up the opening with thinking. About what and why and all that. Just let that be as it -- just let that be, and keep it open, keep it clear, and that means above all you keep your ego out of it. I am the way and the way is me are not the same thing."

"Which one is the good one?"

"I am the way. I'm the one who needs the way the most. I have to have it. I'm dead anyway if the horizon closes. So are you. So's everybody. ... Am I wrong?"

"... No."

"You have a better way?"

The way he's asking, it's a real question. If I had an answer, I might help him somehow.

My mind is at a standstill. My mouth opens, then closes again. I shake my head a little. Grant nods.

"Let me know if you think of one."

―――――

... Prompted by a sudden nervous impulse, or perhaps only by a tic, I lift my head and, in the same moment, catch sight of the obnoxious cow who accosted me about the Figure, eyeing me cautiously from a spot downwind.

"Oh! It's you."

"I thought I might find you here today."

"Did you learn what you wanted to know?"

"Not quite."

She advances toward me.

Her nearer proximity has a bizarre effect on me -- panic and arousal vie with each other, and my thoughts are instantly scrambled. My feet begin to prance under me -- she's chasing me! I'm running, she's chasing!

"Hey, come back here! Come back! Come here!"

"Get away from me you crazy ya-pp-ppl -- you crazy cow!"

She chases me up the slope and back down again. I run without looking where I'm going, in a frenzy. I think I'd throw myself off a cliff to get away from her. Instead I plunge into a stream and charge with the current down the valley. She's following me along the bank.

"You can't lose me! Stop!"

"I can try!" I say, in a strange voice made almost human by the cold creeping up into me from the water.

I jump out of the stream and run past her, back up the slope.

"Would you stop?!"

My terror gives me wings. I zoom right into the middle of a swarm of bulls, all stare, slobber, stride, to and fro and to and fro, showing their horns, their sloppy balls, their rolling prismatic eyes, their liver colored, froth-flecked tongues.

The cow has stopped. I catch sight of her as I turn and turn again. She doesn't seem to want to enter this mob of weird bulls. She watches me, between two long forelocks, one peering eye.

The black bull and the grey-brown cow have emerged from somewhere or other, already speaking levelly to us even from a long way away, in extended, steadying lines, telling us all to be calm, to hearken carefully to them, and their coaxing words become our actions. To an observer, we appear to be sizing each other up, challenging each other, with here and there a preliminary sparring match, but, while outwardly we are doing exactly what we did yesterday, we're actually conducting the rational rut today. I am gradually becoming more and more aware, through the nerves in my feet, of the pulses of my fellow yaks communicating through the ground, and with them the minute tremors of cellular respiration in the grass, coordinated to strictly regular waves of solar radiation I never noticed until now.

The reason all around me is like a speeding roller coaster; it incessantly recalibrates an equilibrium between the cellular metabolic action of grass and weeds and bushes with the soil and the worms, the beetles, the birds, and yaks. Dimly aware that I am in motion, describing with the other bulls an abstract knot of invisible paths, our tongues lolling from our gaping mouths, our eyes blank and stupefied, sizzling hormones burning our reeking acetic bodies and frothing up into our brains, I hear the sound of grass inhaling my breath mesh with the sound of planets orbiting above me.

All this order is making me crazy, these thoughts are thinking themselves because reason doesn't need me to be reasonable to set off a frenzy in me that makes yesterday's aggression look like kicking out in my sleep. We are all there, wild for order, for light -- I see reason -- I see myself -- I see the novel -- I think I even see the one who reads me -- are these the writer's thoughts? This maniacal logic? And now at last the real rut can begin.

I'm vaguely making my way to the other side of the site, following a dirt path halfway up the ridge line, paralyzed with thoughts of AC in her white lace.

Behind and above Chalo, the Narthex croons, strutting atop the spirit glass. Lapels in his hands, head flung back, he soaks up Chalo's shameplume.

AC comes up on me out of nowhere, like a conjuration from the earth, and still in the white dress all cattywampus over her normal clothes, and my breath catches in my throat and stops.

The Narthex catches sight of AC and his breath catches in his throat and stops, cutting off his little ditty, eyes riveted on her and fingers snatch in the air for the cigar he drops, and behind him the Nave picks up the song without missing a beat, singing it through a complacent grin, spreading, sun-dappled, and damp. She picks up the cigar.

"Hey Chalo, they need you over at the causeway. Everybody's looking for you."

"What's happening?"

"Fire! The great hall!"

Right now there's nothing to the great hall but the columns that will suspend it off the ground and the ramp leading to the entrance in the base. The causeway ramp folds around, reversing on itself, and becomes the ramp, and at the moment about half the wooden scaffolding supporting the fold structure is burning. A wave of nullity falls on me when I see it.

All we have to dump on it is seawater. Seawater makes the concrete grow. If the concrete grows now, just there, *why did we use it for that and not regular concrete* if it grows now and there the entire entry ramp will be ruined setting us impossibly far back and if we let it burn out then the concrete will subside and the entire entry ramp will be ruined setting us impossibly far back.

I run toward the fire --

... Agony. Burning. On fire. Running all over. Pain biting and boring into me in a dozen places. My face raw and smarting. My eyes like two craters. People all around me. Flames leaping on me, sucking and twirling. I see two figures dimly before me, throwing out their hands, turning me away from a slope covered in dry brush. I'm grabbed from behind, thrown sideways to the ground, hands are all over me. Rolling me in the mud, pounding me with jackets and blankets. Then water dashes down on top of me.

People are saying all kinds of things to me. Am I all right?

My face is in mud, there's mud in my mouth, in one eye. The other eye looks at nothing while evil skates around me.

⊏━━⊐

"Did it come down?" My voice -- the tone cuts in and out, I'm so hoarse.

"No, still standing."

I'm told Gorgio tried to stop me, that I was crying and shouting, that I drove him back nearly into the fire, so that the heat forced him to release me.

They tell me I went into the fire, wetting my hands with own tears I wiped from my eyes, that I used my wet hands to grab burning timber, rip it off the frame, and throw it into the concrete-lined fountain pit.

They say I went right into the fire, swinging my arms to keep it off my face, that I made directly for the point where the burning section of the frame joins the rest, that I wrenched and tore at that point until I got myself into it, then drove the burning section back, away from the part was that wasn't burning, ripped it free, lifted it over my head, carried it, and threw it into the fountain pit.

I can hear hammering.

A kind of raw agony is blazing up all over my arms, my back.

"Are you s-shoring --?"

I'm screaming too loud to hear what they say, but I see Gorgio pointing, nodding.

They tell me that I ran around on fire, raving, and nearly ignited the brush trying to run from the flames burning me. Eventually they got me on the ground and put me out.

I scream into their horrorstruck faces. The scream slips in and out of a whisper. It means "thank you."

⊏━━⊐

... I can only watch mountains rise around my bed like groans. I lie staring up at the jagged well mouth above me. The ghost of the fire that burned me stands upright in my injuries. I hear the ghost's muffled voice chanting the syllables of an incantation. The chant is implacable and meticulous and endless. It is the spell or it is the prayer that is gods not instead of, with the sound of a prayer learned by rote and repeated until it becomes empty and its holiness takes on the cast of resignation; no, it's pain, and indifference to pain. My own lips are shaping the words. I realize that I have to keep my lips moving, or the fire in my injuries will race up my body with terrifying speed and attach itself to my lips, burning my mouth, and strangling me with fire. It doesn't matter what words I say, they all mean the same thing. I have to keep forming words or like-words. The words arrive before their meaning does, although they're already too late to say it, but they aren't a code. I want to pronounce silence into burns to quench them.

... Propped up in my bed I am like a big impassive religious authority, nominated by bodily misery. Bandages hide my hands, swath my arms, and muffle my head. I have bandages all around my torso. Beneath them, harried reconstruction work is ongoing.

... My bed is positioned so I can blearily make out the work on the great hall through my window. Tears of gratitude fill my eyes when I think of them, the "migrants," hurrying to replace the burnt section of the frame. I think of the concern on their faces as they took care of me, and for a moment it seems like my gratitude might expand so far that it becomes a new body to restore me.

... Nobody knows how it happened, but we can all see it -- first water, then earth, now fire. The elements. I'm in too much pain to think any more about it but isn't it obvious? Even the illusion of a world fights back.

⊏⊐

... "Oh prince of a noble heritage" keeps coming back to me. Or is it "noble lineage"?

... Mist, broken in clots, wanders past me, up from the valley, following the slope, ignoring the terrain. The day is dim and grey, the air is wan and thin. Me unrutted. The rut hasn't started yet. I thought it had. It's closer than ever before, though, I know that.

When the rut is as close as this, all the yaks, male and female, turn away from each other. Each of us drifts, or rebounds, toward meditative isolation. The rational rut, the clashes of bulls and the practiced disdainful gestures of the cows all turn themselves over in our minds, despite the absence, the inattention, the exhaustion. These memories toss like restless sleepers. If I'm any kind of example, you can feel the way they are trying to become you, behind the scenes, and it makes you nervous, wearily anxious.

... I wander off for some mechanical grazing over by one of those natural rock piles that attract me. I like to look blankly at them and see how accident has fitted the stones on top of each other. It's architecture designed by glaciers, or avalanches, to be ogled by groggy yaks like me.

Suddenly -- it's *that* cow. She's panting, her jaw is drooping, steam trickles from her whole body, and her eyes are popped, as if she'd been running for a long time.

I throw back my head and fart protractedly, almost noiselessly. This translates to:

"I'm tired."

She stares at me. Then she waggles her head like a corkscrew and whacks her nose twice with her tongue. This means:

"*You're* tired. Ha ha."

Now the impression is that she did not run a long time -- that she might be sick -- but most likely she somehow generated all that heat, steam, and fatigue, just standing in place, thinking. She walks right up to me and her panted breath and her steam make me more alert.

"I don't know what you want from me."

"I want to know what you learned from the Figure."

"Didn't you see it?"

"Yes, but I need to look at you now."

"Why me?"

She sighs curtly before venturing an answer.

"I think I'm too ... actively looking to be able to receive anything directly from the Figure. I think what the Figure means translates better for you, because you passively receive it. I'm not sure you even want it."

I was about to say the same thing, as far as wanting it is concerned.

"I don't want it," I say, but -- that's strange. I don't feel as if I'm telling the truth, somehow.

"You must have an idea about what you expect it to be. What you would learn."

"Yes, right. It's getting in the way of what it is."

I think she takes what I said as an answer instead of the question I was asking, as if I'd just told her that her preconceived ideas were preventing her from seeing what was there.

"What did you think it would be?"

"What did it tell you?"

"What did it tell me? ... I don't know how to explain it. It wasn't a secret; it was just wisdom. It was about being alive."

The cow is right beside me now, looking me intently in one eye. She's so near that all I can see of her is a wall of hair with a planetary eye in the middle, blinking away flies. Yaks never get this close, eye to eye like this, on purpose. It's uncomfortable. One eye, like a brown and white moon in a shaggy sky. The restriction of vision on just one side, when the other is panoramically open, is disturbing, even painful, when the obstruction is another yak. Our eyes are so big and so open that to gaze directly into another eye that's just as big and just as open makes you, dizzy; it's like standing on the edge of a cliff. Dizzier, since we yaks don't get dizzy on cliffs. There is something a little pleasurable about this feeling, though, maybe only because it's so unusual, surprising.

In order to communicate with her up so close, I have to do everything I would normally do with my whole body using just my head, or as much of one side of my head as she is likely to see. Somehow I try to convey to her the idea that the Figure is an ambassador of sorts to this world from inside, not from any outside, and that it is inside us, that it wants us to be as alive as possible, that it is the blooming and dying, something like that.

The cow keeps her eye fixed on mine so steadily that I begin to forget myself. I think she is seeing something in me that isn't there. So, actually, not seeing. Gradually, her eye recedes, although I don't perceive it getting any smaller, and the rippling wall turns into the cow again. She raises and lowers her ears without moving her head, which means, come with me. I close my eyes as she turns, because I can't look at her ... from behind ... in my current ruttish condition.

... I walk upwind of her, and off to the side, as she climbs the slope to an escarpment all overhung with strange-smelling vines. From time to time she sniffs, smelling me, and a flicker of scorn comes across, which means she's as ruttish as I am. We both jingle inside. We're full of galloping sleigh horses.

... She stops again as we're about to top the ridge line, in a level spot below the top of the escarpment, and looks at me again. She pulls up alongside me like a ship and returns her eye to a position only inches from mine. The vertigo and pleasure come back instantly, and stronger than before. She's taking me to her place, which is up on top, but first she's checking again to make sure she isn't making a mistake. She could be someone like me. Always kind of someone else who is never all here, always inwardly listening with one ear and inwardly looking with one eye for the glamour and the language from further within the horizon, separated, and calling *that* living.

"Wipe your feet."

She moves away, keeping her eye on me.

As I scrape my feet, one by one, on a patch of gravel, she says:

"And don't make any mess up there. If you need to vomit or shit or urinate, do it here -- not up there."

I tell her I'm good.

"It's very important," she says, a little nervously. "No shit up there."

I tell her I'm all shitted out. She watches me a moment more before turning to bring me the rest of the way up.

The top of the escarpment is an open crater, broad and flat, flooded with vivid twilight. A thick carpet of fiercely-green moss covers every inch of exposed ground, which is dotted with a million small pools of still water, milky with reflected light. The pools are all exactly alike, each one the same asymmetrically round shape about four human feet across, and they are evenly distributed over the crater floor for as far as I can see.

She indicates that I should walk around the pools, and never step in the water.

"Don't even touch it. And for goodness' sake don't drink it!"

There's a broad ledge that curls elegantly down the reverse side of the ridge to the crater floor. We take that down. My foot touches the moss. My coat bristles, a cold pang goes all through me.

"You feel that?"

My skeleton is turning to ice inside me. My entrails are cold pulp.

"Don't stand still."

Her ears and tail flick anxiously.

"Walk around the water."

She goes over to one of the pools at the edge of the crater floor.

"I'll start it here."

She indicates another pool at the edge, about two yak-lengths from hers.

"You start there. Now, watch how I go, do everything the same as I do. Try to keep one row behind me. Never catch up, and don't pass me."

I look down into the pool. I see my own face. I see the bottom.

The cow is watching me. When she sees I'm not about to mess with the water, she begins to walk, without looking at me, in a winding way around and about the pools. I reproduce her movements easily. It's only walking. Our paces match step for step naturally. Following her as closely as I am, I'm not able to follow myself, but I don't think I'm doing it wrong. The more steadily I watch her, the less like a real cow she is, and the more she is like the only cow.

... Newts and salamanders are crawling from pool to pool. Dragonflies dart past my face, sewing up the air with laces of rose perfume. We meander over toward one side of the crater, which is lined with stone cabinets. There are no loose stones on the crater floor except for a few small white pebbles that glow white against the green moss, made more green and white by the grey light, which lifts from the pools like music, and goes nowhere, but gathers. Stone cabinets. Like actual cabinets, immersed in some petrifying stuff.

Look into a pool. I see my own face. I see the bottom. The

animals are invisible in the water. All those newt and salamander looking things are seeing me out of one eye. A pool.

... She's just up here, layering systems of walks on top of each other. This is what she does all day, I guess. The crater is a place for her walking-systems. The ponds remind me of limp hands resting on dimpled bedspreads. I'm beginning to think that nothing is really happening, but the pools are lining up, bringing the two of us separately to a scenic vista. Even though I've watched and followed her, so far as I know, without interruption, we're now pretty far apart, and I wonder if I've deviated, and if I should correct course. I guess I won't. Everything here is under the numb sway of thought, so the actions lead to other actions the way thoughts lead to other thoughts, by sneezing, through tiny gaps that both open the way like holes you can crawl forward through, and also prevent you from knowing in that moment what you are doing. I wonder if this is a pat walking system or a new one, and whether she saves them in her memory or forgets them and wings it each time.

"Did you know that's exactly what I call them? Walking systems?"

I tell her I didn't.

We step out together onto a crescent-shaped ledge, shaggy with new grass and the valley opens below us, illuminated by a glowing cloud of irony that sheds layers like an unravelling onion. The valley is a mathematical arrangement of colored smears. While they are nothing alike, they move the way the newts, salamanders, and dragonflies did, and the way we moved around the pools. It must look different from my point of view. Whatever I hate to love is the world; it loves to love me with hate. This makes sense to me.

The grass around my hooves is jumping with lice. The cloud of movement detaches from them like bodily static and siphons inside me. I'm breathing through my mouth and watching childlike phantoms of music escape down the meadow paths, running away beneath the somber, drunken tree gloom. There's that same brown light I've seen before, beneath those trees. A part of me is threatened, reasserts itself, bunches itself up like a muscle. The planet vanishes beneath me and my heart stops. I see space, the onion leaf sun and the Earth, and the far-off sound of a huge ocean.

... The cow gets my attention. I'm back with her, as if the planet had never disappeared, and she tells me at once that as long as we're here, her point of view is my point of view. There is only one point of view here, but it's very large, it can accommodate any number. Any number of viewers. Which of them is a real yak?

This is another question in our investigation. I think to myself, in disgust:

"This is the self I get? This trash?"

... With her here, I am more alone than ever, and nothing is happening to me. I think that's true of her, too.

... There's a shining chrome-yellow smear, a brightly flashing nailhead the sun hammers. It travels above the ground and splatters the grass and the pathway with color, veering to avoid the invisible force columns of her certainties. Something tells me it's my heart I see. It belongs to the landscape now, and it'll be the rotting sun for one day, now mostly over, things mostly not done. I feel its gravity sharply. It is surrounded by a nimbus of trembling faces cut from tracing-paper, yellow and orange, and it belongs to a landscape of finalities, decisions, certainties. If I could draw with my hooves, I could design columns, arches, walls, windows, cupolas, plazas, fountains, cloisters, spires, of finalities, all saying goodbye forever by standing there in that arrangement and no other. The pattern being in me, and it means goodbye. This is final.

The landscapeprocess ponders, reflects, in a scintillating heavy warble all around us; constant, like the dawn chorus, and like a fireworks show that feels like the last. Surrounded by a million gentle voices chanting formulas in rapture, turning in and out of nature, telling me over and over that this is the end of each instant eternally dead hereafter. One more time, to say goodbye. It all feels totally familiar. An endless succession of irrevocable rational decisions being made around and through me, and with me. An ... an ...

At a loss I turn to her --

She tells me it always feels like the end here, and looks at me in a certain way. Desire looks like hate on her face.

... An abrupt blemish in time happens. It jars us together. The nailhead flutters with an arrhythmia that's getting more violent as the landscape, only becoming more vivid, drains into it. We go up to the highest spot, which is the lowest we are willing to go. She calls me down into the glen. What happens is a kind of music of without me and her, the partial separation of the anemone petals folded in abolitions while pure sleeps twine and blend, meshed like light, coming to an end, outliving, taking a position among the pains of going away forever, outlining touched icons, daylight murmurs against windlight, spread above roving sun dapple spangling there with checkered carillons all around, ghosts of a skin within some hearing come out frisking, humming out from day to vanish over and over among the heads of gold, our stories, our heavyheaded grain wafting in beads of green that show through them, curled in soft-ened gold each checker, stumbled over, soared, ambered over and waited, in deepened heaviness, abolished petals still coiled, silence beneath each even lamentation, returning and coming to an end. Watching the insouciant grass and birdsong crossed by chimes like little comets. Being at the bottom of the sea of daylight, where millions of years heap up for swimming in, for austere birds' reminders and momentary states. Warping with one another in cloudlike motion without a shadow, surrounding birdsong without rights, for cascades of dawns, spasms in tiny cataracts of dusks. Dawn pops dawn open. Dawn, coming finally to rest.

"There's the big boy, there's the big boy," he says out of breath, mopping his swimming face with the white towel around his neck, stepping around the door and pulling up a chair by the bed.

"Huge man," he says in a low, creaking voice, drenched in sweat, stepping in behind him and standing up straight beside him.

"I used to think I was fit," he says, shaking his dripping head. "Then I came here."

"Oh, man," he creaks. His red face is steaming.

"Whew!"

"I mean ..."

"It's just like ..."

"Yeah."

"I can't believe the rules ..." he creaks.

"Ohh ... so many ... amazing!"

"Awesome."

"So awesome!"

"Like, so technical ..."

Chalo is resting. The two bankers have beards and beads and white ponchos with the hoods puckered around their faces.

"When the El comes --"

"Not El, bro --"

He blinks.

"The Elemental then -- what's wrong with El?" he asks, without fully turning his head.

"False ety*mology* bro."

"Ah ... What was I saying?"

"When the --"

"When the Elemental comes ..."

"Oh, children ..."

"You've got to be there, bro, planted in the earth."

Chalo says:

> "Mountain wind
> stirs the grass
> in the canyons ...
> to no sound
> but
> birdsong."

Raising his arms and curling his body, Chalo adopts a surfing posture and surfs past them in midair.

They jump up full of admiration.

"Bro is *advanced!*"

Chalo flashes out of sight through the window, a dwindling phantom surfer.

On the ground, under the sky, with bandaged arms and face. He turns to look at the construction site, and there's Wilson right in front of him, his hand out, smiling sheepishly, wearing an oversized black t-shirt with the words "WHATEVER WORKS" emblazoned across it in plain white font. Chalo waves him away in irritation, pushing past him to take a look at the site.

"OK, man, OK, OK ..." Wilson shrinks behind him with a steady, patient eye.

Chalo makes the rounds of the construction site. How long has it been since he was last here? Progress has been phenomenal. Unfamiliar shapes -- buildings he designed -- stand in various states of completion around the great walkways, the water-walled concourse to the center. A woman passes him speaking into a phone she holds flat before her mouth, like an hors-d'oeuvre.

"He started saying stupid shit and I argued, I said ..."

"Acres of flooded land,

Be-gemmed with dragonflies," Chalo says after she passes.

Now he seems confused. Stopping for a moment, stumbling a little, he looks over his shoulder at the sky, the cosmos it implies. Something has changed in their rapport.

He presses his hand to his forehead, eyes on the ground. The raw soil is stamped with the prints of work boots. The paths link buildings under construction. Chalo timidly begins to speak to himself.

"Thhhhhe m-moon ..." he says and stops immediately.

He looks up, and the hand that had clasped his forehead now grabs his lips and cheeks, squeezing them.

After a few minutes, his eyes become dreamy again, and he resumes his tour of inspection. The living concrete sits in rubber-lined moats of sea water, drinking audibly. Chalo stares at these incomplete shapes out of his own imagination with joy in his eyes. Then he notices that, in some places, the concrete has thrown off some sort of polyp along the ground; there are faintly discernible spots on the concrete where sproutings have clearly been knocked away and the surface planed down. Arginaldo Cardito is visible nearby, carefully chipping a growth from a white concrete bulb that will one day be a flying buttress propping up the dormitory. Chalo examines the polyp, which forms a flat whorl at the end, like a pad of congealed wax.

Dust has collected in minute folds in the surface. Chalo studies these folds, his head craned over onto his shoulder, stooping, and walking around the whorl. He awkwardly gets down on his knees, tosses some more dust onto the concrete, brushes the surface, leaving only what clings in the folds, and studies what he sees. It is an image of himself, sitting in the health food restaurant opposite Grant, whose head is almost completely obscured in the steam from his teacup. The figures are all swirling like something from Gaudi or Mucha. The image pivots as he moves his head. When he leans to the right, the figure of himself swings around to face him. When he moves to the left, Grant swings around to face him. When he leans in close, he can see the individual wisps of steam wreathing Grant's face. He can see something in his own eye. He leans in close, prostrating himself. Chalo's eye in the image has a figure reflected in it. He brushes more soil over the concrete, but the details become elusive and the image dissolves into a chaos of meaningless lines.

... Chalo eventually abandons his investigation of this dollop of concrete, and he turns to go on in no special direction. There, behind the little shed the "migrants" built for the bulldozer, Wilson and Rachel are talking without their usual vagueness, without the fog of ambiguity -- Rachel is not aloofly silent and Wilson isn't sketchy. It's like they're different people. Rachel is the first to see Chalo and the next instant sketchy Wilson is turning to him with that aw shucks grin and his hand out, and she is skating away under her headphones lost in her perennial teenage fantasy. Chalo raises his hand in disgust or outrage and an astral spearhead of brown light chimes from his palm, making Wilson wince, blink, and stagger.

"The riddling vetala escapes on the wings of your own intelligence,

be these juggling fiends no more believed," Chalo says sadly.

He waves Wilson away. Wilson pinches himself across his eyes with one hand and disappears around the shed.

Arginaldo is passing, holding a sort of diorama of concrete

against his chest. Chalo peers at it, and Arginaldo explains that these things have been forming spontaneously out of the concrete. He puts it on top of a heap of stone slabs, piled up nearly chest-high. The diorama is an eye-shaped loop, encircling something like a crystal ball filled with distortions.

Chalo leans in, and watches as the irregular, partially transparent zones of color, drawn from the landscape beyond and from the air, and perhaps also from his own reflection, resolve into a bizarre lenticular image that unfolds into a brief, segmented narrative as he moves his point of view from one side to the other.

The sage awaits the Black Mass of the daemon. He sits in a Faustian study, surrounded by alembics wreathed in green steam, architectural plans, and Sanskrit writings; his forked beard reaches to his stomach; his bald head is fringed with long white hair. Between his long hands is the demonic missile -- a rod of grey glass fletched with oily black daggers and tipped with a pyramid of gristle, all covered with uncouth daemonic emblems. The old man's face is lined, haunted, lean, austere, hollow-eyed. His eyebrows rise together and meet in a nest of wrinkles, and all his features, motionless as the image is, nevertheless seem to swim with anguish. Move a little, and now you see him entering the dark chapel, head lowered, the missile clamped tightly to his chest. The chapel is deserted.

Only a shaft of moonlight illuminates this scene, shining down from a shattered stained glass window. Tiny motes glitter in the shaft. The light that rebounds up the statues of the saints from the floor gives their faces a ghoulish, wanton quality. Now move a little more, and the old man is at the altar, performing the mass. Black candles burn in a ring around him, their pale light carving deep shadows into his miserable face. His mouth is open in the midst of his beard like a black pit overgrown with rank weeds, and it's clear he is intoning the daemonic words. The missile stands on the center of the altar, a dead, dripping spark mouldering away its fuse. Move a little more, and the scene is engulfed in the darkness of a horrifying presence that is obscured by shadow. The missile has lifted off, is nearly out of the frame, and the shadow is cast by the column of black, rumpled smoke beneath it. The old man is prostrate within a magic circle, clutching his bare head with his hands, quailing in terror. The moon is gone, the candle flames have become long thin lines of poisonous white. Between the old man and the figure, a large diamond lies on a rude wooden dish where the missile had stood.

Move again. The only change now is that the Figure is touching the diamond with the middle finger of its greenish-yellow hand, leaving a dark stain on the clear stone. It seems the old man is trembling, clutching his skull, the backs of his hands are corded with tension and his eyes are tightly shut.

Move again. Now the old man is back in his laboratory; he leans down to peer intently at the diamond, which he has placed on a brass tray. In the next scene, he is cutting the diamond carefully. He has wrapped his hands in moly and rosemary, evidently to avoid any contamination through the instruments. He has cut the black portion from the rest of the stone. This black portion, which is shaped like a faceted, slightly irregular ball, does not rest on the brass plate, but floats an inch or so above it. The old man is measuring it with calipers, his hands wrapped in herbs. Hands still wrapped in herbs, he sets the black portion onto a balance, where it displaces no weight at all, since it will not rest on the scale. He produces a branch of sagebrush and breaks off a certain amount of it. The sage weights the black mass of the diamond. He now works that mass, turning it into what appears to be a typing element -- the ball of raised letters from selectric typewriters -- covered in Tibetan characters. Chalo is now at the concrete rim. He steps around to the other side and peers in, but the story simply unfolds again in reverse until once again the sage awaits the Black Mass of the daemon.

Arginaldo points toward a concrete piling with a white carbuncle growing out of it, similar to the bulb in front of them, then walks off to attend to other things. Chalo investigates the pylon and examines the carbuncle, which has a shining square of some greasy material set into it like a fingernail -- but he finds nothing so unusual about it. He turns and nearly collides with Malinche Azazul, who is smiling at him.

"¿Qué tal?"

. . .

"Showers of bread cascade down the sticky trunks of the banyan tree,

Rain falls into the pool, the surface is still smooth. The water level has not risen."

"¿Quieres saber que pasa en este?"

She slips past Chalo, takes the carbuncle in both hands, puffs a puff of breath onto the shining square, and peers into it, like the submarine captain studying the view through the periscope.

"Esto es un jeroglífico con un viejo, y siete elementos: la noche, el amanecer, el suelo, la cefalea, la espada, y el espejo. Una noche, tal vez cualquier noche, un viejo consulta un espejo mágico en una juguetería, sosteniendo una espada de juguete en su mano. Él es rodeado por tarros de dulces, la clase típica. Mientras tanto, el suelo fuera de la juguetería es el hervor con gusanos, bichos silenciosos. Cuando ha mirado fijamente en el bastante mucho tiempo de espejo, puede verse ya no en ello. Entonces, se precipita fuera y empuja su espada en el suelo. En la luz de la luna, la espada es ya no un juguete, y la cabeza del viejo es coronada con una cefalea. La juguetería es un lugar sagrado lleno de figuras diminutas, y cada tiene una cefalea también. El viejo se agarra al puño de la espada de una mano. El otro se arruga a su cabeza. Un alambre de oro se quema bajo su cuero cabelludo. Todas las figuras dentro del lugar sagrado imitan su gesto, y su levantamiento de dolores de sus cabezas como chispas de oro, que van en tropel juntos, una masa informe de estorninos diminutos. ¿Qué entonces? Los bichos traen algo como una lata de pastel a la superficie del suelo. El viejo lo toma ambas manos, dejando la espada. Temblor, abre la lata. Una gota negra del humo o diamante se tambalea en el centro. Las chispas vuelan por la azotea del lugar sagrado y se dispersan en todas las direcciones. Amanecer, el viejo mete la mano en poder para tocar la sustancia negra, y el sol creciente se hace pestilencia."

Gorgio, who has since arrived, explains.

"It's a rebus with an old man and seven elements: the night, the dawn, the soil, the migraine, the sword, and the mirror. One night, an old man consults a magic mirror in a toy store, and there's a toy sword in his hand. All around him are jars of sweets. Meanwhile, the soil outside the store is all ... all ripped up with worms. After he stops seeing himself in the mirror, he goes outside and sticks his sword in the ground, and it doesn't look like a toy anymore in the moonlight. And he has a headache. The toy store is a shrine with lots of tiny figures who all have headaches. The old man holds the sword -- with one hand, he holds it, and the other holds his head, where the headache is like a burning gold wire. All the little figurines do it too, and their -- their pain comes out of their heads like sparks that flock together like birds. A certain kind of bird I don't know the English. The worms bring up a like a cake box? The old man takes it, opens it. There's a black blob of smoke or diamond inside. The sparks fly away in all directions. Dawn comes and he touches the black stuff. The sun turns into pestilence. That's it."

Chalo opens his mouth, closes it, then nods and bows a little.

"Want to see another?" Gorgio asks. Malinche stands on one foot, holds the other leg out straight to the side, both arms out to balance, smiles at them both, and then walks off. Chalo nods again.

"Over here," Gorgio says.

He guides Chalo through a little forest of partial pillars. The smooth trunks of concrete are already beginning to show what look like burls.

"The concrete is telling itself a story. It's like it's dreaming."

He pauses a moment to tap a dimpled, braided-looking tumor protruding a few inches from one of the concrete pilings.

"This one will start to show soon. We cut them off and pile them up behind the shed. Once you cut them off, they rot. They stink so bad we have to keep a tarp over them."

Chalo says:

"A lamp swings in the night wind,
the flame never stops pointing up.
Dust thickens on cracked, weatherbeaten tombstones,
dust no one made, in infinite amounts."

Gorgio leads Chalo along a narrow path of stepping stones that weaves among the trees of a little copse. Brown light is beginning to seep up from the ground as the sun goes down. The ground sighs as the heat of the sun begins to subside, and the wild herbs start to smoke. The two men are sweating, blinking.

Gorgio goes over to one of the concrete walls set deep into the ground. Toward one end, the wall has spontaneously produced an art nouveau tendril with a clear globule at its elbow. Gorgio points at it, wipes his brow with his bare hand, and stands aside, holding his kidneys, looking up at the sky with his mouth downturned and breathing out through his teeth.

Chalo looks into the clear globule. What is there to see?

A patient in a hospital bed. A patient in agony. A patient having a heart attack. A tumbling black object, which Chalo recognizes -- a Messerschmitt head, boring through space toward the patient from all directions at once. Suddenly he somersaults over the foot of the bed, and the pain is ripped free of the body as if it caught on invisible hooks. The various pains orbit the patient, pulsing lights like something out of a nightclub. He dances out the window with a crash of splintering glass, and flies pop-locking above the streets of Avalon. The sound of breaking glass is distinct in the twilight air of the construction site; unlike the other scenes, this one is not entirely silent. The frantic gestures the patient is making might be intended to bat away the pains, but they seem to be more involved in precipitating the body through the air. He patient wants desperately to plunge into the cool black Pacific and quench the heart attack there, and he vanishes in black-and-white water.

The tumbling Messerschmitt head rolls out over the waves like the image of an evil planet, with an atmosphere of inky smoke and almost lightless flame. The jaws part. From the gaping mouth shoots a huge cathedral-powerboat, enveloped in shrill screams of terror, its prow long and sharp as a crow's beak. Blood-red flame belches from its rockets, it roars, and lightning from minute thunderstorms flashes over the enormousfaceted engine of greasy iron. The Nave is halfway down the prow, hanging effortlessly on to a guiderope with her left hand, the other visoring her face as she scans the water. The Narthex steers, the Transept is fucking the engine, conducting the miniature thunderstorms like musicians. The Apse deflects spurts of foam with a satin parasol, keeping the seawater out of her martini, while she indicates, with her left hand, the eruption of the latest leak in the boat. The Triforium, dressed in matching wetsuits, hasten to patch the leaks in obedience.

The Nave emits a piercing whistle. Her keen eye has located the flashing pain lights, and her long finger pins them in space. The Narthex turns the boat and accelerates. The boat grinds down into the water, shoving it up in a ramp behind it. Horns emerge from the water as they near the lights. Huge, rolling eyes, long streaming locks of wild yaks. The wave is a green slope, the night is broad daylight, the ocean is mountains, a herd of yaks, a circling horde of vultures, and countless starlike wildflowers. The boat is ploughing up the mountain, full of night in the middle of the day, the daemon eyes glowing like cigarette ends and all around them, not quite below them, are stampeding yaks that swerve in and out of their path like dolphins in a bow wave.

"Find him, Nave! HIC!" the Apse calls.

The Nave's keen eye blinks in the glare of the sun, but even half blinded she cannot fail -- she finds her yak and points it out -- at once the nimbus of club lights reappears around it.

"There he is, Narthex!" the Apse calls.

The Narthex surely takes aim at the yak with the whole screaming boat.

They crest the top of the ridge only a second behind their yak. Broad daylight is night, the slope is a towering wave, the mountains are ocean, the boat pivots over the edge of the wave and spins down the curved front, scarring the water with red scimitar slashes of red fire, out of control and hurtling toward the shore of the burning mainland.

"Please!" the Nave shrieks at the dancing lights, holding out her arms beseechingly.

The Narthex has to throw an arm around her neck to keep her from flying out of the boat. With his free hand he draws his amber pistol with a bullet sputtering light in the chamber and tries to draw a bead on the patient, but the boat is pinwheeling round and round, skipping down the wave. The Apse shrinks into her parasol.

The patient, frozen in the chest-clutching, agonized posture of someone having a heart attack, sails through the sky. Even though it's the dead of night, the wave casts a gargantuan shadow that is drawn over the burning mainland like a sheet being drawn over a corpse's face.

The dream's light fades as the globule goes dark. Chalo recognized the patient.

"It's something, eh?"

Chalo presses his hand against the globule. The cool surface gives like flesh.

"Grant's not looking good."

Chalo nods at Gorgio and hurries off after Grant, scrambling clumsily up a slope of loose earth to the path above. There's no one there.

In one direction, the path extends from the site back to the camp of rheterostylites. There's no one on the path. As the sun sets, music rises from the camp. It sounds like a celebration. The rejoicing song of the true believers. "Ayer maravilla fui ... y hoy sombra mía aun no soy..." ... "Only yesterday, my own existence amazed me ... today I am not even the shadow of myself ..." It meshes with the brown light that trembles in the place where the dusk touches the ground. In the other direction, the path loses itself in the live oaks. Turning to gaze toward the camp, Gorgio stands and listens. The singing rises and falls.

Zeferino Jojobal comes up to him from the direction of the construction site, his arms folded against his body like a rabbit's, his head wobbling on his neck.

The two stand together, looking at each other, without a word, listening.

"How is --" Gorgio asks, but stops when he sees Chalo, running. Zeferino turns to look, then instantly hastens toward Chalo.

"Chalo! Chalo! Did a snake bite you, Chalo? Were you bitten by a snake?"

Chalo's bandaged face is a rigid mask, eyes starting. He breathes heavily through his mouth.

"What happened?" Gorgio asks.

Chalo pants, blinks, shakes his head, rubs his face. He lowers his head, then looks up at the sky. Beyond him, Gorgio sees Grant and Anthony Motion calmly strolling among the trees in the distance. A greyish color is coming into Chalo's face. His shuddering breath catches and his hands wobble.

"What happened?"

Chalo looks Gorgio in the eye. It's as if he didn't understand the question.

"What happened Chalo? What is it? Chalo, what is it?" Zeferino repeats.

Gorgio motions to him to stop.

"Let him get himself together."

"OK. OK. You get yourself together, Chalo. Take your time. Did a snake bite you?"

"Zeferino, please."

Zeferino closes his mouth.

There's a moment of distant singing, distant music. A mourning dove.

"Just yes or no. Are you hurt?"

Chalo shakes his head, and says:

"The w-wind ... traverses the sea unhindered,
The blos-ossom o-opens to receive the worm."

"Something the matter with Grant?"

Chalo nods, squeezing his eyes shut.

"Grant's been bitten by a snake!" Zeferino yells, and runs away immediately, raising the alarm.

"Green foxes watch mushrooms grow by night from menstrual blood,

The star blossoms, pollen fills all of sp-pace."

Chalo tosses his head wildly, eyes clamped shut in frustration. Then he holds up both his meaty hands and shows Gorgio one hand limply and submissively being engulfed and crushed by the other, which closes on it with hydraulic slowness.

━━━

The dusk is an uneven field of lambency softly weakening and strengthening around AC, who sits like a white ember at a stone table beneath the trees, in a paved circle. Rachel takes her shoulder in one hand, then pivots away into the dreamy gloom. Ban, the hoodie man, is squatting not far away, doodling in the dirt with a stick. When AC first encountered Ban at the site, and she recognized him as the cop she'd tossed out a window, the one who fell forty feet and landed on his head, she'd nearly exploded with incredulous rage.

"I killed him! I killed him!"

Then he'd calmly approached her and held out a limp, sticky hand for her to shake. She looked into a grinning, blinking, face, one that twisted and untwisted, and understood. Then she shook his hand.

One of the rheterostylites, a red-faced man of nearly sixty who has been assigned to wait on AC, is pacing unhurriedly in a circle, muttering mystic slogans to himself, irritably correcting frequent mistakes. Various examples of rhetorostylite pottery are placed on the wall that borders the circle like the sides of an ashtray.

AC raises her head and lowers her sunglasses.

"Listen to this," she says, addressing Rachel, who is whispering in her ear. Ban also stops to listen.

Voices without a planet spoke from the metatmosphere of the hellheaven

"Let us destroy the world of numbers and commerce now!"
The ghost of a diamond was blighted and
forty-nine carved heads of alabaster and lead
self-guided,
fell to earth through space
and into the web of the dark conjoinment daemon appointed to
receive them.
When each head grimaced, forty-nine new poisons appeared.
Dark conjoining emanated the heads to the daemon of intoxicated
clairvoyance,
who emanated heads to the daemon of lasciviousness,
to the daemon of temerity and the daemon arrogance.
These ones then prepared ten thousand heads,
emanating them through their own hearts to the numbers and
commerce of human activity.
The smoke of the grimace-poison came from the left ears of ten thousand evil faces.
In the lungs of numbers and commerce,
the smoke of the poisonous expressions formed the forty-nine
enchanted liquids, that suffused the numbers and contaminated the
commerce of human activity.

That bathos was so plangent then,
that the Celestial arose from the bluewhite hellparadise,
"Let us cut the poisoned members away from the dying body of
numbers and commerce."
The ten thousand thousand expressions were transformed into the
ghost of a diamond
with four faces and one hundred and seventeen thousand six hundred
and forty-nine hands.
Languages arose in its core and emanated from its surface.
Gestures emanated from its facets and its many hands.
Air and sea lanes emanated from its four faces.
One hundred and seventeen thousand six hundred and forty nine
times one hundred and seventeen thousand six hundred and forty
nine animals and human beings contemplated time,
because of work.

When one of the rheterostylites humbly asks her what it means, she says --

"I get paid to translate and I do it. You want my opinion? Pay me more."

Ban passes between AC and the sun, stroking his upper arms as if he were cold. The light of the sun does not return once he has passed.

The Figure is standing there, wearing the mask of the Messerschmitt head. AC has never seen this head before, so she does not realize that the wool hat of the original bust has been turned into a rudely-fashioned black crown. Above the head, the blue sky swiftly fades to a foggy circle of black, studded with constellations, and, from one of the stars, waves are coming, that change the appearance of things as they all but impalpably wash over her. Everything is suddenly made of vibrating fine ribbons of black; the colors struggle to escape being imbibed by the ribbons, and, caught and suppressed, their frequencies travel elsewhere, drawn back along the ribbons which she now believes could be black planes viewed edge-on, and the colors are seeping down these folded crevasses, meshing far away into the livid white between the slices.

The Figure is neither entirely immersed in this process nor entirely separate from it. The Figure is composed of little particles collected in billowing filaments of shimmering black and white.

It's as if someone standing behind her were pulling her head back, but it's her own spine that's doing it, compelling her to stare at the wavestar into which all those colors are coiling, and from which come all those evil ribbons -- and there's something else in there.

Something is happening between here and the wavestar, and approaching through those coruscations of black and white -- a travelling detonation, like a scream carried intact through space.

It isn't a scream, AC suddenly understands, it's an order that's coming to them in its own time, which is part of the command, to wait for the order.

I should tell Grant about this, she thinks.

And then, no, I'm not going to say a word to him about it, she thinks.

With what is, by contrast, a loud crash, the hoodie man knocks over one of the shitty potteries, and AC glances, not at him, but down at a freshly-translated passage on the sheet of lined paper in front of her. It's in her handwriting, and her hand is certainly sore enough.

Was she writing? For how long?

AC holds out her arms, indicating the vacancy to either side of her. Without another word, she hurries off in the direction I came from. I watch her as she goes by me, not seeing me, her hair swinging from side to side, taking long paces, so that her dress is pulled taut around her knees, and it's like she's a symbol for more than I ever knew I wanted. I love all of life through her, because she is only a small part of it. I want to be everyone and go everywhere. I want nothing. I want to be this yearning and only this. Instead, I have to turn away and walk to the causeway, rent in streamers that flap impotently after her, trailing behind me like obsolescence.

The brown light beneath the trees and shrubs around me is beautiful. My sadness wavers out from me like candlelight and is breathed in by the brown light, swelling its glow, making me light and transparent to this dusty, herb-scented air and motionless time. Time that grows up and up without passing, like a blade of grass, and includes me. AC is a white blur in the brown light, alive with impatience.

This is paradise. This is an anguish that can never destroy or deplete me, a refurbishing, just because it's infinite, the anguish of wanting everything, loving everything, even my own miserable being.

The Narthex is watching AC go and the Nave is gloating, singing her shame anthem, when a clipped hiccup sounds behind him. The Nave shivers, stops singing, clutches her chest, draws her shoulders together, and turns to face the Apse, draped on her chaise lounge as usual, a weird light sparkling in her martini.

The Nave, convulsed with shame, throws a glance back at Chalo, who burns like a clear brown flame down there. She crawls over to the Apse.

("HIC what haeppened?")

"I-I ... I eh, I don't know."

("You don't?")

"His pet came looking for the maerk, thaet's aell I know."

("You don't know much HIC -- thaet's for sure.")

The Apse winces as the spider shadow of the Crossing falls on her from somewhere in an overhanging cloud. She spills a few droplets of her martini on silver satin. Her face snaps shut in a neutral expression, and she drops her eyes, bracing for a reproach. Only the Transept, masturbating under a nearby tree, is immune to the shame cascade.

"CAME," he repeats drolly.

("Help me up, Narthex.")

The Narthex takes hold of the chaise lounge and heaves it up onto his back. The Apse scans the valley with a silver lorgnette.

("Hmm -- HIC! ... Whaet's the Pulpit up to, do you think?")

It's logical berserking -- the way our bull bodies posit each other. The millions of calculations made per second by our nervous systems ascend into something like its own consciousness, and as I ram my head against my opponent's neck I whisper to him something like a number, and he falters. My number, my quasi-number, is somehow overbalanced by his number and I lose my purchase on him, get a hard whack on the ribs too ...

... We are drawing the sky of the grass and focusing it into our heads, grinding minutes to dust between our mountains -- more and more calculations -- I slip, and he drives in on me counting one, two, three, four, pushing steady, driving me back on my own spine. My back snaps open, my feet are thrown out behind me. I will lose ground if I don't twist, sway my head just so, moving between the beats of his count, throw his head up and his count adjusts to my faster tempo -- all in a haze of instantaneous reasoning that I have to keep forgetting in order to avoid losing myself in contemplation of them when what I have to do is act -- when I remember something I forget what I'm doing, and I slip --

... I have to forget and then I reason in motions and gambits. My body isn't tired or awake, but my mind is wearing out with the effort of saturating itself into my whole bulk and watching the whole body of my opponent, but there in the middle of the world is a burning core, the vaginas of yaks ...

━━━

Today celebrates the completion of the first phase of construction. All of Grant's autodruids and the "migrants" have gathered at the causeway, where the plaza is already surprisingly close to being complete. Chalo thinks symmetry is stupid, so he made the plaza an ellipse with its foci diagonally aligned across the path extending from the causeway to the assembly hall. Before the assembly hall, there's a fountain with a raised platform across the water, and this is now decked out in white gauze and linen, like a bride, heavily bandaged. The fountain isn't complete, but the base, which is a bun of white marble, is installed and the water is rilling over it as intended, so that the stone seems to wrinkle and quaver. The dusk is overcast. This is Chalo's favorite light, this bruised, sourceless light that clings to my hands.

The rascalswashlimities dance, walking in and out and around each other in a complicated arrangement, murmuring, swathed in white gauzes and veils and things. Grant has had them for weeks, he had them take their clothes off, he had them talking to animals, he had them standing still. The "migrants," looking bored, are circling around them waving whirring cords in the air over their heads. Bakarne Bigotes is watching from her high lifeguard seat. Ban is making a big nest of gauze on the platform. No sign of Tarti and Carhart, no whiff of weed. No bankers. Chalo catches sight of the gleam of Anthony Motion's blonde curls -- and starts so violently a reflex makes him grab for his heart.

Anthony stalks past on the other side of the platform and goes down into somewhere, off to one side of the fountain. Chalo's hand squeezes his greasy shirt, comes away shining, grimy. When did he last change this shirt? Will he have to get up there and give a speech or something? Looking like someone just out of jail?

AC and Rachel flash up onto the platform and stop abruptly, eye to eye with Ban. They smile weirdly at each other. The smell of seawater washes over Chalo, and one of the bankers sloshes past him on the left, heading purposively around to some point behind the platform, more or less to where Anthony Motion was headed. Everyone is waiting for Grant to appear.

Somehow he can't bring himself to approach AC. Looking toward the platform gives him a powerful and breathless feeling of flight -- as in run away, get out -- but the image of the world outside is not available. What is it like again? Cars? Jobs? Everything ... not rotten, but spoiled. He can't picture any of it; the campus makes the rest of the world into an irresolvable blur from here.

"We're not cutting ourselves off from the world out here, Chalo, we're cutting ourselves off from the bullshit that obscures the world. This whole Annex is a machine designed to produce some more world."

-- That flash on the horizon, is that lightning?

⊏⊐

... Thunder disturbs the sky above the mountain. A bull gingerly heaves himself up onto the hindquarters of a cow, his enormous head resting on her back. Their eyes are sad and remote. A moment later, he drops back onto his forelegs, his head sliding across her back and flank. I can feel my own face taking on his expression, and with it comes the same yearning melancholy. The two of them are standing alongside each other, facing opposite directions, gazing off into space, waiting, impassive.

The ruts one-pointed fire has billowed out in diaphanous wings. Now we are fully inside it, and the rage to enter its circle dissipates like thunder.

... I approach a cow. I don't know which. The cows have become a ribbon of flanks and bobbing heads, weary eyes, flickering tails, jets of urine, shining horns, panting, wheezing. One of them turns to me. I feel my heart open. Now I am aware of nothing but her, chaffing my head along hers, blanketed in waves of her smell. I walk past her, my nose leading me to her tail. She begins to walk in a circle. I follow her, so we are turning together, nose to tail, wandering in a ring, round and round. We will wander in place together until she stops. Her fragrance, which from a distance had been so sharp and provoking, enough to make my sinuses tingle painfully, is mild and subtle close to her, smoothing out the riot in my blood, lulling me into mating. When we've turned in place so many timesI feel almost like crying with sheer fatigue, she pauses ...

... and now, not knowing what just happened, I feel my forefeet touch the ground, my head slide along her back, light in my testicles, and we stare in opposite directions, like strangers, together. I experience monumental calm, like a powerful sleep. Thunder drops in a coil around us. Then she begins to turn again, and I follow. We turn, and pause, and turn, and pause.

Skies are clear enough now.

Anthony Motion appears on the platform first, standing well back beneath the canopy shading Grant's seat. He walks with the same effortless smoothness as always, as though he were supported by the air and putting no weight at all on the ground. Grant appears a moment later.

Chalo remembers seeing his grandfather's corpse before the funeral. What shocked him then, as a ten-year-old boy, was not the presence of a dead body, but the absence of any recognition. His mind couldn't connect the jovial old man of his memories with the grey-faced thing his father gazed at with a sadness so immense it made his expressive face expressionless.

The Grant who comes on stage is not the Grant Chalo knew, draped in his passenger's seat, casually pilfering a money bag and beaming at him. This man is a sleepwalker. His face is inert. His soul has been eaten by his sunglasses, which are now so black they leave streaks in the air. Behind him, Anthony Motion's own features are obscured by a labile and trembling shadow. Like a veil of grey steam. Grant's veil, changed from green to grey, appropriated by whatever is that inhuman being up there that calls itself Anthony Motion.

Grant commences his movements -- bowing, gesturing, intoning -- with robotic absence. It's sickening. Chalo wants to turn away. The crowd repeats the gestures and words every bit as mechanically, but something is already going wrong. Grant's gestures are becoming half-hearted and vague. It's as if he were shrinking away to nothing under his veil. Gradually he sinks, wavers. Anthony Motion pivots slightly in place, his veil darkening. Grant is shaking. His veil trembles. Is he sobbing? Chalo moves toward him, instinctively.

A cackle bursts from the hanging, veiled head. Chalo trots toward the platform, shoving through the crowd, which is still going through the movements. Blurts of laughter come from the shaking body. There is a terrible irony in them, but, in that laughter, too, there is a ruttish sort of waggery, a kind of struggle is happening in that laughter between bitterness and something more wholesome. Anthony Motion steps smoothly forward and lays a rigid hand on Grant's shoulder just as Chalo mounts the platform. Suddenly Grant throws off Anthony's hand and his veil and sunglasses while rising to his feet in one sweeping gesture, laughing wildly. The trance of the crowd breaks. Grant lowers himself smoothly over the front of the platform and hurries across the plaza, laughing raucously.

Chalo is nearly right behind him, calling his name, while Anthony Motion and the others, seemingly acting on Chalo's cue, follow behind. Grant is shouting with laughter so intense it's frightening. It's like he's gone crazy. It's the laughter of someone who has completely stopped caring, laughter of violent change. It's so fierce he's having trouble walking as he leaves the Annex and climbs one of the steep dirt pathways that lead up to the ridge of the canyon.

By the time he reaches the top of the path, Grant is weaving drunkenly, filling and emptying his lungs as hard as he can. As Chalo hurries up behind him, Grant turns and, seeing him, points rapturously to the sky. Following his finger, Chalo sees -- blue sky, white clouds.

Very blue, very white.

So blue and so white, bluerand whiter and bluer and bluer and whiter and whiter -- Grant sways against Chalo. Without thinking, Chalo takes hold of him, trying to prop him up. Grant is limp, wracked with hilarity, and Chalo is paralyzed by a spasm of grief the moment he touches him, bursting into tears, sobbing aloud, helpless, looking past Grant, following his gaze.

The blue of the sky and the white of the clouds. More and more blue and white, more and more. More and more, and yet more, blue and white, more and more and yet more, like yearning. The sharpness of the soft outline of the clouds, with purple ridges and scalding white prominences, and the infinitely deepening blue of the sky that contains them, is dominion in light and color and space and motion and time.

Everybody but Grant screams when the Special Guest steps casually from behind one of those clouds and begins sauntering down the sky toward them. Everyone but Grant is screaming, screaming at the top of their lungs, frozen in place, screaming at the top of their lungs.

The Special Guest is much closer now. Screaming, eyes brimming, Chalo sees it with supernal clarity. A veiled figure, shaded beneath a black parasol, carrying a swaddled baby. The figure's head lolls drunkenly on its shoulders, as if the neck were broken, the luster of its unblinking eyes and the teeth in its unwavering smile gleam through the veil and the shadow of the parasol.

It walks languidly, dragging its bandaged feet. It's above and all around them, looming up into a well of clouds and blue radiance ensleeving this massive, silent, rippling body, and superimposed on it somehow like the original of the shadow is the same figure, human-sized but impossible to compare with anything human.

The Special Guest is not ten feet away from Chalo and Grant now. Without the least hurry, the figure daintily extends its right foot and touches the planet with one toe.

Very, very small. In me I feel a very, very small change. It's *very small*, but it is the only thing in what I now discover is a boundless emptiness. The Special Guest fades into the glare, but not entirely. Even when I can't see it, it's almost visible. It has left the earth, but it leaves behind the least possible trace of itself for us.

The silence becomes normal. I can hear wind whipping over bare rock, smell fresh grass and a strong animal odor, too. I train my hearing in different directions. I'm not sure how I can do that. Out of one eye, I'm not sure which, I see the Annex in the canyon, all the people there writhing and ...

Out of the other, I see the other side, the ocean, bedded under

white haze, and the fathomless indigo sky. I also see straight ahead --
a steep green slope studded with boulders, the Himalayas, a herd of
yaks. Everything is full of minds, minds, minds everywhere, all the
frantic administrators are converted to become channels for the
teeming syndrome and all the boulders and wildflowers are already
networked and calculating codes. I don't know how I know -- I don't
know it but I can see it -- all the Steves and Stephanies are proph-
esying with fire cockscombs pluming out of their foreheads, all the
Messerschmitt heads are turning into William Blake's death mask.

I look down at a jumble of arms, hair, legs, clothing. The
moment I lower my head to look, I am in great pain. Very enormous
pain, as if I'd been hammered all over and still ringing with it, my
ears ring, my eyes feel scorched, my face is as stiff and crackable as
old leather. My head swivels to and fro on my neck as if I had
Parkinson's. My muscles are burning, my forehead is throbbing, my
crotch feels as if I'd been bashing it with a rock. Staring at that heap
of limbs and clothing, recognizing it without being able to name it,
trying to focus my normal on it -- Anthony Motion. Inert. Collapsed.
The clothes he wore lie neatly folded and wrapped in plastic, brand
new dead stock with tags.

The ringing in my ears is parted now by moans and cries, words
half howled in sobbing voices. I turn my head and a sharp pain splits
down my spine, making me screech -- a bleating, animal noise in my
own throat. Where's Grant? It happened! It happened! Where's
Grant? What happened? It happened. Butterflies, violet and delicate, covered with water, with human silver, bottomless in figure. A
triumphant, pliable form from another future with another past, in
twirling blossoms and flower petals, birds bunching and swooping,
spreading and gathering, all around this figure's black parasol, scattering mirror snow. The figure was long, wrapped in cloth painted
and spangled with bright talismans. The bandaged feet were
covered in saffron powder. Looking at the figure I wanted to fuck
forever in all things. Where is Grant? Did something happen
to him?

... No sign of him.

I go back down into the canyon. Things aren't normal again.
The day is as bright as high noon and as enigmatic as dusk at the

same time. The day is languid, timeless. All around me the rheterostylites are prophecying, with white veils pulled down over their faces, their teary eyes shining behind the veils, hands in the air. Their bodies and their faces are doing different things; they've all got the syndrome. Why not me? Or do I have it, too? I haven't been exactly "in control" lately.

... The canyon is filled with singing birds. In the shady spots among the trees and shrubs, faces of cats and snakes and coyotes flash at us and vanish. Buffalo nod on the ridge line and descend, huge brown blobs arranging themselves on the slopes like musical notes. Faceless whispers with eyes whirl in the leaves and between the flowers.

I cross through bands of sexual light, and see from the horizon clean outlines and bright primary colors, light like wind, wind like color, outlines like caresses. When it sweeps away, the bands of light restore me to the forever brown light dissolving to powder with a humming murmur trembling in billions of human voiceboxes. Afflicted people swim past me like gods; I'm moving like a deep sea diver on the ocean floor, but with none of the weight, not even my own weight. The light and air buoy me up, moving is as easy as breathing and drinking the light and the shade. All around me peace and power are the same. The pains of the landscape have turned into radiant ceremonial posts. Look up at the ridge line -- an all but invisible phantom water is welling up out of the canyon and over-flowing the ridges, spreading out to blanket the island before rolling out to sea and up the mainland shore. Some of the people it contacts will start to prophecy, and their faces will take on expressions that make what they say unbearable.

Look and be shocked, and shocked again. The Annex looks like heaven-art, made of light and shade, clouds, clear water, time, music. AC is sitting absolutely still by the fountain, her white dress is blinding, her face is tranquil, she's become an idea. Seeing her and my transfigured buildings, hearing the murmur, the birdsong and whispering, is like witnessing everything that just happened summed up and happening to believe I know why I am alive just now. The idea frightens me, and oppression fruits out from my fear. Something is singling me out and dividing me from what's happening around me.

I see the plume that swims above the heads of the prophecying rheterostylites retreating from me. It looks like golden cellophane waving kelpy in a strong steady current. A stifled voice, muffled by six feet of soil and maybe by a mask as well, drops a leaden mantle of chanting on me:

"This is you speaking."

It says, coldly forcing me to confront this as I see myself excluded from the magic --

"You are dreaming."

-- and of course I don't know, I can't know --

"None of these people -- Grant -- AC -- and none of these build-ings -- exist in reality --"

The cold pain and weight of that thought I can only say no to is like a blot of shadow battening on me in paradise. I strain to open my mouth. I say --

"The air stirring among the orange blossoms is not wind,
The tree is not wood, its roots -- not wood.
The fragrance of the blossom is not something to remember,
The air is always in motion."

The dry clay at my feet crumbles and bulges. Grinning from ear to ear, a head made of what looks like platinum emerges, dazzling in the muted light, fixing me with its two blank platinum eyeballs.

I see. I didn't get the plague because I've got the plague.

Raising my eyes to the Annex, I see the vision again, standing plain as day, rock solid and real, if not quite complete. For a moment, the platinum face resembles my friend David's face, and something he told me once comes back to me now -- "they say, the home is never finished."

Some of the "migrants" are coming over to me now, apparently unaffected by the plague although I'm not really sure of that. I feel a hand pressed to the center of my back, and I'm being steered away, into the barracks.

The sounds of heavy hoofbeats, of grunts and panting from massive chests, massive stomachs, answer me from very far away. My head swings out in front of my lunging body, driven back and ploughing forward, tossing my horns, snorting, breathing in that crazy sex smell and the baffled odor of bulls' tears and mouths green with grass in a delirium of blue sky and high mountain peaks, beneath the gaze of the imperious and anxious cows.

———

... there was something else I saw -- I don't remember now when I saw it, though I saw it through tears or maybe in tears. I was looking out at sunflakes on the Pacific, all on fire in the setting sun, a field of brilliant platinum lozenges swarming in and out and over each other. There's someone in there. Now, not more than a few yards from the Catalina shore, the ocean rears up a hundred feet in the air -- without a sound. The wave rolls away from me, bearing down on the mainland shore and scaling higher and higher, higher than the highest point on the island. The whole ocean is pulling itself gigantically from its bed to throw itself onto the mainland.

Dwarfed by the wave, one surfer, all in flapping white clothes, is poised at the crest. Masterfully, barely adjusting his board, arms held out, placid, head level, hair flying. Well, guys like that always get away with it.

I see the coastlines eaten up by rising sea waters. I see the abandoned Annex, the grounds littered with trash. I see the senescence of the mainland. I watch everything spoil.

Seawater inundates Avalon, and seethes into the interior of the island, foraging among the clefts and divots in the landscape. It pours into the canyon and floods the Annex, setting the litter in dancing spirals on the turbid brown.

I watch the living concrete greedily drink the ocean. It draws the waves, forms piezoelectric neuronal mycelia, and begins to expand. From a bed of frothing seawater, the Annex grows. Its neural webbing intercoagulates and coordinates the opening and closing of capillary passages, preserving the shape of the Annex. I watch in accelerated time as it doubles in size, then quadruples in size, expanding without changing shape except where alterations are necessary to preserve the overall contours. The Annex stabilizes itself with massive stone-cleaving hooks that clamp it to the bedrock, and by firing pitons like javelins the size of cargo containers, marked with Chalo's name, into the ground: corkscrew buttresses.

The Annex grows so vast that the details of its architecture are plainly visible from Palos Verdes, now itself an island, and, on a clear day, even from the new mainland shore, across Los Angeles Bay, in the beachfront foothills of the San Gabriel mountains. The Annex has formed lattices for admitting sea air to its higher parts, and sunlight-adaptive surfaces to feed electricity into the deep chakras of the buildings. The massive neural network within the concrete achieves a consciousness commensurate with its original purpose, and it begins to chant through its loudspeaker system, rumbling in a voice that makes the ocean buzz for miles around, a steady, dreamlike chanting that is audible from the mainland, and shakes loose a perennial veil of mist from the surrounding sea.

At night, some kind of unidentified flying objects emerge from the Annex and roam through the air over the remnants of Southern California, raking the ground with blazing searchlights. No one has ever been able to catch a glimpse of these things; they're just strange, sort of saucer-like silhouettes against a night sky now much more vivid again in the new, much darker night. The Annex fliers evidently scrutinize every person they encounter with their intolerable beams, select and abduct those that match their unknown criteria, and convey them back to the Annex. I can't see what the Annex does to them. It's like they are half drowned in a sort of cascade of blinding luminosity, and emerge graceful, enigmatic, and different. Some of these altered abductees remain at the Annex and others are returned to shore, to extend the plague.

I see ships and helicopters approach the Annex. I see their crews go wild with the plague and turn their ships and helicopters out, toward the open Pacific. I see drones buzzing the Annex. They are transmitting the Annex chant back to their operators, infecting them with the plague, infecting even their computers with the plague, all crooning, all chanting, with the flame of prophecy dancing over them. The Annex allows certain visitors to land at its sponta-

neously-formed piers, but not many, and they all return to the mainland prophecying with the plague.

People wander dreamily in and out of the broken glass architecture of the former empire. I see myself, drooling in a wheelchair, set
out in the daylight, like a houseplant. From this terrace, I can see the
glinting downtown towers shimmering like a mirage, half submerged
in Los Angeles Bay. Out past that, since it is a fine day, I can see the
Annex -- that I built -- insubstantial and misty as a cloud half-
melting into a summer sky, but also immutably firm, there on the
horizon. The causeway, the great hall, the spires, the plaza, the
dormitories, with walls and ceilings of water that must now be
cataracts, but perhaps still silent, if the design still works at that
scale. It's as if that were my spirit out there, rising or setting, looking
back on my ruined body.

I have to supervise the construction. There is more to be done. The
Annex is not finished. The rheterostylites aren't able to help me;
they have spread the plague across the island, made a beeline for
Avalon and the mainland shore. The "migrants" all have their
dancing tongues of fire now too, but they continue to work, as ever.
The freshness of the air is intense. Girders and two by fours float
purposefully by you in that fresh air with numbers of years ... 1987
... 1998 ... Birds are singing as if that were contributing to the
construction work, or as if the songs were also being constructed.

Look at your body. You can see disease, beautifully organized,
elaborating from your own metabolism and thinking, spreading, and
fractating like the architecture of the Annex, where one detail
spirals out to entail the whole shape, ecstatic fronds of living
concrete sutured around the grid. The architecture of the gardens
geometrically echoes the shapes of the wind as it stirs the leaves.
The people at work look like gold, the people at rest look like prisms,
blissful and ghostly. Or you are, watching as they build your dream.

It's like death. You grieve because you can't feel it more. You feel
so little of all there is, and yourpart in it is so pitifully small and
wishful. There you are, eight years old, with all the same desires you

have now, so feverish you're logical, like when you tore the last page out of your favorite book and threw it away so it could never say "the end" to you. Not to you! Play it again! Why isn't the good part the whole thing?

The roaring peace of the garden of brown light, satyrs temporarily at the weir made of gold rocks,

the many-armed Pains haunting the trees have ceramic mouths full of swearing, riddles, conjurations in an askew tone, gelid shadows stammer in the trembling cruxes of the water curtains as time saturates the Annex, lofty white lessening pinnacles drawing height with the sky wafting along them, the stained irises along the watercolor its tremors, the canyon echoes with the sound of future parades, tumbling roses curtsy and rake the air with their sabres.

Wilson emerges from the gloom behind the storage shed, his t-shirt blazing white and his long face serene, like a statue's. He swings his hand out toward you.

You might have been kept too safe, in no place, until the bright notes of the sadness keep flashing up rejoicing in the color the horizon was when you were eight years old -- blue blue blue infinity, an aquarium full of time where desires vaster than you bent, supple as sharks.

You reach to take Wilson's hand. His face creases in a smile as he whips his hand away before you can take it. He closes that hand into a fist, with one pointing finger. Pointing up. His eyes on your eyes.

You look up. There's a Messerschmitt head perched on an arm of living concrete, directly above you. It's the one they called "The Artist As He Imagined Himself Smiling." The black lead blazes in the sun like platinum, reversing itself blue and white, and it is making expressions. That's when you know you are going.

You look up, and see a four-pound mason's hammer drop from the scaffolding and straight onto the middle of your forehead.

Crack!

ABOUT THE AUTHOR

Michael T. Cisco is a writer and teacher currently living in New York City. He is known for his first novel, *The Divinity Student,* winner of the International Horror Guild Award for Best First Novel of 1999. His novel *The Great Lover* was nominated for the 2011 Shirley Jackson Award for Best Novel of the Year, and declared the Best Weird Novel of 2011 by the Weird Fiction Review. His experimental novel UNLANGUAGE was nominated for Best Horror Novel by *Locus* in 2019. He has published in anthologies edited by Jeff VanderMeer and Ellen Datlow, among others, and his work has been translated into German, French, Spanish, and Italian. His scholarly monograph,*Weird Fiction: A Genre Study,* will be published in early 2022 by Palgrave Macmillan. He teaches at CUNY Hostos in New York City.

ALSO BY CLASH BOOKS

EVERYTHING THE DARKNESS EATS

Eric LaRocca

AFTERWORD

Nina Schuyler

THE LONGEST SUMMER

Alexandrine Ogundimu

DARRYL

Jackie Ess

THE ECSTASY OF AGONY

Wrath James White

HEXIS

Charlene Elsby

LES FEMMES GROTESQUES

Victoria Dalpe

CHARCOAL

Garrett Cook

COMAVILLE

Kevin Bigley

WATERFALL GIRLS

Kimberly White

WE PUT THE LIT IN LITERARY

CLASHBOOKS.COM

FOLLOW US

TWITTER

IG

FB

@clashbooks